"You can tell m
while I lay th

"You want to hear one o

Snapping the reins, Clint set the horse
toward the spot a bit outside of town where Katrine
and her brother had staked their claim. "I like your
stories."

She laughed. "Lars thinks you find them silly."

"They are." Clint laughed right along. "Some of 'em,
at least. But there's a place for silly. We've got all the
serious we need, and then some."

She eyed him, head cocked to one side. "Sheriff
Thornton, you surprise me."

"I think we can dispense with the 'Sheriff Thornton,'
don't you? You can call me Clint."

"Well, then, I suppose you may call me Katrine."

She offered a shy smile. The breeze sent strands of
her hair playing across her cheeks. It looked like spun
sunshine to him—not that he'd ever say such a thing
to her face. Clint swallowed hard and turned his eyes
to the path. "Thank you kindly, Katrine," he said.
"I'll do that."

* * *

Bridegroom Brothers: True love awaits three siblings
in the Oklahoma Land Rush

The Preacher's Bride Claim—Laurie Kingery,
April 2014

The Horseman's Frontier Family—Karen Kirst,
May 2014

The Lawman's Oklahoma Sweetheart—Allie Pleiter,
June 2014

Books by Allie Pleiter

Love Inspired Historical

Masked by Moonlight
Mission of Hope
Yukon Wedding
Homefront Hero
Family Lessons
The Lawman's
  Oklahoma Sweetheart

Love Inspired

My So-Called Love Life
The Perfect Blend
*Bluegrass Hero
*Bluegrass Courtship
*Bluegrass Blessings
*Bluegrass Christmas
Easter Promises
 *"Bluegrass Easter"

†Falling for the Fireman
†The Fireman's Homecoming
†The Firefighter's Match

*Kentucky Corners
†Gordon Falls

Love Inspired Single Title

Bad Heiress Day
Queen Esther & the
  Second Graders of Doom

ALLIE PLEITER

Enthusiastic but slightly untidy mother of two, RITA® Award finalist Allie Pleiter writes both fiction and nonfiction. An avid knitter and unreformed chocoholic, she spends her days writing books, drinking coffee and finding new ways to avoid housework. Allie grew up in Connecticut, holds a B.S. in speech from Northwestern University and spent fifteen years in the field of professional fund-raising. She lives with her husband, children and a Havanese dog named Bella in the suburbs of Chicago, Illinois.

The Lawman's Oklahoma Sweetheart

ALLIE PLEITER

HARLEQUIN® LOVE INSPIRED® HISTORICAL

Special thanks and acknowledgment are given
to Allie Pleiter for her contribution to
the Bridegroom Brothers miniseries.

Recycling programs
for this product may
not exist in your area.

™ LOVE INSPIRED BOOKS

ISBN-13: 978-0-373-28267-8

THE LAWMAN'S OKLAHOMA SWEETHEART

Copyright © 2014 by Harlequin Books S.A.

www.Harlequin.com

Printed in U.S.A.

Be strong, and let us fight bravely for our people
and the cities of our God. The Lord will do
what is good in His sight.
—*2 Samuel* 10:12

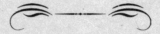

In memory of my dear mother-in-law, Clarice

Chapter One

Brave Rock, Oklahoma Territory
June 1889

Fast wasn't fast enough.

Clint Thornton ignored the knot of iron tightening in his gut. He told his fear to go away, to stop growing colder and heavier with each minute, each uncrossed acre, each dangerous stretch of land between himself and the Brinkerhoff homestead. Oklahoma was hot and dry in June. A fire could turn deadly in a split second. And the fastest fire of all was one that had been set to kill.

He bent over his horse, boots digging into the animal's flanks. *Faster.* Clint's breath tightened to short, hard gasps. If he failed, Katrine would soon be gasping as well, lungs frantic for air, throat singed by the heat, chest bound by the dread of a cabin burning around her. The men threatening the homestead were once soldiers, after all, men trained in the taking of lives. A renegade soldier was a dangerous man indeed. Clint had learned they were seeking to burn a cabin to the ground tonight, but only when he'd followed a gut instinct to check on the Brinkerhoff place had he learned the blood-chilling truth.

Snapping his reins against the horse's sweating flesh, Clint pressed on toward the four torchlights circling the tiny, nearly finished dwelling in the middle-of-the-night darkness just over the hill.

Katrine had nothing to do with any of this, but that wouldn't stop the cavalrymen or the flames they were about to set. They were looking to kill her brother, Lars, the witness to their crimes, and if she happened to die as well it would be of no consequence to them.

Clint yelled out to the men, hoping to distract them and buy Katrine more time, but he was still too far away for them to hear. The knot in his gut seemed to constrict around his whole body as he watched the leader of those men. In a cruel trick of moonlight, Clint saw Samuel McGraw casually, almost amusingly, touch his torch to the roof of a shed next to the cabin. Air fled Clint's lungs in a helpless whoosh that seemed to say "too late."

No. It could not be too late. Clint yelled, "McGraw!" once, then louder, jabbing the horse with frantic boot heels. "McGraw!" Some survival instinct took over from there, turning his voice to one of conspiratorial indifference even as his insides were going off like cannons at the thought of Katrine trapped in the smoke. Even as he watched embers float lazily from the shed to settle and ignite on the homestead roof. "McGraw, it's Thornton. Hold on there!"

Finally he was close enough to see McGraw's face as he handed his torch to another man and peered in Clint's direction. "Thornton?"

Clint kept at full gallop the last few feet into the homestead yard, even as the fire began lapping up the structure's roof. "There's men behind me," he panted, hoping his breathlessness would come off as strain, not fear. "Just up over the ridge. Go." He pulled on the reins as his horse made uneasy circles, spooked by the growing fire. "Get yourselves gone. I'll cover. I'll say the place was burning when I came up on it."

He needed them to believe he was on their side if his plan to infiltrate the Black Four gang would ever work. But he also needed them to leave so he could save Katrine. McGraw, evidently one to see a job done, didn't seem too eager to be gone. Clint's heartbeat pounded ice against the heat now flushing his face. The ice threatened to swallow him altogether when he heard the sound of a bang from inside. It did swallow him when he saw the plank the soldiers had nailed across the homestead door.

"Get on out of here," he insisted as hard as he dared. "I've reason to be here, you don't. I'll cover for you but it won't do one lick of good in five minutes if you're not gone."

"He's right," Bryson Reeves, another of McGraw's cronies, said as he tossed his torch into the little set of rosebushes Katrine had optimistically planted along the east wall. Clint felt them burning as if the flames nipped at his own throat. "Let's get gone, Sam."

Clint flung himself down off his horse with what he

hoped looked like indifference. Every inch between him and that barred front door yawned long and deadly. He gestured over the ridge he'd just rushed down. "Land sakes, McGraw, are you waitin' for an invitation? Go!"

McGraw considered for an excruciating moment, Clint's throat turning to knots as he heard yet another sound from within. The Brinkerhoff homestead held no windows, no way out but the door barred behind him. He thought he heard a cough and imagined Katrine sinking to the floor, her pale hands clasping at her throat. He felt the heat of the flames prickle the back of his neck. The urge to rush over there and physically push McGraw off toward the river nearly overpowered him. He heard a small, insistent thud from the side of the house away from the men and for a terrible moment imagined he was hearing Katrine's body hit the wall.

Then he remembered the logs. The loose two logs on the far side of the house, the ones Katrine was always complaining let the wind in to chill the room. He heard more thuds and realized she was trying to kick them out. *Kick,* he pleaded to her silently as his hands fisted in frustration. *Keep kicking.*

"I'm handin' you a gift here, McGraw. Are you too dumb to take it? You've got four minutes, maybe five afore those men behind me catch up and see you standin' here with torches while this shack burns."

"Fine!" McGraw pronounced after what felt like a year, turning his horse and waving his henchmen to ride off.

Clint forced himself to stand and watch, shoving his weight back on one hip as if the burning house was just another prairie brushfire. The kicking behind him had slowed and stopped, halting his blood right along with it. Just twenty more feet. That's all he needed.

Because God have mercy on him if he had to watch one more person die…

It was as if the walls of the tiny cabin had come alive, creeping toward her like prowling animals. Katrine's eyes stung, far more from the smoke over her head than from the tears wetting her cheeks. The smoke made it impossible to shout, so she'd tried the door, but it would not open. She'd heard voices—there were men outside, but they did not open the door. They were not here to save her. The Black Four had struck again, had come to burn down the house to push her off her land. Her brother, Lars, had worried the terrible gang might someday stoop to killing, but she never imagined they would begin with her. *I'm not ready for Heaven,* she begged God, even though she knew He would welcome her. *I'm not brave enough to die.* Not like this, not trapped. Not alone.

Not yet. Turning in frantic circles, Katrine scanned the four stalking walls, searching for any help. It was so hard to see, so awful to breathe. *My Lord, my protector, save me.* She pulled in another scorching breath, seeing the edges of her vision curl in and grow dark. How could even the Black Four bear to stand out there and watch a soul burn to death?

Stumbling to the table more by feel than by sight, Katrine found a dishcloth, then the Mason jar that still held black-eyed Susans from the supper table she'd set.

The supper Lars had not come home to eat. She pulled the flowers from the jar and stuffed the dishcloth inside, the water feeling cool against the growing heat of the room.

For a stunned moment Katrine wondered why she could suddenly see, why the room glowed orange. Then, pressing the blissfully cool cloth over her nose and mouth, she peered up just in time to see a flaming chunk of the roof fall with a hollow *whoosh* and settle on Lars's bed.

Had they found Lars first? Was he already dead? Katrine's heart froze at the thought that her brother, who'd saved her from how many dangers since they'd come to America, might no longer be alive to save her now. *No, he must be alive,* she declared silently. He must live and make a future for himself in this new town, maybe a family… Her thoughts were coming in tangles now and her eyes stung so badly. Where was Lars? He'd know what to do. He'd built this cabin for the two of them; he'd know how to keep it from being their tomb. *Think, Katrine, try to think.*

The beams overhead gave a dreadful groan and Katrine backed away from the noise, grabbing the jar of water as she did. She stuffed the dishcloth into the water again, but its paltry contents didn't help much against the smoke and heat now filling the room. Why, why hadn't she fought harder with Lars to make windows? He said they would only let in the cold, but the drafty corner did that already.

The drafty corner. The pair of loose logs on the corner of the house. Oh, how she'd cursed those cracks, how they seemed to welcome the flies and dust into the room. Lars had not yet fixed them; they still wiggled when a boot kicked them hard enough. Katrine crouched down and crawled over to the corner, not caring how the split-log floor snagged on her nightshift or scraped against her knees. Behind her, gold light burst out into the room, and Katrine turned to see Lars's coverlet consumed in flames. It gave her just enough light to find the logs and shift around to start kicking.

Her shifting knocked over a chair, but she merely pushed it aside and continued to slam her bare feet against the loose wood. It shifted, but not enough. *"Flytte!"* she yelled, commanding the logs to give way in her native Danish as she kicked them again. Behind her the fire's crackle and growl seemed to come closer. Katrine moved up and began kicking with both feet, not caring about the growing pain on her heels—what would that matter in a few minutes as she lay gasping? The air seemed to race away from her, stealing the breath she needed to keep kicking. She could feel her efforts growing weaker, feel how the smoke robbed her strength.

Keep kicking. Her leg wobbled as she forced it against the log, and somewhere through the thickness of her mind she heard a voice. She thought she heard crumbling, imagined the log was pulling itself from the cabin, coming to life to save hers.

"Katrine!"

She couldn't actually say whether the voice was real or imagined. Everything was spinning into a black hole in her mind, like water draining through the bottom of a barrel.

The rush of night air hit her face like a slap, clear and startling. She heard a man's growl of effort as another log shuddered loose and fell onto the floor beside her. Air. "Here! Through here!" the voice called. Without thinking, Katrine turned and reached through the ragged opening, clinging to the hands that grabbed her outstretched fingers.

The change in air was astounding. Yellow sparks swirled against a dark violet sky as she felt herself pulled from the menacing heat. Katrine sucked down a huge draught of air, only to curl over in a cough that seemed to tear her throat into pieces. Before she could catch her breath, the hands dragged her across the cool prairie grass as the most dreadful, most unearthly sound filled her ears. A wind-filled echo, an evil rush of air such as she'd never heard before. Katrine looked up to see her home, her cabin, sprout flames from every corner and tumble in on itself, spouting in a volcano of smoke and sparks.

The fire burned hot and bright in all directions, throwing sharp light and flickering long shadows into the night. She coughed again, tasting coal and acid, and felt a hand on her back. Turning to look, she saw the face of Clint Thornton. She was safe in the grip of the town sheriff, thank goodness.

Fear widened his dark brown eyes, sweat glistened on his cheek even as it plastered the front of his dark hair against his forehead. "Are you all right, Katrine? Are you hurt?" His voice was tight and dark with worry.

Was she? She wasn't sure she even knew. Too parched to speak, Katrine managed a weak nod, giving over to the shivers that suddenly took her. She hugged herself and drew up her knees, appalled to remember she was in nothing more than a summer nightshift.

Sheriff Thornton kneeled in front of her, shucking off his coat to wrap it around her shoulders. He took each of her hands and arms in turn, checking them for cuts and bruises. His touch was quick and reassuring. Her feet throbbed and felt as if they were covered in scratches, but she could move them. She started to say, "I'm fine," but the words only became another cough. When he went to stand up, Katrine grabbed his hand, stopping him until he looked at her.

"Thank you," she managed in a thin whisper that hurt with each word. She squeezed his arm again. Sheriff Thornton was Lars's good friend. Surely he would know about her brother. "Lars? Is Lars alive?"

"Yes…and no."

Katrine felt her fear surge back up. "Whatever do you mean?"

"Lars is safe, but only if no one knows."

She blinked up at him, confused.

His dark brows furrowed. "I have a plan, Katrine, but you may not like what it is."

Chapter Two

Katrine began to come undone by the time Clint managed to get her to his brother Elijah's house. She looked up at him one more time as he brought her down off his saddle.

"You're sure there is no other way?" He hated that she was near to tears again.

It felt cruel to ask something so big of her just now, but there simply wasn't another way to keep her and Lars safe. Not that he could see. "Yes, I'm sure. This will work, and it will get me in with the Black Four so I can put them away for good. I'll convince them you were gone tonight—say you had an argument with Lars or some such thing—and that they got Lars in the fire."

"Why would they believe you?"

"Folks are always ready to believe what they want to hear." Life had taught him that, over and over. Even here in Brave Rock, people were too ready to believe the broken fences and other "accidents" that had happened in the past month weren't anything more than hard times.

This time he would make blind assumptions like that work in his favor. "They already think I'm on their side since I told them I'd cover their tracks. I've needed this chance—I can put it to good use—and it might not come again. The best way to bring the Black Four down is from the inside." He caught her elbow and felt her shiver even under his coat. "I know it's hard, but Lars would agree, I'm sure of it," he pressed, even though this was far beyond the plan he and Lars had crafted mere hours before.

"I don't like lying. Not about this." She shook her head more firmly. "How can I tell everyone he is dead?"

Clint stared hard into those big blue eyes now rimmed in red and soot. He did hate putting such a load on her like this. After what she'd just been through, it didn't seem fair. He'd seen enough of her spirit to know she was strong enough to handle it, even if she couldn't quite see it now. "You like to tell stories, you're good at it. This is a story to save Lars. To save yourself. Can you be brave, Katrine?" He dared to use her first name as he took both her shoulders. "Can you trust me in this?"

She softened a bit under his hands. "You promise me Lars is well?" Katrine sniffed, and he could feel her clutching at his arms even through the sleeves of his coat that hung down well below her hands. "That you need this story, and only for a short while?" She looked frail, as if she'd sway any moment.

A trickle of panic skittered down Clint's spine. He knew how to protect, but precious little about how to comfort. Lije was good with people, Clint's other brother, Gideon, was good with animals, but Clint had neither of those gifts. He was the sheriff here, and despite his fondness for many of the folk in Brave Rock, that meant he kept a certain distance. By personal choice and by profession. All that neighborly comfort business? That was his pastor brother's corner.

Still, as much as Katrine needed Godly comfort, he couldn't let her into Lije's house until he'd gotten her to agree to his plan. That meant that for now, he'd have to venture into those emotional waters and try to tell Katrine what she needed to hear. Looking into those impossibly blue eyes, it wasn't hard to find a soft spot from which to pull the words. Tall as she was, she felt tiny and frail under his hands, and the urge to keep her safe needed little encouragement. Those eyes could drive any man to feats of heroism, especially when framed with wet lashes and looking up from within the confines of his own coat. "I promise Lars is safe. And will be." He meant every word, gruff and hoarse as they came from his sooty throat.

She blinked back more tears, and something unknotted inside Clint. He couldn't leave all the comforting to Lije; after all, he'd placed Katrine in this spot and it was up to him to help her endure it. The compulsion to tighten his grasp on her shoulders became irresistible. He wanted to hold her up, to lend her some of his strength despite how out of his depth this all felt. "Give me a little while," he said, amazed at the unfamiliar tone of his voice. "Give me some time, and all will be well."

He saw the light come on in Lije's window. Hang

it, he didn't have time. The lawman side of him knew what had to happen now, kind or not. If he didn't get an agreement from her right this minute, all would be lost. "But this piece cannot wait. Say yes." He forced the command back into his voice, hating the flinch he felt in her shoulders. "Now, Katrine. You must say yes to this *now*."

Her eyes fluttered shut for a moment, as if the weight of her agreement pressed down on her spirit. Of course it did—he'd pressed it there himself—but he couldn't think about that now.

"Yes." It was a whisper. A frail whisper with an edge of fear he felt right down to his gut. Still, it was an agreement, and that's what he needed right now. "I understand," she went on, nodding, her voice gaining a tiny sliver of strength. "We will do this. For Lars."

"Clint?" Lije's voice came from the door as he pushed it open. "I saw flames. What is…" His expression changed as the light from the window illuminated Clint's and Katrine's soot-smeared faces. "Land sakes! Are either of you hurt? Where's Lars?"

Katrine looked back to Clint with wide, panicked eyes. For the delightful storyteller Katrine was, this tale seemed beyond her right now. Could she really do as he asked? He looked at her hard, his stare saying "Lars needs you to do this," but she blinked and wobbled a bit as if she'd just had the breath knocked out of her. He spared her any further answer by turning toward his brother and slowly shaking his head.

Clint watched as the realization spread over his brother's face. Losing Lars would be a huge blow to this community—it was precisely why he had to be "lost" now so that his life could be saved. "God have mercy. No. Not Lars."

Clint nodded even as Katrine seemed to wilt. He held her upright by the shoulders, sending her strength through his grip. This was asking a lot of her, but he knew her. She was stronger than she knew, even if she couldn't have been prepared for tonight's shock. The fire's trauma still pounded through his own blood, for that matter. How could it not still hold her in its grip? "The house went up like a matchstick," Clint said, focusing his thoughts with the facts he could safely relate. "It's a wonder I could get Katrine out through the back wall."

"You saved her life, Clint. Thank God for that."

Lije's brand-new wife, Alice—they'd just been married the first of the month—came out from behind her husband, wrapping a shawl around her nightshift. "It's dreadful, dreadful news. Bring her in here, Clint. The two of you look awful." She pulled Katrine from Clint's grip, brushing aside the blond locks that had frayed out of Katrine's long braid. "You're sure you're not hurt?"

"Ja," Katrine said meekly, lapsing for a moment into her native tongue. "I am not hurt. Not much." She coughed, hiding her face in her hands.

"No need to talk about it further. Come inside and let's get you cleaned up. Clint, you, too. I want to look at that hand." She nodded to the bloody gash on Clint's left hand inflicted by the splintered logs as he had pulled Katrine to safety.

"Give me a moment with Clint," Lije said, grabbing Clint's elbow. "I'll be inside in a minute."

"I'm *fine,* Alice," Clint insisted when Alice gave her husband a questioning look. "A bit worse for wear but nothing serious."

Alice held up a pair of fingers. "Two minutes. Then I want you inside to get some antiseptic on that arm."

Clint turned to his brother as the door shut behind the women. "Before you ask, no, it wasn't an accident. It was the Black Four."

"Lars was murdered? By the Black Four?"

Life took harsh turns out here in the territories, but Clint had learned that the four men who had come to be called the Black Four were helping things along by ensuring certain weaker settlers met with more bad luck than others. Worst of all, Clint now knew that Samuel McGraw and the other members of the local "Security Patrol" were the men behind the name. As the Black Four, these cavalrymen had done exactly what they were out here charged to prevent: cut fences, set fires, let livestock loose and a whole host of other crimes. Acts designed to intimidate folks out of their land. As a result, scared settlers had sold their stakes at cheap prices—right to a convenient buyer Clint was pretty sure was in McGraw's back pocket. Greed was alive and well in Brave Rock, Oklahoma, but all Clint had right now to prove McGraw was behind the Black Four was Lars's eyewitness testimony. The witness that the Black Four had thought they killed tonight.

Clint ran his hand down his face, still feeling the gritty soot he'd tried to wipe off several times already.

The image of that private's lackadaisical stance made his stomach churn. Evil was alive and well—and in the last place most people would think to look. "Keep this between us for now, Lije, but they nailed the door shut with her inside. McGraw set his torch to the place as easily as if he were lighting a cigar."

Lije placed his hand on Clint's shoulder. "Lord protect us." Clint saw grave worry darken his brother's eyes. "These men have people fooled and must be stopped. Clint, you have got to prove McGraw is behind everything. Any way you can."

He'd begun to do just that, hadn't he? "I intend to. Men like that will kill again if it suits them, and more easily as they go. They're going after the easy claims now, but it won't stop there. Pretty soon no one will be safe. I know how much I need to bring them to justice." After a pause, he added, "I owe that much to Lars. To his memory." He didn't like keeping Lije in the dark this way, but there was nothing for it—the fewer people who knew Lars lived, the more chances the Dane had of staying alive.

As if she'd heard his thoughts of her brother, Katrine's quiet sob came though the cabin window.

Lije's hand tightened on Clint's shoulder. "Not all was lost. You saved her life."

The skitter of panic returned and Clint pushed away the black thought of what might have happened if he'd been even five minutes later. "Barely."

"In these parts, barely's enough. Come inside and let Alice tend to you. The fire's out, and there's nothing to be done until daylight."

It must be near two in the morning, but even though every bone in his body ached, Clint was sure no sleep would come to him tonight. He couldn't leave Katrine right now. Not only wasn't it wise until he knew she could maintain the deception, but a part of him felt responsible for her now. He'd saved her life. He'd inserted himself into a crime and had thrust this simple, gentle woman into a dangerous game. He'd tangled with the cavalrymen by choice, in order to see justice done. Katrine? She'd only been in the wrong place at the wrong time.

He pushed through the door to find her slumped and still shaking at Lije's table. He'd always thought her quietly strong, but she looked to be made of glass right now.

"Are you hurt?" Clint asked as gently as he could. He didn't think she was, but *Are you all right?* wasn't even a question worth asking.

"Her feet are badly bruised from kicking," Alice offered, gathering up the ash-blackened cloths that sat beside the wash bowl. Katrine's hands fared no better, for red scrapes marred the too-pink skin of her scrubbed hands. "It's awful." Alice's voice broke. "Poor, dear Lars."

Clint caught Katrine's eyes and silently told her to hold on just awhile. "I'll bring Lars's killers to justice," he declared to her more than anyone else. "So help me I will."

Even though daylight came through Elijah and Alice's windows, Katrine felt as if she were still surrounded by darkness. Sunshine did nothing to bring her peace. She wondered how she would get through another hour—much less an entire day—of telling people Lars was dead. Already she had watched them mourn her brother and offer her comfort. Much as she trusted Sheriff Thornton's judgment and wanted to keep Lars safe, these few hours had fed Katrine's doubts that this plan would work.

Breakfast was barely finished before Alice resumed dabbing more disinfectant onto one of the deep scratches. The woman who served as Brave Rock's nurse offered a sympathetic smile. "Nasty stuff, isn't it? Trust me, an infection would be a lot nastier. And hurt more." Alice peered at the wound on Katrine's arm once more, then began to wrap it in a bandage. "God was watching over you last night. I know you've lost much, but you haven't lost your life."

Katrine looked at the cabin's table. Already it had begun to fill with food and other gifts of comfort from the good people of Brave Rock. "I have lost Lars," she whispered. It wasn't as hard to say as she feared. After all, it was true, at least for now, wasn't it? She didn't even know where he was, only that Sheriff Thornton had promised he was safe. She had prayed all night that it was true.

Alice sat down opposite Katrine and took her good hand. "I'm so sorry, Katrine. We all are."

"Thank you." Katrine didn't know what else to say. She wanted people to leave her alone, but she didn't want to be alone, either. Fears and worries tumbled around her head, muddling her thoughts when they needed to be clear.

"Lars would be glad you were spared though, wouldn't he?" Alice was trying hard to make her feel better, only no one really could accomplish that. She and Sheriff Thornton were alone in bearing the truth of what had really happened. "He'd be glad Clint was able to save your life," Alice went on when Katrine failed to reply. "Maybe in time you will be able to let that give you comfort."

The only thing that gave her comfort right now was that Sheriff Thornton had told her he was going to see Lars. Soon Lars would know all that had happened; soon he'd know to remain wherever he was and stay safe. When this was all over, Lars would be safe. Sheriff Thornton had told her to hang on to that thought, and she desperately needed to do so.

"I think it comforted Clint to be able to save your life. He's lost his good friend as much as you've lost a brother. The whole town will feel the loss, but you two most especially." Alice packed up her medical kit, nodding toward the kettle on the stove in a silent invitation to have more tea.

"Yes," Katrine agreed, but for different reasons than Alice meant.

"Our good sheriff," Alice said, a sigh in her voice. She brought two cups to the table and returned to her seat opposite Katrine. "Clint is a fine man. Oh, he can be a bit surly, and not a little bit lost, but he's as loyal as the day is long." Alice raised an eyebrow. "And not so bad to look at, hmm?" Katrine saw Alice's thumb run across the shiny gold band of her new wedding ring.

"It's good to have a loyal man in your life. Especially one who saved your life."

"I'm grateful to him. Really I am." Katrine would have to be blind to miss the glow in Alice's eyes. The new bride was so happy.

"Just grateful? Nothing else?"

Sheriff Thornton was a fine man to look at, but he seemed hard and dark and some days he seemed far beyond the ten years older she knew him to be. Every once in a while, at town gatherings or the many meals he had shared with Lars and her, she would catch a glimpse of something warm behind his eyes. A long look, a detail noticed, a fragment of something beyond friendship. Even Lars had said something once, but with such an air of dismissal Katrine could easily guess Lars would never approve should the sheriff display open interest of that sort.

No, Sheriff Thornton's regard for her seemed far closer to bafflement than anything more familiar. In truth, Katrine felt as if Sheriff Thornton had a long list of ideas of how the world should be and couldn't decide where she fit on that list. More than once, the tenor of his regard had made her wonder if he'd somehow learned her secret. That wasn't possible, of course, but he was a lawman, and maybe they had ways of finding things out she didn't understand.

It was true—Katrine was lots of things besides grateful, but none of those could be put into words. Certainly not this morning. Today words felt like her enemy— at least every word that wasn't from Sheriff Thornton about Lars. Katrine was grateful a knock on the front door kept her from having to continue this conversation.

Alice raised an eyebrow, silently asking if Katrine was ready to accept visitors. She hadn't faced a single one yet.

"No." Katrine shook her head, left the tea in its cup and fled to the bedroom. It was easy to convince Alice that she was too upset to receive condolence calls. *Father God, help me. I don't know how I'll lie to all these good, grieving people.* The whole thing tangled her stomach up in such knots that it wasn't much of a fib to say she was feeling poorly.

As she heard Alice talk with someone about what a fine fellow Lars was, Katrine sat on the bed and remembered what it felt like to be pulled from death's smoky clutches. Her throat seemed to tighten at the mere memory of that awful, acrid smell. She'd bathed again this morning and still felt as if she couldn't wash the scent from her skin. *I will choose to be thankful. For my life. For Lars's life. For Sheriff Thornton's bravery and for trust in his wisdom. You have made this way, have given us a chance to protect Lars's life, and I will do it. But You must know how hard this is for me.*

"I agree," she heard Alice say. "He was a hero indeed. I am glad he is sheriff, too. These are perfect and much needed, thank you." And then, in a lighter tone of voice, "Why yes, we're very happy. Thank you for your good wishes. I'll be sure to let her know you came by."

Katrine could barely rise up off the bed when Alice opened the door. "Everyone has such kind words for you, and such fond memories of Lars." She lifted up one skirt from the armful she held. "Deborah Kincaid is much closer to your size. These will fit you so much better than my clothes until we can get new ones."

So much generosity and compassion. Brave Rock was going to be a wonderful place to call home.

But home was gone now, wasn't it? No, she would try not to think of it like that. Just the cabin was gone. The cabin with those blessed, blessed loose logs she'd complained about so often.

"Alice, I'm not sure I can go."

"Where?"

"This afternoon. Sheriff Thornton said he'd bring me back to the cabin to see what was left, but I don't think I am ready." She used her good hand to wipe away the tears, which seemed to come so easily. "We only had a few things from Mama and Papa to remember them by, and they will be gone."

Alice put a gentle hand over Katrine's. "They may, but they may not. Wouldn't it be better to know?"

"I don't want to see our home in ashes." Katrine felt the words burn her throat all over again. "I don't want to see what those men did to Lars. To me."

"Elijah and I will go with you and Clint, if you'd like. You'll have to go over there sometime. Perhaps it's best to get it over with right away."

Katrine shook her head. If Elijah and Alice were with her, Thornton could not talk of Lars. Nor could they talk freely here. No, if she wanted to hear of Lars, she had to go see the cabin. What a gruesome bargain that was. "If twelve people were to come with me it will not help. I must find a way to be brave, *ja?*"

Alice straightened her shoulders and took Katrine's hands. "You are brave. And strong. And God is braver and stronger still. Hold on to that. Can you do that?"

Without Lars beside her? It seemed impossible. "Alone? I don't know."

"That's just the thing, Katrine, you're not alone. Not even close."

Chapter Three

"Well now, look what the wind dragged over the prairie!" Sam McGraw scraped a match across the bottom of his boot and lit the thin cigarette that hung from his lips. Most frontier men rolled their own tobacco, but somehow McGraw and his partners in the Security Patrol always managed to have fine store-bought cigarettes. Clint had wondered more than once how men of a lowly private rank came by such luxuries, but he'd seen enough of how government worked to know sometimes hard jobs came with special privileges. And Clint was no stranger to just how hard it was to keep folks in line before and during the Land Rush.

The fact that he felt McGraw had done a mighty poor job of it, well, he'd just have to keep that to himself a while longer. A uniform didn't automatically earn a man respect in Clint's view, but it was clear that's how McGraw saw the world.

The private tipped his navy blue cavalry hat farther back on his head and squinted up at Clint in the late-morning sunshine. "I was laying odds we wouldn't see you again."

"Funny," Clint said as he swung down from his saddle. "I had the same notion about you." He slapped the dust off his hat. The ride down the riverbank from Brave Rock wasn't that far, but it had been hot and dry. "I couldn't rightly say I wouldn't have just kept on riding after that fire. Or worse yet, if you were simply going to circle back around and shoot me where I stood. Loose ends are bad for business."

McGraw laughed. "Well, some loose ends do indeed require a snip." He raised an eyebrow at Clint. "Others are useful enough to leave hanging."

"Hanging? Or swinging from a gallows?" McGraw looked to Clint like the kind of man who wouldn't think twice if a lynching served his purpose.

McGraw waved the match out and flung it to the ground. "You are a funny one, Thornton. Sending men to the gallows is your job, not mine."

Actually, law and order decreed it was the county judge who condemned men to hang, but Clint didn't really feel like arguing the point with the likes of this man. Clint had seen enough in life that very few things repulsed him, but everything about Samuel McGraw set Clint's gut to churning. McGraw gave him that slanted smile of his, and all Clint could see was the loathsome grin the private had given him as he rode off last night. As if the whole world tilted around the Black Four and his every whim. Every second Clint spent in these men's company felt ten seconds too long.

Get on with it, Thornton. Finish the job you and Lars started. "Thought you ought to know, he's dead."

McGraw took a long pull on the cigarette. "The foreigner?" He spat the word out like an insult, in the tone Clint's childhood guardian, Cousin Obadiah, had used for varmints and beggars.

"Brinkerhoff's dead and gone." Clint didn't like putting such a casual air into his voice when discussing murder. "The cabin went up like straw and him in it. No body to bury, even." He pulled a canteen from his saddlebag and took a long drink, then sat down on the rock beside McGraw. He kept his eyes on his boots as he stretched his long legs out. It was easier to fool a man when you weren't looking him in the eye. "Nothin' left to save by the time anyone could have gotten there to try. No one'd seen you, neither. I asked around just to be sure."

McGraw settled his hat back down and made a self-important show of inspecting his cigarette. "Bein' all friendly-like with the sheriff does have its benefits."

"I done you four a mighty big favor." Clint leaned back, the heat of the rock feeling much better than the cool, oily sensation talking to Sam McGraw always gave him.

"A fact which does not escape my notice, Thornton." McGraw inhaled with a dramatic flourish. "Go on."

"And where I come from—where we *both* come from—debts get paid. Alliances can be highly useful. A man of your position can appreciate the value of a well-placed partnership." Clint made sure to give McGraw's position an air of admiration he didn't truly feel.

"Indeed." McGraw blew a series of complicated smoke rings that hung in the hot air like targets.

Clint leaned in. "Let's not beat around the bush, McGraw. I've a notion of what you're up to. Seems to me certain claims are falling into certain hands in a very convenient fashion. Might just be poor luck on the part of folks who aren't suited for life out here, or it could very well be something a bit more...deliberate. Four black somethings—or someones—to be exact. Makes me think it could serve a man well to be on your side of things."

"Deliberate? What exactly are you implying?" There was no defensiveness in McGraw's tone. In fact, he sounded more like he was playing a game of cat and mouse that he very much enjoyed.

"I've found it pays not to put any stake in coincidence in my line of work." Clint then offered a short list of the properties that had met with Black Four "mishaps" to scare their original owners into defaulting or selling. "It don't take much to see where things are headed. Stakes go for cheap when the owners get scared. Stakes that might not go for that low price if things had gone well for those same owners. You might say a man of opportunity could turn a tidy profit by being the right buyer comin' along at the right time."

"You might say that." McGraw looked out over the horizon, blowing out a long thin stream of smoke.

"I've seen enough to know that you might be that man. That, and I just got a whiff of how you treat your enemies."

McGraw laughed out loud at that. "Well now, we

don't charbroil everyone who stands in our way. Some of 'em just up and get shot." He gave Clint a sideways glance that belonged on a rattlesnake, not a government soldier. "Fences fall. Animals die. Wells sour."

"Accidents happen."

"Yes indeedy. It's a cryin' shame how accidents do happen."

"That's how folks view what happened to Brinkerhoff. A stray ember on a dusty night—it ain't too hard to explain away. You're the peacekeepers here, after all. But folks aren't all that dumb. Unless you're careful, someone might catch on. See something. Best to have someone pointing suspicions away from you. Someone folks are ready to believe."

"And that'd be you now, wouldn't it? The good sheriff at our disposal."

"The well-paid sheriff as your inside man," Clint corrected.

McGraw pinched the edge of his considerable mustache. He played to character with such a sense of drama that Clint couldn't help but wonder at how much McGraw relished it all. Power did that to some men. Clint had seen it dozens of times in the war. It turned men cruel, brought out the predatory animal hiding under civilized uniforms. "What sort of arrangement do you have in mind, Sheriff?"

"Nothing you can't afford—if my suspicions are correct. And I'm hardly ever wrong."

McGraw gave a dark chuckle and stubbed out the last of his cigarette on the rock between them. "I like your confidence. Okay, Thornton, you're in. By the way, what about the other one? The foreigner's pretty little sister—Katie-something, isn't it? She go down with her brother?"

Clint now tasted the bile rising in his throat, and fisted the hand McGraw couldn't see. "What do you care what happened to Katrine?"

"I found her rather fetchin', that's all. Be a shame if the world lost a pretty face just because it was in the wrong place at the wrong time. I'd be sort of sorry."

He'd be nothing close to sorry. "She wasn't there. She and Lars had a falling out the other week and she was up in Brave Rock staying with a friend for a few days."

"How fortunate for her." McGraw drew the word *fortunate* out in a way that made Clint's stomach churn. "I'd hate to have her meet with any kind of accident on account of her knowing...unfortunate facts."

A protective resolve settled around Clint's spine, cold and hard and straight as north. He would draw his last breath keeping this snake away from Katrine Brinkerhoff. "She's of no consequence, McGraw. She doesn't know what Lars saw and she'll be no trouble to you." While it bothered him to do so, he added, "She's not too bright and her English is worse than Lars's was anyways."

"Land sakes," McGraw snickered, bumping his shoulder to Clint's like they were barroom buddies. "It weren't *conversation* I was looking for anyhow."

It smelled like death.

There wasn't another way to put it. To Katrine, campfires had always smelled of home and cooking and good people gathered against the night. Today the wind blew sour, acrid scents against Katrine's face as she stood looking at what remained of the home she'd shared with Lars. *"Tak Gud,"* she whispered, forcing herself to remember no one had died here.

"Pardon?" Sheriff Thornton stood squinting into the wind, his jaw set with a kind of anger she knew he reserved for criminals. Lars had often said, "I'd never want to be an enemy of Sheriff Thornton's," and today she could see why. He would stop at nothing to see justice done. She prayed such determination would be enough to keep Lars safe.

Katrine felt her cheeks flush. "I was thanking God for our lives." As she said the words, they struck her anew. Clint Thornton had reason to be thankful for his life today, too. He had risked his life to save hers. She believed that to be an enormous thing even if he didn't seem to recognize it. "For *all* our lives." That truth—coupled with the secret they now shared—seemed to bind her to the sheriff in unsettling ways.

She walked a mournful circle around the pile of rubble, feeling as though coming here solved nothing. Half of her wanted to run, to look away and never remember the home that had stood here. Another half, equally strong, wanted to claw through the wet, black timbers to find something—anything—worth saving. A wave of fear washed over her as she came across what was left of their front door. Their *barred* front door.

She gave a small, whispered yelp at the sight, and in seconds Sheriff Thornton dashed over to stand next to her. She heard him swallow hard. "Don't think about it."

How was that possible? Threats of harm were an old, evil menace for her, a tie back to a time in her life she tried hard to forget. It seemed unfair that in one single night all the peace she'd fought so hard for had been taken away.

The sheriff reached down and lifted up a curved piece of metal. Katrine recognized it as the decorative iron latch that had been on their door—one of the things Lars had brought from home. It was covered in soot, wet and bent out of shape.

He'd meant it as a hopeful gesture, but it made Katrine recall the terrible moment when she'd realized the door wouldn't open. The remembered feel of the door refusing to give way sent ice down her spine even now.

He saw her response. "Okay, then talk about it. Don't swallow it. It won't help."

Katrine didn't want to talk about it, but when he took a bandana out of his pocket, wiped down the latch and handed it to her, it was as if the words burst out. "There is an old Danish superstition that you must leave a window open when someone dies. To give the soul a chance to fly to Heaven. I know faith is stronger than such things, but I thought about it when I knew they had nailed the door shut. I thought, *how will my soul fly to Heaven?* We had no windows." The tears, never far from the surface all day, brimmed her eyes again.

"No one died."

"I keep telling myself that but it is not working."

"Then keep repeating it. Out loud when you can, in your head when you can't." He nodded at her, cueing her words.

"No one is dead." Her words were wobbly and insufficient.

"No one is dead," he repeated for her. Katrine found herself stunned by the compassion in his eyes. There were wounds behind those eyes. She could see their shadows before he broke the gaze and turned away.

There was a moment of raw silence until he caught sight of something and walked toward it. "Try thinking of last night this way—you made your own window."

She wiped her wet lashes to watch him turn over a log with his boot, the recognition hitting her as fierce as the wind: the corner log. He must have tossed it far enough from the cabin when he pulled it out of the wall, for it hadn't fully burned. When he bent to another, she knew that both logs of her "drafty corner" had somehow survived the fire.

Sheriff Thornton squatted down and inspected the logs. "You should save these," he said, turning to her as she walked closer. "Build them into your new home."

Katrine recoiled at the thought. "Why?"

"Lije says the strongest people make peace with their scars. You were brave to fight your way out last night, and you're being mighty brave to do this now. It'd be good to remember."

Remember. Was it worth it to remember when all the ashen pieces of home were blowing away in the wind? A black flake of charred wood settled on her hand and she flinched as if it still burned. "I think I might rather forget. Or not. I just do not know." The tears threatened again.

To her surprise, the sheriff rose and carefully settled

the logs on one end, like an odd little row of order in all the destruction. He extended a hand. "Maybe you don't have to know yet. Lars would want you to see what else can be saved. Maybe it's more than you think."

She let him pull her closer to the blackened pile, still smoking in some places. With a tenuous smile, he pulled a pair of gloves from his pocket and began picking through the debris. She watched him for a moment, then began walking around the collapsed house, trying to feel Lars's encouragement but failing miserably. She spied half a blackened bowl and swallowed hard. The two new bowls brought by neighbors couldn't really replace it. New wasn't always better, was it?

"Well now, look here!" Katrine raised her gaze to see Sheriff Thornton holding Lars's favorite tin coffee mug, the blue enamel still visible under spots of black soot and a considerable dent. He used his glove to wipe away some of the soot. "He'll want this back, I reckon."

He said it like a secret. He'd said over and over that this deception was necessary, that it was the best way to keep Lars safe, and Katrine wanted to believe him. Neither Lars nor the sheriff truly knew why this was so hard for her, but that had to stay a secret, as well. She lifted her chin to the sheriff. "I want to see him."

Thornton came down off the pile and stood in front of her. "You know I can't do that."

Katrine felt the urge to stamp her foot in a childish fit. All the pain and loss was boiling up inside of her, and he'd told her not to swallow it, hadn't he? "You could find a way. Do you know what it is like to sit in your brother's house and hear people talk of Lars dead?

They bring me food and clothes and they cry over my loss. It is awful. I want to run away, but…" She flung out her arms at the mound of ashes in front of her. "I have nowhere to go now, do I?"

"You could build a mansion out here and it'd be no good if men like McGraw are free to take it from you!"

She spun on him. "So it was McGraw!" The shouts from outside the cabin that horrible night clicked in her memory. Lars had hinted that he knew something about the men, but wouldn't say outright, claiming she was safer not knowing. That hadn't proved true, had it?

The sheriff kicked a fallen beam. "Hang it, I wasn't supposed to say." He pointed at her. "You forget you heard that. You're in enough of a spot as it is."

She had to agree with that. "I don't like the way he looks at me."

"Well, I don't either," he said quickly, then ran his hands down his face as if he hadn't wanted to admit that. "It's gonna be fine. I'll get him. I'm already in with the load of 'em. We just need to get through this part until I have enough proof to put the Black Four away for good."

"I need to see Lars." She knew it was pointless, but she couldn't help saying it. Without hearing Lars's voice, without looking into the strength of his eyes, she wasn't sure she could keep up this dangerous game. She waited for Thornton's temper to rise at her childish insistence.

He sighed instead, walking over to hand her the battered mug. It wasn't much of a peace offering, but he was trying, she could see that. "How about I take him a message? Write him a note, and I'll bring you back his reply. Will that help?"

It wasn't like seeing Lars, but it would have to do. "Yes. Yes, it would help very much."

Chapter Four

An hour after returning Katrine to Lije's house, Clint rode out of town toward the Cheyenne reservation. He wandered through the open prairie, following the hunting trails Lars used, deep into the wilderness where only those most familiar with the countryside would venture out. He watched the stones along the path until he began to see piles of three stones—carefully laid so that they looked natural and would not catch the eye of anyone not looking for such clues. When Clint saw three piles close together, he stopped his horse along the series of rocks Lars had marked and gave a long, low whistle. He waited, watching a hawk loop overhead, then gave the same whistle again.

A minute later, a long low whistle floated down from the rocks to his left. Lars was here, and Lars was safe. He'd known that, of course, but he was still relieved to see his friend's face peering out. All the talk of death and mourning he'd left back in Brave Rock made it a double joy to pull the pack of supplies off his saddle and climb up to shake Lars's outstretched hand.

"It is good to see you, Thornton!" The man looked strained and tired as he accepted the pack from Clint. "How does our plan go?"

Their original plan had been for Lars to "lie low," to be out hunting for a while just to ensure McGraw and his men didn't try anything rash. They hadn't been sure McGraw knew Lars had witnessed them planning to go so far as to burn down a home.

Up until last night, there was still a chance Clint and Lars were wrong. That chance had burned with Lars's home. Clint considered it a blessing Lars was far enough out of town not to see the flames or smoke. For all Lars knew, Brave Rock had spent a quiet night.

"Not well. Not well at all." Clint took a swig from his own canteen he'd brought up with Lars's supplies.

Lars froze, his hand stilled inside the pack. "What has happened?"

No sense beating around the bush—there was no good way to deliver the news he bore. "I'm in with McGraw's men."

"That is good, *ja?*"

"Not the way it happened. Lars, you need to know that Katrine's safe, but I've had to tell folks you're dead."

"What? Why?"

"Sit down, this is gonna take a bit of explaining."

Lars motioned them into the small cave he'd often used while hunting, lifting the leather flap that served as both door and disguise. The shelter within was cool and comfortable, fitted with a makeshift pallet, rock table and stacks of supplies. "I do not understand," Lars said, gesturing for Clint to sit on the pallet while he sat on another rock. "Why should I worry about Katrine and why are you telling people I am dead? This was not our plan and I am very sure I am alive."

"You were right—McGraw was planning to burn a home down. *Your* home."

"Our cabin?"

"Burned to the ground last night. Meant to burn you down with it, near as I can tell. That tells us for sure he knows what you know. Somehow, he's found out you saw enough to link him to the Black Four. That means you're not safe until they're behind bars, so I thought it best to let him think he'd succeeded in killing you."

Alarm widened Brinkerhoff's bright blue eyes. "And Katrine?"

"I got her out in time." The remark felt like putting that terrible night in too simple terms, but Clint would rather avoid the details. It would do Lars no good to know how cruel McGraw had been. The Dane did not need to hear of bloody feet or choking gasps or how the door was nailed shut. If Lars pressed him for details, he'd simply couch it in terms of Katrine's desperate, brave escape. "But all of it burned. Katrine is staying with Lije and Alice. She's fine enough, and she knows you are alive, but...well, I'm sorry." Again, those two words didn't seem near enough for what had happened, but Clint didn't think this was a good place for particulars.

Lars muttered something in Danish. "I had expected trouble, but not this. Dangerous. These men are more dangerous than we thought. This is not a fence or a well.

These were lives. To seek to kill like that." He looked up at Clint. "To kill me."

"That's just it. If they thought you were still alive, they'd try again. Surely you can see that. You've got to know that you and Katrine are safer this way."

Lars's furrowed brow—altogether too much like his sister's—told Clint his friend wasn't quick to agree. "This was not our plan. I don't know."

"It's not a perfect plan, and it's hard on Katrine, but…"

"And Winona—she does not…"

In all his planning, Clint hadn't thought to consider Winona Eaglefeather. The Cheyenne woman and Lars had been growing close during her many English lessons with Lije. Lars spoke the Cheyenne tongue fluently, and while Clint had always put their closeness down to the language, it was clear now that feelings between them ran deeper than mere translation. This plan was getting more complicated every minute. "Look, Lars," he reasoned, "it can't be helped. She can't know." He started to say, *We're playing with fire as it is,* but stopped himself to simply utter, "The more people know you're alive, the more dangerous this gets."

"Winona cannot think I am gone," Lars argued. Then, as if his feelings for her weren't reason enough, he added, "And she can help."

She could, in more than just practical ways, but it was still a bad idea. "Not yet. Not until we know what we're dealing with." When Lars only offered another frown, Clint added, "We'll get you back to life as soon as possible, but for now you'd best stay dead. For your own sake as well as Katrine's. And maybe even Winona's."

Lars blew out a frustrated breath. Clint waited until the Dane came around to his line of thinking. Finally, Lars turned and asked, "They believed you? Truly?"

"I made it in their best interest to believe me. After you and I talked about them likely burning down someone's home, I got a bad feeling."

"You and your hunches." Lars was forever kidding Clint about his gut instincts where crime was concerned, and how funny he found the American term for it.

"If McGraw had any inkling you were on to him…" Clint shrugged off a chill despite the hot day. "I couldn't shake that hunch, so I rode by your cabin on the way back to town just to be sure." He looked away from Lars, not wanting his good friend to be able to read any of last night's dread in his eyes. "That's when I saw the torches. They were setting your shed on fire by the time I got there. They weren't even trying to make this look like an accident. McGraw's gotten so cocky he wasn't even wearing a black bandana." The use of dark clothes and black bandanas had earned the mysterious gang its name. Clint forced the sound of the crackling rosebushes as well as the sickening thump of Katrine's kicking from his memory. "It came to me in a flash, but I had to act right then and there. I had the perfect chance to show I'd be loyal to them, to get in close enough to be ready for whatever the Black Four planned next. I took it."

"It was a big chance to take." Lars shook his head.

"Katrine is safe with Elijah and Alice. Lije, Alice, Gideon—they all think you're dead. They're taking it pretty hard, actually. Folks have brought Katrine food and supplies and all kinds of comfort."

"Of course they would. Brave Rock is a good place with good people."

"Well, tomorrow morning, you're Brave Rock's first funeral."

Lars gave a shiver. What man wouldn't at hearing talk of his own funeral? "It is not an honor I enjoy."

"I don't like it any more than you do, but a chance like this to get in with McGraw may not come again. This is the safest place for you to be. You just need to keep your head down until I've got enough proof to expose McGraw and his men as the Black Four. It's our original plan, and it still holds. It's just a mite more... complicated now."

"And Katrine? You are sure she is not in danger?"

He wanted to give Lars an outright no, but found he couldn't. "I hope not. I've convinced McGraw she doesn't know anything important." She surely knew enough to be in danger now, but he left that out. He also left out the near-lecherous tone the private had used when discussing her. Lars was protective of Katrine, but Clint was about to double those efforts. That louse would never get within a mile of her. "He's got better things to do right now, anyways." Clint leaned in and held Lars's gaze. "He's plotting more 'accidents,' and I aim to know what they are so we can catch all four in the act."

Lars's eyes narrowed. "Brave Rock will be no place to call home until they are gone."

Clint suddenly remembered the most valuable provision he'd brought. "Here. It's a message from Katrine. I told her I'd bring one back from you. She'll be just fine if she can hear from you." Clint handed over the folded note, envying the eagerness with which Lars snatched it from his hands. Family meant everything out here.

Ducking out of the cave to give Lars some privacy, Clint surveyed the landscape. If a man had to carve out a future somewhere on this earth, Oklahoma Territory was a fine place to do it. The rolling green plains begged for homesteads, the clear air gave a man space to think. Plagued with growing pains as it was, there was a brand of fierce hope out here that Clint had never found anywhere else. The kind of hope that made a man feel capable, almost unstoppable. It egged a man on to grabbing his slice of the future with both hands.

Clint's two brothers, Elijah and Gideon, had surely grabbed their futures with both hands. Not only had they settled lands, but settled their hearts, as well. The iron-clad trio of the Thornton brothers was still there, but it had widened to include two women—wives, now, actually. Lije and Gideon had wives. Within Clint, marvel battled with a hefty dose of envy. He'd never quite forgiven God for making him want a big family—a whole noisy passel of sons and daughters—and then taking away his ability to do so. Back when Cousin Obadiah told him that disease "cursed" him to never be a father, he'd been too young to understand what a curse it truly was. Now he was old enough to feel its weight every single day.

Lars's groan behind him pulled him from such thoughts. "She is not telling me everything, Clint. She is very upset and picking words with care. Watch over her for me, will you?"

"Just a while, Lars. She's strong enough to hang on that long."

Lars came and stood next to him, handing him a reply to bring back to Katrine. "I want your word, Clint, that you will protect her."

That was easy to give. "You have my word, Lars. On my life, she'll be safe."

The oath took a bit of the strain out of Brinkerhoff's face, but not all of it. "I will hold you to that, friend."

Clint grasped his friend's arm. "One thing I'll ask in return."

"Of course."

"When you build your new home, give it windows. Two."

The Dane's brows shot up. "Windows? Why?"

Clint allowed himself a slip of a smile. "It's a long story for another time."

The next day Katrine looked up from taking in a skirt that had been given to her—thankfully long enough for her tall stature but big enough to fit her and Lars inside, it seemed—to see Clint riding up to the house. The sight was a mixed blessing; she knew Clint would bring news of Lars, but it stung to know Clint could visit him while she could not.

"I've found something over at the homestead you ought to come see," he said, more for Elijah and Alice, who were bent over a box of new medical supplies Alice had received. The way he caught Katrine's eye, she knew that remark to be a ruse in order to bring news of her brother.

"Of course I'll come," Katrine said, then winced at the thought of how falsely cheerful she sounded. She was truly delighted to hear how Lars fared, but her words sounded unnatural.

"Take the wagon," Alice suggested. "And while you're at it, take some of that ham Mrs. Gilbert sent over. There's enough food in this house for a dozen church picnics. In fact, take a whole picnic and go sit by the river before you go." Alice cocked her head to one side and eyed Clint. "You're too thin. When's the last time you ate a good meal that wasn't at our table?"

"Alice, leave him be," Elijah chided with an affectionate smile. "Thornton boys have survived life long before wives fussed over us."

Clint looked as if he didn't care for the scrutiny. "I'm survivin' just fine, Alice. Don't you worry none."

"Still, a picnic sounds nice." Katrine put down her sewing. If she was careful, she could pack several extra things that Clint could take to Lars. "I could use a pleasant task."

Knowing looks shot between Alice and Elijah. The hour before, Katrine had sat with the couple and set the order for Lars's memorial service. The task was far from pleasant and made Katrine's heart feel sour and heavy.

The minute the wagon pulled out of earshot, Katrine let out the frustrated sigh that had been building all day. "How much longer?"

Clint needed no further words to know the subject of her question. "Can't truly say. Longer than you'd like, I know."

Katrine looked at the sheriff. "How am I to get through the service tomorrow? All those mourning people? What will they think of us when they learn their sadness did not have to be?"

Clint pulled the horses up and turned to face Katrine. "They'll be glad you did what was needed to keep Lars safe. They'll be worried for you and wanting to help you get back on your feet—which you'll need to do no matter what. You can't stay with Lije and Alice forever."

"Certainly not." Katrine shut her eyes at the thought. Elijah and Alice were wonderful—compassionate and helpful—but their affection and closeness had only served to make Katrine more lonely for her brother. More lonely in all sorts of ways.

Clint looked surprised. "Everything been all right? Lije and Alice treating you well?"

How could she talk of such loneliness with Sheriff Thornton? "No, no, they are wonderful. It is just…" There weren't even Danish words for the tangle of her thoughts.

"They're hard to be around sometimes," Clint offered. "All that happiness wears on a person."

"Yes!" Katrine let her relief whoosh out in the single word. She could almost laugh at the pained way Clint made a face.

She did laugh at the oh-so-accurate imitation Sheriff Thornton did of his pastor brother's besotted smile. "All that 'dear' this and 'darling' that." He joined in her laughter, and Katrine felt the weight of grief slide off her shoulders. She had not laughed since the fire, and it felt wonderful to remember there was still joy to be had in the world. "Still, I'm glad to see him so happy. He's a good man and they're good for each other, I think. Not everyone's suited to be on their own."

"Yes," Katrine agreed, more quietly this time. "That is true."

"He's fine, Lars is." Clint turned the cart down the path that led to where her home used to stand. "Worried about you. Worried about Winona."

"Winona." Katrine had not seen the Cheyenne woman since the fire. Word was she had stayed on the reservation since that night. "Lars cares for her, I think."

"I think so, too. He asked me to tell her, especially since she can travel easily between the reservation and the…where he's hiding out." Katrine could tell Sheriff Thornton was taking care not to offer clues to Lars's location. She liked that some part of him considered her strong and brave enough to venture out looking for her brother.

"Someone else who can see Lars while I cannot." She failed to keep the frustration out of her voice.

The sheriff looked down at her. "I told him no." There weren't many people in Brave Rock who could tower above her like that, but it was more than his height that gave Clint Thornton his air of command. "Lars is going to have to do this alone. Don't be thinking this isn't as hard on him as it is on you. He wants to come home, too." As he said those last words, the wagon pulled next to the ashes. "Well, when home is…"

Suddenly Katrine did not feel at all like picking through the remains of her house. "I think we should have that picnic now."

The sheriff looked puzzled. "You do? I figured that was just a way to scuttle off some food for Lars."

So he had come to the same plan as she. "Well, yes, but…" She stared at the pile of charred timbers, then pulled the napkin off the basket in her lap. "I would rather eat ten muffins than deal with that today."

An amused smirk filled the lawman's often-serious features. "Ten, huh? How many did you bring?"

"Too many. I made too many. I needed something to do."

"Lars told me you bake when you worry." He bit into a muffin. "They are fine indeed. But I'm fond of that bread you make, too."

"Kartoffelbrod?"

"That's it. Tasty, in a different sort of way."

Katrine smiled. "It is Lars's favorite."

"Well, I'll be sure to go on about it when we get back to Lije's. That way you can make me two loaves and I'll be sure to pass one on to Lars."

It would feel good to be able to send bread along with her next message to Lars. "I'd like that."

"See?" the sheriff said as he swung down off the wagon. "This ain't as hard as you think. Just requires a bit of thought and patience, that's all. Think of it like making up one of your stories."

This was nothing at all like making up charming stories to entertain. This was life-and-death and dark secrets that could get Lars killed.

Chapter Five

Friday morning, Clint stared at the back of the building that would become the church of Brave Rock and watched the shadows of the people who had just filed out of Lars's memorial service. He'd known Lars would be mourned, even prepared himself for it, but was not ready for how the sorrow would cut him to the quick. People were downcast, buckling under what seemed a gruesome tragedy, yet still clinging to their faith. It was the first time he felt as if the weight of this plan might be too hard to bear.

"He was good to many, but an especially good friend to you." Lije's voice was as close as the hand Clint felt on his shoulder. "I know you would have saved him if there was any way. We all do. I'm so sorry."

He'd kept the truth from Lije for an essential reason, but still he felt the wedge it placed between them. There always seemed to be a gap between Clint and his brothers, but today it yawned wider still. His life was forever destined to be different from theirs, solitary even if it was full of purpose.

Sitting next to Katrine hadn't helped. It was both soothing and unnerving to be near her since the fire. The truth they alone knew made him feel close to her—and yet that closeness managed to open up a black hole of lonesomeness at the same time. The sad service had shown him how much Katrine would need to lean on him while this plan played out. Only, Clint wasn't the sort of man who could offer that kind of support. She would need someone else—some person other than him to turn to for comfort. It'd be easy—but wrong, and dangerous—to pull in Lije. Clint needed someone who could ride out of town often without raising any eyebrows.

Lars was right; he needed Winona's help. She'd spent a good deal of time with Lars, didn't interact much with most of the Brave Rock folk, and rode back and forth between town and the reservation many times each week.

Lije seemed to follow his gaze to the Cheyenne woman as she stood with her nephew Dakota. "I'm glad Winona felt welcome to come. You were good to invite her. I want her to see how faith takes away the sting of death for those of us who believe."

Leave it to Lije to paint Clint's actions with the brush of faith. He'd extended the invitation because Clint knew Lars was fond of the young woman. Lars also confessed to a soft spot for Dakota, the half-white boy who had been abandoned by his white father. Lars had talked in admiring terms of how Winona had stepped up to take the boy in, how it took courage to do so.

Well, it would take courage to step into this dangerous circle he'd drawn around himself, Lars and Katrine. Clint nodded at his brother. "I was thinking she'd be good company for Katrine. She's started to attend services regularly, and Katrine will need someone to sit with her with Lars gone."

"There is no doubt I see her drawn to our faith, and she's taken to English like lightning—even though I have to say I credit Lars for that much more than myself." Lije eyed his brother with one eyebrow raised. "Still, I can't help saying how much I think *you* are good company for Katrine."

Clint frowned. "I think not."

"Why?"

"You know why." Lije never did understand Clint's reluctance to take a wife, forever pushing him in the direction of relationships that weren't to be. Despite his endless compassion, Lije seemed blind to how the subject felt to Clint like God's cruelest burden. Lije could start a family whenever he wanted, had even been engaged once, but had lately insisted on being single until Alice stole his heart back in Boomer Town. In contrast, Clint wanted nothing more than a big, noisy houseful of young'uns but could never sire children. The childhood disease hadn't taken Clint's life—he knew he should be grateful for that when so many in Pennsylvania died that winter—but it had taken almost more than Clint could bear. Lije couldn't see how a wife but no children could never be enough for Clint, how it was less painful never to marry at all.

"She needs a friend," Lije replied. "That's all I'm saying."

Clint could not be a friend to Katrine. The tiny part of him that had come to think of her in ways that went beyond friendship had taken firm root the night he pulled her from the burning cabin. His mind strayed to the beautiful statuesque blonde too much lately.

"Which is exactly why I brought up the subject of Winona."

Lije shot him an older brother "you're not fooling me" look and began stacking hymnals as if they were discussing something ordinary rather than the long-painful subject it was. The church was nearly complete, with some walls up all the way and others still sporting bits of tent tarping to keep out the blazing June sunshine. The fact that Lije had enough hymnals to stack was a minor wonder in itself. "Katrine looks at you the same way you look at her—when you aren't looking of course, or when you think I don't see. But I saw it. Alice did, too."

Clint began stacking hymnals just to give his hands something to do. "So you and Alice are in on this together, are you?" Sometimes Lije could be too much the elder brother, all full of "sage" advice when Clint would prefer he kept to his own on some matters.

Lije offered him one of those "I know better than you" smiles just then. "Actually, Alice brought it up first. Once I was looking for it, it wasn't that hard to see." Thumping the last stack down on the church's back bench—still without a laid floor, the church sported rows of benches where pews would one day sit—Lije planted his hands on his hips. "You mind telling me what's so awful about the prospect of you and Katrine Brinkerhoff?"

He was going to make him say it, wasn't he? "Stop."

Lije's sigh was long and weary. "Not every woman pines for a family, Clint."

As if he didn't know that. As if he hadn't considered the foolish notion that somewhere out there might be a woman who would welcome a man with his particular set of shortcomings. The war had filled the world with pretty young widows, already-made families in need of fathers, but he wasn't the sort of man who could take that on.

"This one does. I've heard Lars speak of it, and her, too. Besides, a body can't hardly make it out here without a big family, even you know that." He let out a sigh ten times wearier than his brother's. "It ain't to be, Lije. Leave it alone."

"God crafts families in many ways."

He'd heard that line before, too. He'd heard every single platitude on that subject. "I said *leave it,* Lije." He walked out of the church, needing to put some wide open space between himself and his brother's meddling.

Of course, Lije followed him. "Well, then, let's talk about Katrine. She's alone now, and missing a heap of provisions besides. You just said how hard it is to make do out here with a few hands, let alone all by herself. So how do we help her? If what you say about how her place burned down is true, how do we keep her safe?"

Hadn't he done nothing but worry about that very thing for days now? "You do your job, I'll do mine. Seems you got half of Brave Rock corralled to get her settled with provisions. I'll get the homestead built back up as fast as I can while I see to her safety." It would be so much easier to tell Lije this was just a temporary solitude for Katrine, but that wasn't smart. Not until he knew more. Maybe he could keep her in safe company until this was all over. "Can't you keep putting her up in the back of the clinic for a while yet?" Alice ran the Healing Hearts medical clinic right next door.

"Of course we can. But even if you do get her cabin built back up, I'm not much for the thought of her living there all alone."

He'd thought of that. He'd spent too much time thinking on that, actually. He gave Lije the same argument he gave himself: "She spent plenty of time on her own while Lars was out tracking or on the reservation. She's made of stern enough stuff. She'll do all right once the grief clears a bit. But that might be where Winona can help, too."

In that moment, he caught a glimpse of Katrine standing off to the side of all the folks gathered remembering Lars. She stood tall and strong in the sunlight, the hem of her borrowed Sunday best dress whipping in the wind, the band of black fabric standing out like a gash against the sky-blue of her sleeve. Even her bonnet couldn't hide the strained and lonesome look he could see in her eyes.

"Winona might be good company for her, but *you* need to watch out for Katrine, as well."

Clint was never the kind of man to shirk his duties—most especially in a matter like this—but Lije didn't realize what he was asking.

His reluctance must have shown on his face, for Lije put a pastorlike arm on Clint's shoulder and said, "It's the least you can do for Lars. He'd have wanted you to take care of her, don't you think?"

Was the whole world conspiring to keep Katrine Brinkerhoff at his side? "You know I'll protect her. She'll come to no harm, I promise." He cast his eye back to the woman. She was wiping one eye with a handkerchief—one he knew to be one of the pale blue ones Lars always carried. Around her neck, on a black ribbon, she wore the pocket watch they'd found yesterday amongst the homestead ashes. Even now, her hand came up to finger the old timepiece—their father's, she'd told Clint—as she gazed off in the direction of the reservation.

Did she guess that Lars was hidden out over that ridge? Could she feel him the way Clint could sometimes sense the presence of his brothers? Families were strong like that—it's what held the world together out here where there was so much to overcome. He stared at the set of her chin and told himself again that she'd come through this okay. She'd push on through to build a fine homestead, find some good man with as much faith as Lije, and raise up a passel of children to listen to the harrowing tale of "when Uncle Lars had to disappear for a while."

He'd stay close enough to see her through. He'd bring Winona in on this dangerous game because that was the only safe thing to do. Then, when Lars could come home, he'd return to his place in the background of her life—doing a disappearing act of his own.

Katrine sat down on the rocking chair outside Elijah and Alice's home after all the congregation had gone, weary inside and out. She stared off into the horizon, wondering where Lars was and if somehow he could hear all the lovely things that had been said about him today.

"I wished I had a jar."

She looked up to see Gideon's wife, Evelyn, sitting next to her. She hadn't even noticed that the woman had sat down in the adjacent rocking chair. "Pardon?"

Evelyn offered a sad, knowing smile. "When my grandpappy died, I wished I had a special jar that I could catch all the fine things said about him at his funeral. I was so tired and sad I was sure I'd forget most of it. The stories, the compliments, that sort of thing."

"Lars was a fine man." Oh, how she hated using *was.* Her mind would shout "He still is!" every time she had to refer to Lars as if he were truly gone. Today seemed stuffed full of "was."

"Of course, I had no such jar," Evelyn continued. "But I didn't forget them, you know. Oh, maybe one or two—and there were a few stories grandmammy would have groaned to hear—but I remember all the fine words as if it were yesterday."

Katrine let her head fall against the tall back of the rocking chair. It was so soothing, to sit here and rock. *I will want one of these in my new house,* she thought, bemused to remember she had no such house at the moment, much less a chair or a porch on which to rock. "I am glad to know. I feel too weary to remember my own name right now."

"Grief is tiresome business. It wears on a soul to lose ones we love. And you've lost much more than that." She placed a brown paper package on the arm of Katrine's rocking chair. "I wanted to give you a little bit back."

"Me?" Evelyn was becoming one of her closest friends here in Brave Rock. She loved to look at Evelyn's talented sketches, and Katrine had often enjoyed telling stories to Walt, Evelyn's charming young son.

"Walt is fond of you. Now that he talks again, he has tried several times to tell me stories like Miss B's." Back when Katrine first met Walt, the trauma of his father's death had rendered him mute. Now, finding a new father in Clint's brother Gideon, Walt was an endless stream of chatter and generous affection. He loved Katrine's stories, but they'd had to resort to Miss B when Walt couldn't possibly get his five-year-old mouth around Brinkerhoff.

"I am fond of Walt." She fingered the twine on the package. It was too soft to be a book, too small to be yet another must-be-altered item of clothing. She undid the knot to pull a beautiful linen pillowcase from the wrapping. Delicate and soft as a cloud, it was embroidered along the side with familiar yellow flowers with six long thin petals. "Star of Bethlehem!" she exclaimed.

"I asked around town to see if someone had a book that would show me a flower that comes from Denmark. I thought you needed an extra touch of home. Did I get it right?"

Katrine brushed away a new wave of tears. "It is perfect." She had never felt so welcomed, so part of a community in all her years in America. If she had ever had doubts that Brave Rock was her new home, today had erased them. "Thank you so much."

"I thought you might like something that is all yours. A soft pillow is one of life's great luxuries. And a good night's sleep makes everything better." Her eyes took on a shadow of memory that spoke of experience. Evelyn had lost her first husband on the day they staked their claim here in the territories, and the land been at the center of a long argument between herself, her three contentious brothers and Gideon Thornton. The worst fights sprung from contested claims out here, where two settlers claimed rights to the same land. It had been a heated battle—one which became as much about the decades-old feud between the Thornton and Chaucer families as it was about good land. Katrine only knew the bits and pieces Evelyn chose to reveal—something about land and the war—and what her brothers and those who listened to them muttered or whispered. Despite Evelyn's loving relationship with Gideon, that rift had yet to heal. So, when Evelyn spoke of needing softness at the end of a trying day, Katrine could believe she spoke from experience.

How many sleepless nights would pass before Lars could come home? "I miss him terribly," she admitted, running her hands across the sweet yellow flowers. It had become the safest thing to say; she did truly miss him.

Evelyn only nodded. While it was clear to everyone who saw them together how much she loved Gideon, something in Evelyn's eyes told Katrine her first husband had not won her affections so deeply. When she married, Katrine wanted to miss her husband desperately whenever he was gone, even hunting. Lars was fine company, but a brother was not a husband. And a sister was not a wife. They had come to the Oklahoma territories to build whole new lives for themselves, not just to acquire land. For Katrine, that new life had always meant a happy family.

"I think you will tell your children wonderful stories about their uncle Lars one day. He was a good man, and you are a wonderful storyteller. Until then, you may tell Walt as many stories of Lars as makes you happy." She leaned toward Katrine. "In fact, I will be grateful if you steal his attention now and then. Five-year-old boys can be such a handful."

Katrine felt just enough of a laugh bubble up to let her know the day's tensions were indeed slipping from her shoulders. "I will tell him endless tales of how Lars Brinkerhoff always minded his mama." That made Evelyn laugh, as well. "I'm afraid not all of them will be true, however," Katrine went on, "for I must say Lars was not at all good about minding his mama."

"So I've heard." The deep voice startled Katrine, bursting the small bubble of happiness she'd formed with Evelyn. "Lars was fond of boasting how he was no end of trouble as a child," Clint added.

"It is true," Katrine said. "He was..." it took her a minute to choose the right English word "...precocious as a boy. What you would call a rascal, I believe."

"Now now, Katrine." Evelyn's voice was warm even though her words were chiding. "Let us not speak ill of the dead."

Evelyn's words stole the smile from Katrine's face. This was how it went every day; for seconds—when Clint was around, especially—she could allow herself to remember that Lars lived and would return. Then, like a splash of cold water, someone or something would remind her Lars needed to appear dead. The contrast was difficult to endure, exhausting at times. It made her crave time alone with Clint where she could talk about her brother in terms of life, of safety and of his return. To think just seconds ago she was giving thanks for what a supportive home Brave Rock had become. Just this moment, she would have given anything to ride out of town and hide with Lars wherever he was, away from all the compassionate, suffocating mourners.

Clint picked up on her distress and turned to Evelyn. "Could you give us a moment? I have some delicate matters to discuss with Miss Brinkerhoff. I'm sure you understand."

"Of course." She turned to Katrine. "Please forgive my earlier remark. I wasn't thinking. Lars was a rascal, I'm sure, and knowing what I know of young boys, I can hardly count it speaking ill in any case." She laid a hand on Katrine's arm. "Anything. Anything at all, you call on me. I want to help."

"I know," Katrine said, holding the soft, beautiful pillowcase tight against her chest. "I know."

The second Evelyn left, Katrine slumped back into the rocker, feeling twice as weary as she had before. She propped her elbow on the chair arm and let her forehead fall into her upturned hand. "This is too hard."

Clint sat on the porch at her feet, looking up at her with an expression of regret that caused a lump in Katrine's throat. "I know." She kept forgetting that this necessary charade was as difficult for him as it was for her. Still, he seemed so strong, so in control, where she felt like a weed tumbling across the prairie in hapless gusts of wind. "You need someone to help you."

She couldn't help it. "I need Lars." She tried not to whine the words, but the weariness had stolen all her good behavior. Evelyn was right, she hadn't slept well since the fire. She looked straight at Clint until he looked right back into her eyes and then she whispered, "Tell me he lives. I need to hear the words out loud."

"Katrine." His eyes darted around them, careful for nearby ears. "We'll go out to the cabin again tomorrow."

"I can't wait until tomorrow." She stood up, pacing the porch. She needed to hear someone else speak the words, to know she was not so fogged up in thought and pretended mourning that it was still true. To know she could call her dear brother a rascal and not be speaking ill of the dead. She turned and simply demanded it of Clint. "I cannot."

He took one look around, and for that moment she resented his role as protector. She did not want his cautionary nature. Then, to her surprise, he walked toward her. He took one of her hands and pulled her close to him. One strong hand wrapped around her shoulder, the other held her elbow. Not the full, protective embrace he'd offered her after the fire, although she could feel his desire to do so, but a careful, much-as-could-be-allowed gesture. His face hovered just above her head, close and startlingly tender. "He is alive." His words were as filled with emotion as any she'd ever heard from the sheriff. "Lars will come home."

Chapter Six

Not half an hour later, Clint found Winona Eagle-feather standing quietly on the edge of the Gilberts' property where she kept a tepee with Dakota. The Gilberts had become good friends with Winona, as they had watched over Dakota when he first arrived in Boomer Town before Winona had arrived, looking for the boy.

She still had on the plainclothes dress she had worn to the service. When she came from the reservation, she wore Cheyenne dress, but many times in town she dressed in the manner of other Brave Rock women. It was late in the day, but after talking with Katrine he knew the news he carried could not wait until tomorrow.

"I'm glad you came to the service." It didn't feel like the right greeting, but Clint couldn't find other words. "Lars spoke highly of you."

"Your fun-e-ral—" she worked the new word carefully on her tongue "—is so strange to me." When Winona had first come to Brave Rock, she could only communicate in English on the most basic level. Now, only three months later, the language came much more easily. That had a lot to do with the amount of time Lars had devoted to teaching her. Lars was an excellent instructor—already Clint had learned a great deal about the area and tracking from the Dane—but Clint knew their motivation to communicate went deeper than a grasp of English.

"Strange?" he inquired. A funeral for a living man was oddity enough, but since Winona could hardly have known that, Clint was curious about her reaction.

"Yes." She circled one hand in the air, as if reaching for the right word. "So…quiet."

He'd never had cause to see a Cheyenne funeral, but Lars had told him of the tribe's colorful spiritual ceremonies. Solemn rows of folk in black couldn't be further from costumes and fires and sacred dances. "I suppose it must look that way to you."

"When the Cheyenne mourn their dead, we place a body up high to speed them to the Great Beyond. There is much wailing and crying. Singing and telling stories."

"We tell stories—you heard Reverend Thornton tell a few about Lars as part of his message—but mostly to each other more than part of the ceremony." Lije had indeed told several heartwarming tales of the help and support Lars had given people in Brave Rock. Clint had felt his soul warm to the fact that in three short months, this prairie settlement had become a true community. He and Lars were fighting to keep that community safe, and Lars's own memorial bore truth as to why that was worth the current cost. "Lots of people stopped me in town or after the service and told me stories of Lars. People see it as a way to remember."

"And headstones." Her eyes squinted up in consideration of this unfamiliar custom. Brave Rock had no graveyard yet, but even Lije had mentioned they'd need one soon. "Reverend Thornton tells me your people put the bodies down in the ground."

"That's true, usually. Only there is no body to bury in this case." He found his words ironic, given what he had come to say. Still, it wasn't the kind of thing he could just blurt out.

"You wear black," she went on, then motioned to her own dark clothes. "We wear red." He noticed that the elaborate beaded decorations she always wore in her long black braids were a bright red today. Even in American garb, she managed to retain her Cheyenne identity. Maybe that was why Lars felt such a connection to the woman—she had a gift for moving between the two worlds of her life. Lars was little different; he seemed to slide with ease between his Danish heritage, his American future and his time spent learning hunting and tracking on the Cheyenne reservation. It's what made him such a good role model for young Dakota. Half white, half Cheyenne, the boy was struggling with who he was and where he belonged since his mother had died and his father, prior to his death, had never even acknowledged the boy's existence. The more Clint thought about it, the more Lars had in common with this aunt and her nephew. Clint would be glad to put an end to their mourning.

"We are so different," she went on. "And yet death is

sadness everywhere." He did not need to see her wipe a tear from her eyes to know she mourned Lars deeply; it was clear in the tone of her simple words.

"Can we take a walk, Miss Winona? I need to talk to you about something important. Private. To do with Lars."

She looked at him with curiosity, but turned as he gestured away from where Dakota sat working with some leather outside the tepee. "I have told you all I know. I do not know how I can help you, Sheriff Thornton."

Clint made sure they were a safe distance before he turned to her. "I have not told you all *I* know." He took a breath, fully aware he was bringing danger to Winona's door but also aware that Katrine could not go on without more support. "Lars is not dead."

Winona's eyes, already dark and large, popped wide open. "I do not understand."

"Lars is alive, but in hiding. He did not die in the fire, but we thought it best to make it look as if he had died. The men who set that fire were looking to kill him for something he had seen, and we didn't want them trying again."

"He lives?" she whispered. Her hand went to her chest, confirming Clint's suspicions that Lars had come to mean much more to her than an English tutor.

"Yes. Only Katrine and I know this, but I fear it's too much for her to bear alone."

Winona's eyes glanced over Clint's shoulder back in the direction of the church where so many people had mourned just hours ago. "A great lie."

"Yes, but a necessary one. And only for now. Lars's life is worth saving at any cost." After a moment he added, "I know you feel that way." Lars had known the reasons Clint could pull her into this; she understood the cost, and her heart would make her willing to pay it.

She paused a telling moment before saying, "You speak the truth."

"He needs supplies brought to him where he hides. And messages. I've told Katrine she can write to him but for her to visit is too dangerous. I suspect certain folks are watching her—folks who might aim to finish what they started."

"Katrine is still in danger?"

"As I said, I believe her cabin was set on fire on purpose. To kill Lars. By the same people who have been setting other fires and doing other damage." He paused a moment before adding, "Lars and I both believe we know who the Black Four are. I am trying to catch them even now, so that Lars can come home and everyone can be safe."

"A heavy task."

"One that is my job as sheriff. Only it makes it hard for me to help Lars. You, though, you slip in and out of town every day. And he is not far from the reservation." Clint was used to telling folks what to do, to giving orders and planning strategies. It felt odd to be asking, pleading even, for assistance. "Will you help?"

The Cheyenne woman did not need time to consider the weight of his request. "I will do all I can. My people owe Gaurang much, they will be glad to help."

Clint could never understand the complicated Cheyenne language which came so easily to Lars. How could an odd name like Gaurang be any simpler than Brinkerhoff? Still, he knew that was how the Cheyenne village referred to Lars, and the affection with which Winona spoke the name needed no translation.

"No one else must know, Miss Winona," he warned. "No one. I feel bad even asking you to keep this secret. There are…dangers."

"Life has many dangers, Sheriff, for red skin and for white." Her own sister, Dakota's mother, had died. Lars had told him many harrowing tales of the harsh life the Cheyenne community faced. Winona probably knew more of life's darkness than many women in Brave Rock.

"Yes, but every person who knows Lars is alive makes it harder to keep him safe. I need you to promise no one else—in Brave Rock or your village—will know Lars lives. Can you do that?"

"You have my word. Where is he?"

Clint gave details of the place where Lars was tucked away, glad to discover she knew exactly the spot he described. Her people had taught Lars all he knew of hunting and tracking in these parts—of course she knew the countryside as well as the Dane. "It is a good spot," she agreed, nodding her head. "Near water, far from eyes, good shelter."

Clint found his eyes wandering up to the ridge where he knew Lars sat hiding today. What must go through a man's mind knowing his friends and neighbors were just a mile or so away sitting at his funeral? The cost of this plan seemed to rise higher with every passing day, but still no other option presented itself. "I'm hoping he doesn't have to hole up there long. I've a mind to bring the men who tried to kill him to justice as fast as I can."

"Then I shall pray for just that," she said, folding her hands in front of her with the serene grace her people always showed. "Your brother tells me God cares about all things—large and small—and this is a very large thing."

"Whopping huge, Miss Winona." Big enough to press down on Clint's chest every waking moment. "I'm glad for your help. Miss Katrine will be, too."

Winona Eaglefeather walked up to Katrine an hour after supper, and without a single word Katrine knew Clint had spoken with her. A glow of relief spread through Katrine's chest that one more soul knew Lars was still among the living. "A hard day." Winona took Katrine's hand in both of hers. "But I have spoken with Sheriff Thornton to learn it is not as hard as I once thought."

"Yes." The reply was simple, but it held the full weight of the truth they now shared. So much had to be left unsaid, and yet Katrine felt a powerful urge to speak Lars's name, to talk of him, as if the conversation could keep him tethered to the living.

"Shall we take a walk together and remember our friend?"

"I'd like that very much." Katrine found her hand straying again to the pocket watch on its somber black ribbon. Grief—even pretended grief—was an exhausting business.

Winona led the way quietly toward the edge of the churchyard, walking toward the setting sun. "It is a good thing to watch the sun go down on a day of sadness."

Katrine rubbed her sore neck. The sky was splashed with orange and purple tones, the relentless wind settling a bit as it did every dusk. Even before all this strife, dusk had become her favorite time of day. The birds, always so loud and combative during the day, seemed to ease into softer songs. Oklahoma's continual buzzing torrent of insects died down as the sun set, but the dogs and wolves had not yet started in on their night howls. Sunrise often spoke of possibility, but sunset always spoke of peace. "I am glad to have this day finished." Katrine sighed, feeling far too little of that peace. "It has felt twenty days long instead of just one."

"Still, it is good to see such honor paid to your brother, yes?"

"Sheriff Thornton told me to look at it that way as well, but I couldn't. All those tears. All that sadness. I know it is to keep Lars safe, but it feels so cruel."

Winona nodded. "My people mourn him, too. He was kind to many of them. I will be glad when I can tell them Gaurang lives."

"Gaurang?" Lars had never mentioned his Cheyenne name.

Winona offered a bit of a smile. "While we have words that are as long as your name—" here Winona offered a cumbersome pronunciation of *Brinkerhoff* to prove her point "—it is too hard on the tongue of many of my people. Gaurang is our word for Man of Fair Skin.

It is better than the word for Corn Hair, which is what Dakota called Lars at first, don't you think?"

Katrine welcomed the laugh that sprung up at the thought of Lars answering to that name. Lars had talked of how many of the Cheyenne found his flaxen, straw-straight hair odd, but Corn Hair? "Oh, I shall have to tease him with the name when I see him again." She couldn't help but add, "It feels so long until I will see him again."

"He must miss you. He would know the pain this is causing many, and I am sure it weighs on him."

Katrine looked at the woman's dark eyes. She cared for Lars, it was clear. "When you see him, tell him I am going to be fine. We are all going to be fine." She fingered the watch hanging from her neck. "Tell him we will have a grand party when he comes back from the dead."

"His own Easter, yes?"

Well, of course it wasn't quite like that, but Katrine had to smile at Winona's grasp of the Christian faith. Easter had fallen just the day before the Land Rush, so it had barely received notice this year despite Pastor Thornton's efforts to keep the holiday. "Lars has told you of Christ's resurrection from the dead?"

"And Pastor Thornton. He has told me, as well. It is a powerful story."

"It has all the power in the world to us."

Winona folded her hands. She was a graceful, peaceful woman. Katrine couldn't help but think the Cheyenne beauty had handled today with far more calm than she had even before learning the truth. "Your Christ also said 'blessed are they who mourn,' did he not?"

"He did."

"Then many of your people and my people are blessed today."

Katrine pulled in a deep breath of the cooling air. No matter how hot and dry the day, the evening always brought a welcome breeze. It had taken her a few days to make friends with darkness again—the horrors of that night clung fast to her memory—but she could welcome the end of this day in the peace of knowing the hardest part was behind her. "You are a very wise woman, Winona. Yes, we are very blessed today." She took Winona's hand in hers. "Thank you for your friendship. I'm glad you will be keeping Lars company."

Winona returned her grasp with strong, weathered hands. "I am glad to know the sheriff is watching over you. He is a good man, as well. Strong and full of honor."

Katrine couldn't help but ask. "What name do your people give him?" For some reason, Katrine expected Winona to say something dark and serious, something like Face of Stone or Silent Guard. She couldn't imagine even the Cheyenne children giving the somber sheriff a name as funny as Dakota's initial choice of Corn Hair.

Winona's face split into a broad smile. "We only call him the sheriff, the same as you."

Katrine laughed. "Well, I think Corn Hair might have a thing or two to say about that!"

Winona's eyes were soft and warm, but they settled down to a more serious gaze. "The sheriff saved your life. My people believe that binds you in many ways. More than just the friendship he shares with your brother."

Katrine turned her gaze to the river, wrapping her shawl more tightly around her, even though the evening breeze was gentle. "He was doing his job, that's all." She almost winced at how false the words sounded.

"Did you feel close to death that night?"

Close to death. The phrase made Katrine shudder. "Far too much. The sound of the room coming down behind me—I do not know if that will ever leave my memory. When I felt the sheriff's hands pull me, I…" She closed her eyes and clenched her teeth for a moment. "I am grateful to be alive." She turned to look at Winona. "I want those men brought to justice. Whenever hiding Lars feels too difficult, I remember how much I want them brought to justice."

"The Cheyenne believe a warrior who has faced death is stronger for it. You are stronger for this, and the sheriff has the strength of facing death many times." She placed her hand over her chest. "The brave have strong hearts. My father always taught me that one strong heart knows another." Her face took on a slight glow when she added, "I believe it is true."

Katrine touched the woman's shoulder. "You believe my brother's heart is strong, don't you?"

Winona nodded, but did not speak. Even without words, her eyes betrayed the affection she had for Lars. Katrine marveled, for a moment, how very different Lars and Winona were. She could not think of a culture further from the Danish world than the Cheyenne, and yet some things were never bound by country or language, were they? "Does he know?"

Winona only blushed and lowered her eyes. "We have not spoken of this."

Yes, some things were universal across every people. "He speaks of you with warm words, Winona. I know that to be true. When all this is over, I will ask him how…how 'strong' his heart is, if you would like me to."

"No!" Winona's eyes grew wide and the hand that had been on her heart went up to cover her mouth. Katrine could only smile at her alarm, revealing as it was. "Such things come in their own time, do they not?"

"I couldn't say," Katrine offered. "But I will say nothing to Lars unless you ask me to."

"We must bring him back from the dead first. Then, as my father would say, we will let the river flow where it wishes to go."

What an astounding place the Oklahoma territories were that a Danish man thought to be dead could grow sweet on a Cheyenne woman who came to church. Some days it was easy to believe anything was possible out here on the frontier.

Chapter Seven

Saturday morning was a busy shopping day in Brave Rock, but Clint watched only one citizen as she made her way down the main street and into Fairhaven's Mercantile. He slipped into the store and stood across the room, keeping an eye on Katrine but granting her some time on her own. That is, until Clint saw Sam McGraw saunter up to her and dangle a yellow ribbon.

"Suits you, don't it? I do hope you'll allow me the pleasure of buying it for you. Seein' as you've lost so much in the fire and all, it's the least a gentleman can do."

The genteel tone of McGraw's words, the ease of his false gallantry, churned in Clint's gut. Looking on, shopkeeper Polly Fairhaven seemed totally taken in by the uniform and the gush of fake charm. She beamed at the soldier's gesture. This was why McGraw would be so hard to convict—he had everyone fooled.

Katrine's shoulders held firm and straight, even though Clint could see the white-knuckled grip on her basket from his position across the shop. "I am in mourning, sir." She pointed to the black band on her arm. Since most folks could not afford the luxury of full black mourning clothes out here in the territories, a black ribbon on their sleeves was the most practicality would allow. How very like McGraw to exploit the fact, offering bright finery to the very woman he believed he'd sent into mourning. Every time Clint felt he'd seen the depths of McGraw's menace, the man sank to new lows.

"The time will come when you no longer mourn," McGraw said. Then he added, "With all due respect for your loss, ma'am, life does go on." He held the ribbon up as if admiring how it went with her complexion. Mrs. Fairhaven tittered from behind the counter and made some comment about the cavalryman's generosity.

Clint had heard enough. He began walking toward McGraw, determined to come up with any diversion to get that snake away from Katrine. "McGraw! There you are."

McGraw laid down the ribbon with a dramatic reluctance. "Another time then, Miss Brinkerhoff. You be sure and let me know if you need anything. Anything at all."

"Lawrey down at the land office was looking for you right away." It was true, but not with the urgency Clint assigned to it. "Some trouble with the two claims down by the river."

McGraw tipped his hat to Katrine. "Ladies, I'm afraid duty calls." He leaned in to the shopkeeper. "Give Miss Brinkerhoff a helping of coffee and sugar and put it on my account. Even a woman in mourning can have her coffee sweet on my watch."

"Such a kind man." The shopkeeper sighed as she watched McGraw swagger out the door in the direction of the land office.

Katrine merely caught Clint's eye with a pained expression. Clearly, she found McGraw's display as distasteful as he. The day that man was exposed for his true nature couldn't come quickly enough. "You'll be needing a heap of nails come Monday when the timbers are ready," he said to her, just to keep his teeth from grinding against each other in anger. "Walls'll be going up and it'll start looking like home."

"Shall we walk down the street to the smithy's and put in the order then, Sheriff Thornton?" Katrine looked eager to get away from the prying eyes of the shopkeeper.

"Oh, and here's your coffee and your sugar from Private McGraw along with the rest of your order," Mrs. Fairhaven called, her knowing glances now eagerly matching up McGraw with her current customer.

Clint took the basket from Katrine's hands and unceremoniously plunked McGraw's "gifts" in with the other goods. "Your hands are still scratched. Let me carry that for you."

Katrine pushed out a breath the minute they were out of the shop. "He has everyone fooled." She shook her head.

"That's what makes him so dangerous. Folks will never suspect the likes of him until we have solid proof."

"More proof than the word of my brother." Frustration clipped her words short.

"I'm afraid so." Clint settled his hat farther down on his head. "Much as I hate to admit it, he'll be believed over Lars if it comes down to word against word." When Katrine sighed, he added, "But I aim to change that as fast as I can, you know that."

"I know."

"Let's order your nails and then ride out to the homestead. I've blocked out the foundation. I meant it when I said it might help you to see the cabin on its way back to being built. Besides," he added, knowing it was still hard for her to go to that place, "I have news."

"News?" Her eyes lit up. The blue of her eyes never ceased to startle him. He'd never met any Danes other than Lars and Katrine, and sometimes he wondered if everyone in Denmark had such rare blue eyes.

He gave her a cautionary look. "Not here."

As they walked down the bustling town street to the smithy's, Clint watched her look over her shoulder more than once. It made him regret not stepping in between her and McGraw earlier. That man could insert himself where he wasn't welcome with a slippery, genteel ease. Even though Clint had overheard the conversation, he asked, "What'd he say to you?"

"Private McGraw? He wanted to buy me some ribbon. It was nothing."

It was far from nothing. Clint didn't have to catch the man's every word to read what McGraw's expression said loud and clear. "That's all?"

"He looks at me as though—" she waved her hand

in the air the way she did when she was reaching for the right English word "—as a hungry man would look at bread."

Clint would have put it in coarser terms, but her comparison was accurate enough. "He's a man used to taking what he wants. I don't like him anywhere near you."

They reached the blacksmith, and Clint put in the order for the amount of nails he would need. While it would take until midweek for the full order to be ready, the smithy could give him half the needed nails now. That was good, because Clint was feeling the need to take his anger out on a few logs this afternoon while he and Katrine were out at the homestead. Not only could he see that the constant stream of sympathy from townsfolk was wearing on her, but McGraw's leers had doubled Clint's resolve to keep Katrine in eyesight every second he could. On a last-minute impulse, he bought a small basket of apples, a jug of cider, some bread and a chunk of hard cheese two doors down.

"Saturday luncheon?" Her eyebrows arched in curiosity as he piled the food in the wagon alongside Katrine's dry goods.

"Let's just say I think it's a good idea to keep you out of McGraw's sight for the weekend." He handed her up into the wagon and swung up beside her on the seat. A steady breeze had kept the usual June heat at bay today, and there was a pleasant enough tree beside the homestead to host their meal in shade. He nodded to the red leather journal he'd seen in her basket. "You can tell me one of your stories while I lay the corner timbers."

Clint could almost see her flinch at the mention of

corners. The sooner he got Katrine back into a solid home of her own, the faster she could put that awful night behind her. "You want to hear one of my stories?" She forced a casual tone into her words Clint could see she did not feel.

Snapping the reins, Clint set the horse to a gentle trot toward the spot a bit outside of town where Lars and Katrine had staked their claim. "I like your stories." It was true. On the many evenings when he had shared supper with the Brinkerhoffs, Katrine had often entertained them with stories. Normally he wasn't much for such fanciful things, but the way her blue eyes darted over that little red book of hers as she read aloud had caught his imagination, despite his best attempts to stay away.

She laughed, and he was glad for the sound. "Lars thinks you find them silly."

"They are." Clint surprised himself by laughing right along with her. "Some of 'em, at least. But there's a place for silly in the world, don't you think? We've got all the serious we need, and then some, if you ask me."

She eyed him, head cocked to one side. "Sheriff Thornton, you surprise me."

He gave in to a whim as they pulled out of town. "I think we can dispense with the Sheriff Thornton, don't you?"

"Pardon?"

"When we're out on the homestead, you can call me Clint if you like. Sheriff Thornton is a mouthful anyways."

He watched her make a decision. "Well, then, I suppose you may call me Katrine when we are here."

She offered a shy smile, laughing when the breeze pulled the bonnet from her head and sent strands of her hair playing across her cheeks. Her hair had always looked like spun sunshine to him—not that he'd ever say such a thing to her face. Clint swallowed hard and turned his eyes to the path. "Thank you kindly, Katrine. I'll do that," he said, trying—and mostly failing—to say her name with a casual air. "I'll do that." The truth was her name sat sparkling on his tongue, as potent as it had lodged in his mind since the fire. He stole another look at her, feeling awkward when their eyes met.

Yes, spun sunshine—that's exactly what her hair looked like to him.

While Dakota sat with Pastor Elijah going over some new words and phrases after services on Sunday, Katrine was glad to see Clint motion for Winona and her to join him in the empty infirmary. Alice had invited Winona and Dakota to stay for lunch, and was in the cabin getting things prepared. The situation being what it was, the three of them had to grab the opportunity to exchange information whenever a private meeting place presented itself.

"How is he?" Katrine asked the second the door had shut behind Clint. Every detail was a gift to her, every letter an absolute treasure, even though she had to hide them carefully.

Winona spoke, smiling at Katrine's enthusiasm. "I will see him tonight." She understood Katrine's hunger for information much better than Clint did, and Katrine was glad for the Indian woman's companionship on this strange journey. They had even prayed together for Lars's safety, something Katrine cherished. "I have food, another blanket and one of the books I borrowed from the reverend."

Katrine went to her cot, pulling a small bundle wrapped in a napkin out from under her pillow. "Alice and I made these cookies yesterday evening for Sunday supper this afternoon, and I snuck half a dozen away for Lars. He has a sweet tooth."

Winona's brows furrowed. "Sweet tooth?"

"It means he likes sweet things like cakes and cookies," Clint said, keeping one eye on the window in case Alice should return. "I'm glad you can go, Winona. I'm not able to get out to Lars until tomorrow, or even Tuesday."

I would find the time every day. Katrine was surprised how the sour thought roared up without any warning. Try as she might to keep such feelings at bay, Katrine always felt a sharp stab of jealousy when Clint and Winona talked of seeing Lars. It hurt to be the only one who knew Lars was alive but was unable to see him. Her brain knew better. As a young woman, she had no plausible reason to ride out alone into the wilderness. Her sensible side knew such action would only raise suspicion. Her lonesome sister's heart, however, refused to accept that truth. Every day, every hour, she yearned to make the journey to Lars's hiding place no matter how foolish it was. Just yesterday she'd spent an hour trying to dream up a reason to "pretend" to visit the reservation, only to surrender to the fact that it just couldn't be.

So, she settled for what was possible, even though it felt woefully insufficient. "Here," Katrine said, handing a thick fold of papers to Winona to deliver along with the cookies.

Winona looked at the stack. "Very many."

Katrine could only sigh. "I was missing him. Writing is all I can do when I miss him."

Clint's eyes softened from their watchful glare. "This will end. He will come back. Remember that."

But you both get to see him, Katrine wanted to wail. No matter how silly she told herself it was to shed tears of grief over a man who wasn't dead, the tears came anyway. She missed Lars so. "I try, but…" None of the many ways to finish that thought seemed to make any difference.

"Your burden is heavy," Winona said. Lars had told her the Cheyenne woman had such peace in her eyes, and she could see that peace now. "But you will lay it down soon."

Katrine wiped her eyes. "Soon. That is my favorite word today."

"Lars worries about you," Clint offered. "He knows this is harder on you than the rest of us. Just keep reminding yourself this is to keep him safe. When he returns to Brave Rock, he will be a hero for all he has done. Take that book of yours and start writing down plans for a hero's welcome, if that helps."

"Your letters mean much to him," Winona said as she tucked the stack into the pocket of her skirt. "He reads them over and over. And talks of you often."

"Nâháa'e!" Dakota's impatient voice came from outside. "Aunt, where are you?"

Winona gave Katrine's hand a final, compassionate squeeze and walked toward the door. "In here, child." She opened the door but turned to raise a hand in goodbye. "Soon," she said to Katrine.

"Soon," Katrine whispered back, the word becoming an endless prayer.

"Soon," Clint echoed. He pulled in a deep breath. "For them, too, I suppose."

Katrine looked up at Clint. She never expected him to realize what was between Lars and Winona. "Them?"

Clint looked a bit flustered. "Well, it just seems that they…the two of them…the way he talks about her…" His voice fell away.

So he *did* know. "Has Lars talked of Winona to you?"

Clint pulled his hands down his face. "A man doesn't come out and say such things. It's more in how he acts that shows…well…you know."

Katrine tried not to be amused at Clint's befuddlement with matters of the heart. "My brother is very fond of Winona, is he not?"

Clint found a roll of bandages suddenly worthy of his inspection. "I'd expect you to know that best of all."

"Only I cannot see him now and you can. If it is how a man acts, as you say, what do you see?"

Clint looked like she'd asked him to reveal some great secret. "Don't he write to you about it?"

Truth was, while Lars had never come out and spoken directly of his feelings for Winona, she had already noticed the actions Clint mentioned and had read between the lines of his recent letters. Still, the curiosity—and amusement—of hearing Clint's version proved irresistible. "He writes to me of many things."

"Well…" Clint looked up at the ceiling, as if the right words could be found in the rafters. "He does seem to be mighty glad for her company. He was even before all this, don't you think?"

She nodded but didn't offer any words.

"And he spends a lot of time up on the reservation. And I think Dakota's taken quite a shine to him, as well. And him to the boy."

"My brother has a big heart."

"Only, they're different. That counts for something."

"Not for all things, but yes, for some."

Clint put the roll of bandages back in the basket on Alice's table. "I expect he's wondering just how much it counts, and has a lot of time to ponder it up there in those rocks. Seems to me he might come back down knowing the answer."

She had come to nearly the same conclusion. "You know Lars well. You are his best friend." When that pronouncement raised Clint's eyes to meet hers, she ventured, "What do you think of them…as a pair?"

Clint shook his head. "Don't really matter much what I think, does it? He sure has never asked my opinion."

He really was evading her questions. "But *I* am asking." For an amusing second, Katrine wondered if she might need to stand between him and the door in order to pull the answer from the sheriff. She cocked her head as if to say "I can wait all day," and crossed her arms over her chest.

"Well. She makes eyes at him, that's plain enough to see. And I've seen him staring after her, that's for certain. I think it might be…hard…parts of it, but they both seem the kind to stand up to whatever comes. Out here, folks could be welcoming if they should…take a fancy to each other." That seemed to cross some sort of line for him, for he looked relieved. "So, yes, I suppose I'd be glad to see him happy if Winona is what makes him so."

Katrine let her smile broaden. "That is how I feel, as well." Just because Clint looked so uncomfortable having broached the subject, she added, "But we will not yet share our opinion, *ja?* It is for them to work out. And we have too many other worries for now."

Clint looked at her with a curious expression—half smile, half frown. "Yes, ma'am, too many."

Chapter Eight

Katrine was surprised to feel herself anticipating Monday's visit to the site where the cabin had burned. It was sad to pick through the remains of her home, but every little piece of her life that she uncovered from the ashes offered a particular solace. She spent her time wandering through the black remains, sorting her findings into little piles that made no sense to anyone but her. Out here, she did not have to apply a mask of grief. Out here, she could say the words *Lars is* instead of choking on every *Lars was*. If Clint had not insisted he be with her every time she set foot on this property, Katrine would be here every day.

Clint, however, treated the site in an entirely different way. As he worked to clear the charred timbers and cut new ones, something huge and powerful drove him. He swung the ax like an angry man. She'd seen Lars do it—take his fury out on logs by chopping wood—but it looked so different on Clint Thornton. Lars just seemed to be burning energy that had nowhere else to go. Clint—and oh, how odd it felt to call him Clint, even in the quiet of her mind—seemed bent on conquering the wood. She could see the strain in how his neck corded as he brought the ax down. His purpose tightened his grip on the ax and cast dark shadows over his eyes. She'd always thought of him as strong by virtue of being sheriff, but watching him out here showed his strength as a man. *If I were a criminal, I would fear him.*

It struck her, as surely as if he'd brought the ax down on her thought, that she *should* fear him. After all, Clint saw the law in pristine, sharp edges of right and wrong. She had come down on the wrong side of that edge more than once in her difficult years. Would he be so fierce in his protection if she told him all she had done?

No, she would not waste these precious hours of mourn-free afternoon thinking such things. She leaned up against the tree that once sat in her and Lars's front yard, soaking in the pampering sensations of the splendid breeze across the speckled shade. *Lars will come home here. We will live safe lives here.* Katrine watched Clint split a log, feeling something warmer than admiration for the power in his broad back and his muscled forearms. *Clint has saved me. Clint is strong enough to keep me safe.*

And she did feel safe—out here. Katrine hadn't realized how tense she'd grown surrounded by the mourning folk of Brave Rock. It required so much energy to keep up appearances, to fight the knot in her stomach that formed anytime McGraw or one of his men were around. After making a list of all the small pieces and trinkets she'd found, she'd switched from her writing papers to her private diary. She wanted to write Lars a long letter, and such a task was nearly impossible at Reverend Thornton's house. Dipping her pen, she started a letter in Danish, knowing it ensured that only Lars read her words.

Dearest Lars—
I worry so much for your safety. Are you well? Are you lonely? Do you count the days until you can come back as much as I? I know Sheriff Thornton will keep me safe.

Lars had said it over and over in the short message he'd sent back through Winona, and she wanted to believe the words. She wanted Lars not to worry about her safety, did not want to add to his burden out there wherever he was. Lars faced dangers with so much courage, something she had never been able to do since—

Katrine laid down the pen, consciously deciding whether to open up that black box of memories in her mind. She'd never spoken of that night to anyone— not even Lars—and for good reason. The Dark Man, as she'd come to call him, had made terrible threats if she ever told anyone. She had been fourteen, and old enough to know that the alley behind the saloon was no place for a young girl to be at that time of night. Still, working at the ale house had taught her the back alley was filled with food scraps at the end of the evening, filled with great stores of food if a smart but hungry girl knew where to look.

She had been looking, but had not found anything to

eat. No, instead she had found a woman, facedown in a pool of red, her neck purple and slit from one side to the other. Death was ugly enough to make her wretch despite the empty stomach, and the sound startled the Dark Man from his place in the shadows. How horrible his face was, coming out of nowhere like that. The only bright thing about him was how the tip of his knife glinted in the moonlight. She could hear his words even after seven long years, sharp with threats and close, as if he still lurked around every corner.

Of course, he'd never come for her yet, but that was because she'd kept her word and never told a soul what she'd seen that night. Not even Lars. Never. Still, despite her kept promise, some lingering part of her always waited for the day the Dark Man would find her and harm her despite her silence. It was a fool notion, as Clint would put it, to think some criminal from seven years ago could find and hurt her all the way out here. Her head knew that for the fact it was. The pit of her stomach refused to let go of the deep-seated old fear.

Katrine left the letter to Lars, turning to a fresh page to write her own thoughts. "Samuel McGraw feels like the D.M." she wrote, still unwilling to put the Dark Man's name to paper after all these years. "Clint would hate the D.M. as much as I do, would know he was evil."

Clint hated wrongdoers. He used harsh words whenever he spoke of Private McGraw and his gang. She disliked them, too, and had avoided them whenever possible even before the night of the fire. Still, even Lars could cite a few benefits these men had brought the community. Clint, on the other hand, gave them no quarter whatsoever. His world divided up into those who upheld the law and those who broke it.

I broke the law. The admission trailed out of her pencil before she could smudge it away. She knew, by the way Lars described Clint's crusade against the Black Four, that the sheriff despised all who had seen the Black Four's crimes but had not come forward. He'd talked over and over about the only way men like the Black Four succeeded was by terrorizing witnesses into silence. He'd quoted sayings about the crimes of good men doing nothing in the face of injustice.

She'd done nothing but keep silent at the crime she'd seen. Not when she was young enough to be afraid, and not when she was old enough to show courage. Not in seven years. She prayed for the soul of that young woman slain by the Dark Man's knife whenever that horrible memory surfaced. "The D.M. has gone free because I would not come forward," she wrote. "Did my house burn in payment for that crime beside Lars's courage to come forward?"

"New stories?"

Clint's voice startled her out of her memories, and she snapped the book shut with fearful speed. She hadn't even noticed him walk over to the shade. He was breathing hard, his forehead shining with sweat under the wandering locks of his thick dark hair. She must have been staring, for he produced a bandana from his pocket and mopped his brow as he reached for the jug of cider.

"No." She was sure her cheeks were pink, her bonnet lying beside her on the cool shady grass. She tucked the book under her skirts, feeling the guilty words glaring out from under the leather covers. She rubbed her leg to hide the action, feigning the soreness that had finally left her injured feet and legs.

"Still hurt?"

"Not so much anymore."

"I'm still mighty proud of your bare feet for kicking out those logs. They're big logs, and more than a bit stubborn." He turned and pointed at the two corners of the cabin walls that were closest to her. Their black smudges set them apart from the other fresh timbers he had fitted along the foundation. She winced.

Clint hunched down in front of her, dragging a shirtsleeve over his chin. "I've no mind to force them on you. If it really bothers you, I'll pull them out of the wall right now. This is your home, not mine."

Katrine stared over his shoulders to the two charred logs. They had been her escape, monuments of her fight to live. She wanted to have the brave new life this territory promised, and perhaps she needed to choose it rather than wait for Lars to bring it to her. "No, keep them there."

He nodded, a gentleness in his eyes she hadn't seen before.

"But I wish to paint them."

Sitting down fully, Clint took a healthy swig from the jug of cider he'd brought with them. It was as hot a day as June offered up on the prairie. "Don't rightly know if that'll work. Burned wood might not take to whitewashing or such. I never had much need for frills like that. Alice or Evelyn might know, though, so we can ask."

"If I can't paint them, then I shall plant rosebushes in front of them."

He chuckled. "You do that. I always did wonder how you managed to get those to grow out here. Never seen things quite like those before you put them in, and I was sorry they…burned."

He did that—hesitate whenever words associated with that night snuck their way into conversations. It told Katrine that the memories sat as uncomfortably on his spirit as they did on hers. "You've not yet told me your news. You said you had more news of Lars."

"Lars is fine and safe. I took you out here just to keep you away from McGraw."

She could not help but feel disappointed. As eager as she was to get away, he did not need to lure her with hopes of word from Lars. Clint need only ask and she would always agree to come out here with him. "Oh."

Clint's gaze fell to his hands, running his right thumb along the gash still healing on his left hand. Every time she looked at the sheriff's hands, her mind shot back to the feeling of grabbing those hands—and of them clasping onto her wrists—and how they had pulled her to safety. Perhaps Winona was right and they were bound to each other now, whether they liked it or not. It was an uncomfortable realization, and yet she could not ignore that his presence did, in fact, make her feel safe. Safe enough to ask, "Why did he do it?"

When Clint looked at her, she went on, "I think I know why McGraw tried to…" she made herself say it "…burn down our house. But you never truly told me why."

"He didn't *try* to, he did it." Clint thunked the jug down on the grass and shook his head. "I didn't mean that so harsh. What I meant to say is that he thinks he can do whatever he wants. Mostly because folks are afraid enough of him to let it happen. Those three others? They don't follow McGraw out of honor, they follow out of fear."

Katrine tucked her feet farther under her skirts. "I do fear him. He makes—how does Alice say it?—he makes my skin crawl." She ventured to say more. "I am old enough to know what he...wants from me when he looks at me like that, but—"

Clint cut her off. "He should *never* look at you like that."

Katrine felt her cheeks redden. "I know I am no great beauty, still I—"

He leaned in, agitated. "But you are. You are a fine woman, Katrine." Realizing the potency of his admission, he sat back again, more flustered than she'd ever seen him. "You'll make some good man a fine wife, raise yourself a fine family and give Lars a passel of nephews to tease. Don't you dare let the likes of McGraw make you think differently." He ran one hand across his forehead. "It's the land he wants. You and Lars are just standing in the way."

"But he has land, does he not?"

"Men like McGraw always want more, better, bigger. He gets to thinking your stake is better than his, or your stake might fetch a pretty price if he could sell it, and suddenly you're not some fine family in search of a good future, you're an obstacle to defeat. So he arranges for your fence to fail so you lose your livestock. Or harm comes to your wagon, or things go missing. Whatever he thinks might press you into selling or even outright walking away."

Katrine thought of all the accidents that had happened in and around Brave Rock. Not all of them had been put down to the Black Four, but what if life out here *was* harder than it needed to be because McGraw made sure it turned out that way? "I have not seen him buying land."

"That's because McGraw is the worst kind of criminal—a smart one. He's found a middleman, near as I can figure. Someone who's quietly buying up the land he scares up, then paying him a percentage of the profits. That way he can sit there looking like a fine upstanding gentleman while he robs half of Brave Rock blind." The sheriff's voice held a terrible contempt, a hatred for such crimes Katrine could almost feel in the air around him. She did not see how a criminal could not be as fearful of Clint Thornton's passion for justice as they were of Samuel McGraw's thirst for power.

"And Lars, he saw this middleman?"

"Lars saw enough to connect McGraw to the Black Four. And that's all you'll hear from me, Katrine. The less you know about all this, the better. I've let you sweet talk me into telling you far more'n you ought to know as it is."

Katrine sat back against the tree trunk and crossed her arms over her chest. "I do not believe anyone can…" she fumbled on his word, finding it too intimate "…sweet talk the mighty Sheriff Thornton into anything." She regretted the words instantly, for they felt too much indeed like "sweet talk." "But I am grateful for your protection," she added quietly, not wanting to leave the conversation at that awkward point. She gestured toward the homestead. "And for your help. You are a good friend to Lars." She hesitated for a moment before adding, "To both of us."

He caught her eyes. Even though she wanted to look away, she couldn't. The breeze tossed his hair across his forehead, and for just a moment he lost the hard edge she always saw in him. He smiled so rarely, he did not seem to carry the joy Elijah knew or the warmth Gideon possessed. He was somehow separate from his brothers, although she could not quite say why or how.

She only knew that the intensity of his eyes made her breath hitch.

The firelight's long shadows gave Samuel McGraw an even more sinister appearance. In Brave Rock, his uniform, finely trimmed mustache and regal bearing made it easy to think him a gentleman. Out here, snickering with a flask in his hand, Clint found it easy to picture the man doing what Lars claimed he had done. The assessment he'd given Katrine had been dead-on: this was a man who would squash anything in his way without a drop of remorse for the consequences. After yesterday's warm and bright afternoon with Katrine, this evening's meeting with the cavalrymen felt doubly cold and dark. A chill dashed down Clint's spine despite it being the middle of summer.

"Evenin', McGraw." The swing down from Clint's saddle felt like a descent into a den of thieves.

"And here's our man with the badge. Sheriff Thornton, so glad you could make it." Convivial as his tone was, Clint had the clear impression a man declining an invitation from McGraw lived to regret the decision—if he lived at all. "Jesse here tells me you're ready to prove your worth."

Clint had made a point of finding Jesse Wellington in the week since the fire, dropping hints and snippets of friendly conversation about his "eagerness" to get in on the private's good fortune. He'd evidently left enough of an impression for Wellington to pass Clint's interest along. That was good—the more people who believed Clint was ready to fall in with this crowd, the more information he could gather. "I am."

McGraw motioned to the bench seat next to him around the crackling fire. He offered his flask, but Clint declined. He'd jailed enough drunks and seen enough men destroyed by liquor that he'd never wanted anything to do with the stuff. "Seems your timing is right on the money, Thornton. We're hatching a plan I think you'll be especially pleased with, given your name."

"My name?"

"Bein' a Thornton, I figure it can't miff you too much to help us take down the Chaucers. The bad blood between you and them been running a long time, ain't it?"

Clint settled himself on the bench. "Things are far from cozy between us, that's true."

"Is it still true? Even with that Evelyn gal hookin' up with your brother?"

Clint gave a disgruntled shrug. "We're learning to live with it. Our beef's with the brothers, anyhow."

Bryson Reeves took a long swig from his own flask, wiping his lip with a shirtsleeve. "It's them we mean. Got some of the finest farmland in the territories, those three do. Don't seem right to have all that good soil locked up by one family."

The Chaucer claims? Were these four really thinking of going after so big a target? "You'd need a whole train car full of money to lure those claims away from those men."

"Now, Thornton," McGraw cut in, "you of all people should know some things don't get accomplished with ordinary transactions. This here is a matter of the proper incentives. And critical timing."

Clint did not like the sound of that one bit. "I take it you have a plan for those 'proper incentives'?"

"Indeed I do. Livestock does tend to wander off in these parts, especially when fences fail. It's such a crucial time for young crops to take, too. A farmer could be wiped out if things didn't go his way, especially if his seed stores disappeared so he couldn't replant. Winter comes quick, and sometimes a man needs to pull up stakes and start over if he's no chance of bein' ready."

Did McGraw realize how he'd overestimated himself? Had his hunger for power blinded him that much? "They'll band together, those Chaucers. You'd be in for a fight, if they gave in at all."

"The art of war, Sheriff, is to find your enemy's weak spot."

Clint stared at the private, wondering exactly what he was threatening. "You mean where to put the bullet?"

"Now, now, I dearly hope it does not come to that. Sometimes, however, tragedies cannot be avoided."

"I'm not killing for you, McGraw."

"No one is askin' you to. We're merely counting on you to look the other way should the unfortunate come to pass. Our aim is to entice them to sell cheap and move elsewhere. They can keep their lives."

He said it as though it were an act of mercy. And here Clint thought his disgust for these men could rise no higher. "Provided they clear out of town."

"You're a Thornton," Ryder Strafford piped up for the first time since Clint arrived. "I'd have thought you'd be glad to watch those Chaucers go."

"I'm not saying I ain't," Clint offered, just because he knew it was what McGraw wanted to hear. "But I want no part of the killing." That was the truth. Life was hard fought for in this part of the world. The casual way in which McGraw considered taking lives to suit his purpose was downright despicable.

"No stomach for bloodshed?" Jesse Wellington teased.

"It's not exactly the kind of thing folks look for in a sheriff. I'll be of no use to you if folks run me out of town right behind the Chaucers' exit. You need me, and you need me seen as trustworthy. That means no blood on my hands." Clint picked up a stick and poked at the fire, applying a casual air to his words. "Just what and when is whatever it is I'm not supposed to see?"

McGraw scanned the sky to the west. "We need a few more days for folks to let their guard down, so I'm thinking Monday night. Unlessen it rains over the weekend. Don't want tracks in fresh mud telling no tales."

Six days. Could Lars and Katrine hold out that long? "True. Are you going to do more than make off with their livestock? Fires, maybe?"

McGraw's gaze snapped back to Clint. "Why do you need to know?"

"There's friends and neighbors who might be near those lands. Say what you want, but I'd prefer to have some plan to keep them safe if you're planning another fire. Besides, if it's prime land you want, innocent deaths are bad for business. Spooking them off their land is one thing, but driving folks away from Brave Rock is another."

"Don't you be gettin' too curious, Sheriff." McGraw sat back, his eyes narrowing. "We can do this with or without you. And as you said, you've seen how kind we are to our enemies. You got some fine land there yourself, come to think of it."

Clint knew he'd pressed as far as he could for now. Treading the razor's edge between keeping close and raising suspicion was a dangerous game. He stood up to take his leave. "So I'm just to make sure my eyes are looking elsewhere than the Chaucer settlements Monday night. Have I got it?"

McGraw nodded. "No, you'll be riding with us Monday night."

Clint hadn't counted on that. "With you?"

"I like to keep my associates close. If you're in, you're all in. We'll all be masked, and we'll give you a fresh horse so as no one recognizes you."

How could he keep the Chaucers safe if he was riding with McGraw's men? "But—"

"Don't worry, son, we won't make you shoot nobody." McGraw's condescending tone brought a wave of snickers from his men.

Then again, what better way to gather evidence against the men than to be with them as they committed the crime? He was already far deeper into this than he'd ever intended. He might as well play it out to the full conclusion.

He must have hesitated too long, for McGraw stood up to meet him eye to eye. "So are you in or not?" The fact that the private's hand was on his pistol did not escape Clint's notice. Sheriff or not, it was easy to believe that the wrong answer might very well get him killed and thrown into the river within the hour.

"I'm in." Just for effect he added, "But I expect to be paid well. If I'm riding with your men, I'm collecting like one of them."

McGraw sat back down, enjoying another healthy swig from his flask. "I do like your backbone, Thornton. You'll do fine."

Clint settled his hat farther down on his head, glad to be on his way away from these men. The sooner he could rid Brave Rock of their kind, the better. Only now he had an even bigger challenge: gaining the cooperation of the Chaucer brothers. These days, that felt about as likely as the sun coming up at midnight.

If only he could tell Lije to start praying.

Chapter Nine

As they walked down the main street that had become Brave Rock's "downtown," toward the smithy's to pick up the rest of the nails, Katrine stared at her arm. Frowning, she tried not to be annoyed by the long gap between the end of her sleeve and her wrist. Tall as she was, most of the borrowed clothes she wore lately fit poorly despite good-intentioned alterations. She knew folks were kind to offer the clothes, but the "make do" tailoring served as a constant reminder that her own wardrobe lay in ashes outside of town.

"Still hurts?" Katrine looked up to find Clint's brown eyes following her gaze. His jaw hardened, and she knew memories of that night tightened his chest in the same way it cinched hers. He clearly thought she was staring at her hands where all the scrapes and scratches had been.

"No." His genuine concern made her complaints feel vain and petty. "It does not hurt. And I should be grateful it does not. Even my feet no longer hurt." She gave a sigh that belied her frustration with her own heart and behavior. "I have much to thank God for."

Before she could think better of it, Katrine looked up at Clint when she said the last sentence. Sure enough, something flashed behind his eyes. She knew it would, even before the words left her mouth. He diverted his eyes for a moment, but then his gaze returned to her. They were walking down a street full of busy townspeople, but were uniquely alone. That night had connected them. No matter how they tried to ignore it, the truth of it kept surfacing at surprising, confusing moments.

It hung in the air now, unspoken, suspended between them. Of all the things for which she should offer thanks, Clint's hands that had pulled her to safety topped the list. Lately, the man himself—his protection, his encouragement, his very presence—topped her list. Feeling the moment too keenly, Katrine squared her shoulders and applied a pleasant, everyday smile to her face.

He could not be fooled. Catching her eyes with a sideways glance that gave her permission to be neither pleasant nor everyday, he simply cued, "But..."

The fact that he could now read her so well felt both comforting and invasive. She knew he would see right through any efforts to say the proper thing. His eyes held only a companionable recognition, not any judgment or advice. Rather than try to hide her silly ingratitude, she simply offered a sad smile and held her arms out straight. The cuffs of her practical white shirtwaist barely came past her elbows. "Everything is too short. Everything." Even her petticoat and skirt fell more to a length suitable for a schoolgirl than a woman of twenty-one years, and she'd let down the hem as far as possible. Wincing, she recognized that the whine in her voice did indeed make her sound like a schoolgirl.

Clint smiled. Not an amused smile, but a softer one that spoke of understanding. Knowing what she knew of his harsh judgments where the law was concerned, his response surprised her. And then again, it didn't—she'd somehow known he would understand. How could this man's actions feel so out of character and yet familiar at the same time? Clint understood her feelings. As they had moments before, his eyes said, *It's all right* even before he spoke.

"I'm the youngest of three brothers," he began, adjusting his hat. "I've spent years grousing about having to make do with someone else's castoffs. Some days it's hard to be grateful."

"You are the youngest. I had not thought about that." The image of Clint as a young boy, shirt cuffs rolled up to fit and pants cinched small enough with a belt, poked its way into her imagination. Its contrast to the man ever in control and now walking down the street beside her brought a smile to her lips. "You are the most serious of your brothers, aren't you?"

He chuckled. "Oh, I don't know about that. Lije has a powerful purpose in life, and Gideon seems to prefer his own company to any of us—before Evelyn, that was—but I don't know that either of them would rank me as the most serious. I was a mite dour as a child, though. Always grousing about how things weren't as they should be." He paused for a telling moment before adding, "Lots of things weren't as they should be growing up."

Goodness, but she knew how that felt. "The world should feel perfect and wonderful when you are young. But it does not always come to us that way, does it?"

"No." Clint's voice sounded as if he was far away in some memory. "Not for me."

She wanted to ask, but knew this was neither the time nor the place to explore whatever sad stories made up his past. She'd heard bits and pieces from Lars or the other Thornton brothers: a father lost to the war, hard times after the plantation was lost, and nearly everyone in town knew something terrible had driven the wedge between his family and the Chaucers. No, Clint Thornton's childhood memories were neither perfect nor wonderful. "Times were hard?" It seemed a weak question, but she could not come up with another.

"Sorrowful hard." He stuffed his hands in his pockets. "Matter of fact, I'm not sure I'd be lying if I told you I didn't own a new shirt or shoes until I was twelve." Then, as if to push all of those memories safely behind him, he raised one eyebrow and teased, "Twenty, maybe."

"Twenty?" She laughed openly, feeling the bitterness unwind from around her heart. "Surely it could not have been as bad as all that."

"Maybe not quite that bad." His mischievous look faded, leaving a dark streak across his eyes. The sheriff had shadows in his past, too.

"At least all my brothers are my size." She could hear him dismiss the unpleasant memories as if he'd wiped them off a slate board. "You can't say the same about those who've lent you clothes. Near as I can figure, you've got half a foot on most of the ladies in Brave Rock."

While she hadn't given the issue much thought in years, she did seem to feel her height every day since the fire. Pulling on too-short clothes every morning made forgetting it impossible. Suddenly she was eleven again, feeling awkward and gangly.

"All of us Thorntons were short until we shot up like weeds near our tenth birthdays. Were you and Lars always tall?"

Lars. It felt so good to be able to talk about him. Most people in Brave Rock talked carefully around the subject of her "late" brother. They were trying to be kind, to spare her from crying and such, but it only made her want to shake folks and shout that he still lived and would come home soon. "Yes, Lars especially. I cannot remember ever feeling short. Such names I was called when I was younger! 'Beanstalk.' 'Tree.' All in Danish of course, but none the kinder for it."

"Young'uns can be cruel. They never count how that kind of thing sticks to you." He spoke from experience—that much was clear—but didn't elaborate.

"I hated being so tall growing up. Even if we had enough money—which we never did—I have had to make my own clothes as long as I can remember. Or add trims to ones I could buy."

"You shouldn't take your height amiss," Clint said, narrowing one eye. "It suits you. You're graceful." Then, as if he hadn't intended to say something like that, he cleared his throat and stuffed his hands in his vest pockets. "Besides, you'd look odd next to Lars if you were all tiny and dark."

His attempt to cover up the flattery failed. He'd called her graceful. He thought of her as such. The genuine compliment—for she knew he wasn't a man of false praise—settled warm and soft under her ribs. Why was he always surprising her with such gestures? "Well, you would look just as odd next to your brothers if you had corn hair."

He burst into laughter at the reference, and she joined him. The world had felt heavy on her shoulders for so long that such frivolity soothed like cool water on a dusty afternoon. How she longed for the days when the hardest thing she faced was how to coax her roses to bloom in Oklahoma soil.

"That I would." Clint suddenly turned completely around, looking back in the direction they had come. Katrine stopped, wondering what had caught the sheriff's eye, but only found him staring down the ordinary-looking street, scratching his chin in thought. "You know," he said after a pause, "Gideon told me Evelyn just got one of those fancy pedal sewing machines."

Katrine shrugged, stumped by such an odd comment from a bachelor. "Did she?"

"She's got one of those contraptions, I'm sure of it." Without another word, he started walking toward Fairhaven's Mercantile. "Come on."

Even with her long legs, Katrine found herself almost running to keep up with him. "Why?"

Clint simply walked into the store and went straight

up to Polly Fairhaven. "Mrs. Fairhaven, Pastor Thornton sent me here to fetch Miss Brinkerhoff some fabric. On the church's tab. She's a need to make herself some new clothes on account of the fire."

"On *my* account," Katrine corrected, not willing to be Brave Rock Church's first charity case.

"On the *church's* tab for now," Clint reiterated with a look so commanding Mrs. Fairhaven nearly gulped. Katrine was afraid he'd gesture toward the star on his vest as if the law required the purchase. "We'll settle up later if need be. Enough for two skirts and maybe a blouse or two of some kind." He flapped his hand between Katrine and the shopkeeper as if declaring a partnership. "Seems to me you ladies ought to know what all that means." Then he looked at Katrine. "I'm off to pick up the rest of the nails and I'll be back in a few minutes."

Katrine planted her hands on her hips. "But—"

"Mrs. Fairhaven, don't you let her leave until she's satisfied with her purchases and don't you let her put them on her account. I've strict orders from the reverend."

"You've no such—" Katrine started to protest, but the door had already shut behind Clint. She was sure she heard his chuckle echo down the street.

She turned back from the door, only to find Polly Fairhaven eagerly hoisting two bolts of good broadcloth. "I've some lovely buttercream for a blouse, and what about gray or navy for the skirts? No sense keeping to mourning blacks all the way out here."

If only she could tell Polly there was no sense in

keeping to mourning blacks *at all*. In time, that would come—she had to hold on to the truth of that. Right now, the prospect of new and finely fitting clothes called to her like the sweetest of confections. Katrine shrugged and offered a smile. "You heard the sheriff. All of it."

"Shall we say grace?"

Alice extended her hand to Clint, as joining hands for dinner grace had always been the Thornton tradition. It wasn't so hard to take at Sunday afternoon suppers with lots of guests around and a groaning tableful of food.

Tonight's smaller foursome for a midweek supper meant Clint had to take Katrine's hand during grace. He tried not to make a fuss about it, but a cannon went off in his chest when Katrine placed her hand in his. He felt the smoothness of her skin alongside the roughness of the bandage that still covered the deepest of his gashes. Even as he tried to hold her hand as lightly as possible, his mind shot back to the night of the fire. He was grateful prayer required him to bow his head, as looking Katrine in the eyes would prove too much at the moment.

"Bless this food to our bodies, keep us grateful for Your provision and Your gift of salvation. In Jesus' name, Amen." Even Elijah's short grace was far too long to be touching Katrine's tiny hand. It twitched a bit in his grasp, and he knew the moment was as awkward for her as it was for him. It had become torture and bliss to be around her lately, like one of her beloved roses—too appealing not to risk the angry thorns.

"Gideon couldn't come tonight?" Clint asked, wishing there were more folks around the table than just the four of them.

"Too busy with his horses," Alice replied. "You know how he is with those animals. Plus, I think his side is bothering him again. That accident with the horse was weeks ago, but I told him he should still take it easy."

"Never did do what he was told," Lije teased, patting his wife's hand. "Don't take it personal."

"He's been paying us no mind his whole life," Clint offered. "'Specially when it comes to animals."

"And Walt," Katrine added. "He is wonderful to Evelyn's boy. They make a fine family." Her voice held true admiration.

Alice handed a basket of bread to Clint. "Katrine made her potato bread, Clint. Lije said it's a favorite of yours." Clint didn't care for the look in her eyes, as if she were making matches where she had no business doing so.

"I did say it was tasty." He gave Alice his darkest *nothing more than that* look as he took a slice and handed back the basket.

"I like it, too," offered Lije, ever the peacekeeper. He took the basket from Alice's hands and gave himself two slices. "Lars must eat—must *have eaten* well." He tried to correct himself before the comment, but there was no way to take it back. "I'm sorry, Miss Katrine, that was thoughtless. I miss him and still can't quite believe he is gone."

"It is how I feel, too," Katrine said. Clint had to admire her careful choice of words. She was smart enough to push a change in subject. "How is the Nelson baby, Alice? She was so tiny. I have prayed for her every day this week." Clint noticed she had barely eaten any food on her plate, and she hadn't touched much of the picnic lunch they had the other day, either. Even though he imagined it was normal for folks in grief to lose their appetites, he wondered if Alice or Lije had noticed how much thinner she looked.

"Oh," said Alice, beaming, "Daisy is just fine. She may be small, but she's got lots of fight in her. I expect she'll hold her own against all those brothers."

"Five brothers," Clint said, catching Lije's eye across the table. "Can you imagine the fights? There were only three of us and we tore each other to pieces twelve times over."

"But we always had each other," Lije said with a warm look toward Clint. His hand covered his wife's. "And good things have come along."

"A big family is a wonderful blessing," Alice added, her eyes on her husband. "Especially out here. Come harvest, Don Nelson will be glad for all those strapping young boys and their strong backs." She dished herself some more potatoes, handing the bowl to Clint when she was done. "I only pity Louise—that's a passel of hungry mouths to cook for and it will only get worse as they grow."

"A happy task, *ja?*" Katrine smiled at Alice. The longing for a home and family of her own was all over her face, Clint recognized. No wonder Lars had spent so much time pondering how God would send her a husband—it was plain she wanted one, and she was of more than sufficient age to be settling down on her own. Clint kept waiting for the day when such a notion of a wife and family wouldn't stab him in the ribs, when he'd find a way to be satisfied with his role as uncle and protector. It wasn't coming near soon enough. The way Katrine kept poking into his thoughts, it had better hurry up and arrive.

"Have you written down any stories since…the fire?" Lije's voice was full of tender concern. "I saw your journals by your cot and hoped you found some comfort in that. It's a marvelous gift you have. Don't lose it."

"Mostly, I write to Lars."

Clint's jaw tightened. Were she Lije or Gideon, Clint would have found a way to kick her foot under the table for the slipup.

"It is my way of saying goodbye, I suppose," Katrine went on, and Clint felt a stab of guilt for his first reaction.

"Well, no one can fault you for that." Clint found himself wondering if Lije had told Katrine the story of his own loss, having watched his fiancée succumb to the same influenza epidemic that took Gideon's wife and child. Yes, sir, the Thornton men were no strangers to grief. Some days that was the only silver lining Clint could find to his solitary future. If a man had no family, he had no family to lose. "Perhaps when we order church supplies we can include more journals for you." He turned to Clint. "Were you able to order all the supplies for Katrine's cabin?"

Clint was glad for a safer subject of conversation. "The smithy's making the last of the nails and hinges, so it's just a matter of manpower from here on in. The foundation's laid, so it's just the walls—"

"And the windows," Katrine cut in. Hang her, every time he got to thinking she was a frail thing she'd go and show him the strength of her spine. It did something to his heart he didn't like one bit.

"And the windows. And the roof."

Alice raised an eyebrow. "Windows?"

Clint parked an elbow on the table and tried to keep himself from rolling his eyes. "Miss Brinkerhoff has insisted the new cabin have a window."

"Two," Katrine corrected.

"Well," said Alice, clearly aware that there was more going on here than the finer points of cabin structure, "windows are a fine thing to have, and I need the good light for nursing. I only wish the flies and the winter wind didn't share my opinion."

Now it was Lije's turn to look beleaguered. "Alice has been after me to get some pane glass for the home and the infirmary."

"What?" teased Clint, glad to feel the earlier tension clear the room. "Before stained glass for the church?"

"I have plans," Lije replied.

"And I have *patients*," Alice added.

"Now all you need is *patience,* my sweet." Lije softened his jest with a tender kiss to his wife's cheek. Clint turned his attention to his plate while Katrine found something important to adjust in her long blond braid. He was happy for his brother—he truly was—but watching all that wedded bliss with Katrine just one seat away stung worse than a whole nest of hornets.

He'd put in twice the hours at the Brinkerhoff cabin tomorrow. For crying out loud, he'd work all night getting Katrine's walls and roof in place just to keep from having to endure another dinner like this.

Chapter Ten

Frustration proved to be a mighty fine incentive, for Clint seemed to do twice the work in half the hours on the Brinkerhoff cabin Thursday morning. It helped that he'd managed to convince Katrine to stay home and make use of Evelyn's sewing machine. It didn't help one bit that he'd gotten the walls up far enough to begin setting the holes for the window—windows, he corrected himself with an unsuppressed smile. The thought brought a whole mess of distraction with it.

He stood inside the walls, looking overhead to judge the angle of the sun. One window facing east, one facing west. Only not directly opposite each other, so as not to give a strong wind too much of an invitation in winter. Squinting to measure against his raised hand, he tried to imagine the best height. She was nearly as tall as he.

Hang it, he knew *exactly* how tall she was. His chest remembered the exact place where her shoulders had fallen against him as they rode from the fire. He knew, without actually remembering if she had ever been that close to him, exactly how she would tuck under his shoulders if he held her. His memory had somehow catalogued the angle of her neck as she looked up at him. It was as fixed in his brain as the sideways glance she gave Lars when she was annoyed with him, or the way her entire face changed whenever she spoke to children.

He pulled a pencil from his pocket, marked a spot on the wall log and went to fetch the ax.

"I hope that's not for me." He hadn't even seen Lije come around the corner of the cabin.

"Very funny."

Lije walked around the half-built walls, giving a low whistle once he'd made the complete circle. "You're in the wrong line of work, brother."

"I thought you were in favor of my being sheriff. Peace and justice, order and such."

"Oh, I am." Lije pulled a bandana from his pocket and wiped his brow. The morning had been hot and windless. Clint's own shirt was already soaked. "Only I never realized how fast you can raise a cabin. I think this is going up even faster than Gideon's did, and there were a whole mess of folks helping out with that."

Returning the ax to its place among his other tools, Clint eyed his brother. "What's it to you? You two newlyweds missing your privacy?" It came out sharper than Lije deserved, but his brother's overflow of marital happiness last night stuck in Clint's craw.

Clint deserved every bit of the scowl Lije gave him. "You know me better than that. And I know you better than to wonder just what it is you're chopping out here."

This was the hard part of having a minister in the

family. Lije was forever tending to the state of souls, and brotherly souls were entirely too close at hand.

"I'm chopping wood." Clint overemphasized the words, as if explaining it to young Walt rather than a learned older brother. "Takes such a thing to make a cabin." Trying to outguess Lije's thinking, Clint added, "And no, I'm not working out my grief over Lars. Although I'm not sure what it'd be to you even if I was."

Lije always looked after his brothers, but now he wore what Clint privately called his "Pastor Face," a compassionate look usually accompanied by a firm hand on a shoulder. "You've lost a dear friend in the worst possible way. No one would fault you for taking it hard."

Clint chose not to reply. Not that it stood any chance of ending Lije's pastoral care, but it was worth a shot.

"Still," Lije went on, "this doesn't look like grief to me."

Clint shifted back on one hip and wiped his chin with the back of his hand. "Really, now." This felt too much like the time Clint cut down one of Cousin Obadiah's apple trees and Lije decided he'd been showing the guardian how much he hated him. Truth was, Clint was just tired of getting stung by the bees gathering outside his bedroom window. Lije was always stuffing emotional complications into simple actions. "What all does this look like, other than a man building a cabin? And if I tell you I don't really want to know, will that change anything?"

"Gideon likes to take things apart when he's frustrated. You, you like to put things together. Judging by the rate of speed here, I'd say you've got a king-size bee in your bonnet."

"I'm not much for bonnets, if you haven't noticed."

Lije narrowed his eye, as if analyzing why he'd chosen to respond about the bonnet rather than deny his irritation. Some days talking to Lije was like poking a path through a field of bear traps. "Bothered by a bonnet, are you?"

"No." Clint nearly growled the word, feeling like the aforementioned bear who tread wrong and heard *snap*. He picked up the ax again, hoping to cue Lije into an exit.

Lije simply removed his coat and picked up a hammer. "Need some help?"

Not from you. It comes with too much conversation. Against his better judgment, Clint nodded toward eight shaved planks and a tin of nails. "Think you can square those up?"

"Miss Katrine's pair of windows?"

Suddenly Clint was sure he didn't want help, not especially with Katrine's beloved windows. Still, if he changed his mind, Lije would be on him like flies to honey. Lije was looking at him funny enough as it was. "Yep. But you won't help me much if you can't square 'em up." He hoped Lije would take his scowl as perfectionism.

Lije put the hammer down. "I have many gifts, but despite the example of our Lord, carpentry has never been one of them."

Clint laughed. It was true. Gideon and he had enjoyed several laughs at Lije's expense over what the

Brave Rock Church would be like if the reverend were required to build it. The structure was coming along nicely, but only because Lije supervised rather than lent a hand. "I think God sets fine stock in men who know their limits."

He immediately regretted uttering a sentence with the word *God* in it. There were no short conversations about faith with Lije. "I think God sets fine stock in men who save lives. Still, building Miss Katrine a new cabin doesn't have to be your penance for not being able to save Lars."

Clint didn't look up, but sunk the ax blade into a log to start the notch that settled it into the log underneath. "That's what you think this is?"

"I think you're working too hard at something others could help you do. I don't know why you think you have to do this alone."

It hadn't struck Clint until just this moment that he had, indeed, taken it on himself. Only it wasn't as Lije thought—it wasn't some self-inflicted punishment. It felt more like the only true part he could play in Katrine's life. There was no "have to" about it—this was a "want to" kind of thing. "You know I like doing things on my own." It sounded like a weak excuse even to his own ears.

"No, I don't think you really do. I've seen you at our table, at church, with folks. Gideon may prefer the company of animals, but you *deny* yourself the company of people. I think you believe you have to do things on your own because—"

Clint cut him off with a mighty swing of the ax—so

hard it split the log instead of finishing the wedge cut. "That's about enough, Lije."

"I know it's not—"

"I said *leave it.*" He kicked the log off the rack that held it in place. "Go tend your flock however you like but I'll ask you to back down off this *right now.*"

The look in Lije's eyes, however, held little yield. A silent standoff began between them, Clint shifting his grip on the ax and Lije holding irritatingly still. Clint hated when Lije got this way—it always made him feel as if his private feelings weren't all that private.

"Lars's death is not your fault." Lije's words were low and steady.

Clint came dangerously close to shouting "Lars's death isn't even real!" Short of his own blood, Lars was about the only man whose safety would drive Clint to the extreme of keeping such truth to himself. Honestly, if Lije stayed one more minute, Clint couldn't be sure if he would tell his brother, or sock him. Instead, he did the only thing he could think of to do: he turned his back and walked away.

Let Lije think it was guilt that drove him to work so hard. Clint knew what it really was. And he knew why it was so much worse.

Some June afternoons Katrine found the Oklahoma territories to be as close to Heaven as she could imagine. When the heat let up and the whole prairie turned out in freshly sprung color, Katrine could tell herself the happiest of stories. Almost without effort, she could build a picture in her mind of a big noisy family tending a bursting vegetable garden, of pink roses turning their faces up to fluffy white clouds like the ones that filled Friday's wide blue sky. Days like today she could almost lay aside the dark images of their burned house, replacing them instead with the vision of a white board cottage with blue calico curtains fluttering in the breeze. Someday—soon, she prayed—Lars would come down out of his hiding place and back to life. They'd put this whole awful episode behind them and make new lives. Big, wide-open-space lives filled with happiness.

Years ago she and Lars had talked about such details, dreaming together about the families they would raise side by side. Of course, back then it had taken much more imagination, and never had she dreamed it would be so far out west as Oklahoma. Still, she and Lars had invented their futures together often—it had served as their favorite diversion on the nights when that future felt far away. Their sharing had offered distraction from hungry nights back east when all they'd had to eat was what she could scrounge together from scraps at the saloon. They had sat on the floor of the tiny, dingy boardinghouse room and taken turns describing their houses, losing themselves in complicated, flowing Danish descriptions, never having to reach for the right English word. They'd shared stories again as they ventured out west, using the same distraction when hunting was poor or Lars's traps would come up empty. Now, she used the diversion to keep her from loneliness or worry.

"Pjusket blå gardiner," she wrote in her journal, forced to dream of "ruffled blue curtains" in writing rather than aloud because Lars was hidden away. She

went on to describe a table set with sunflowers, piled high with big white pottery bowls bearing blue-striped trims. A bursting table groaning under heaps of food, set to feed a dozen people at least—her and Lars's great big American families. Giggling, she expanded her story to write of a tall, handsome American cowboy riding in off the range to this well-deserved supper. In the American family of her daydreams, Katrine's husband was far from Danish in his features; she would cast her imaginary hero as ruddy and dark-haired with a thick stubble and a cowboy swagger to match. And their children—all eight of them—would be a mix of features. Her imaginary sons would have dark, American eyes while her daughters would have big blue Danish eyes to bat at their many beaus.

"Do you write in that?" A different dark-eyed male—eight-year-old Dakota Eaglefeather—stared at her from the edge of the tree's shade. He nodded toward Katrine's journal as though writing were a puzzle he could never hope to solve.

"I do, Dakota." She offered him a smile. As the son of a Cheyenne and a white cavalry officer, Dakota suffered too much scorn from too many of the full-blooded Cheyenne boys. Winona had reason to worry about his future among the tribe of Cheyenne. His lighter skin was no fault of his own, and Katrine could see that Winona did her best to give him confidence, but it was a challenge. It didn't help that there had been enough people back in Boomer Town ready to look down on his skin for being too dark. Lars had said more than once how glad he was that Brave Rock was not home to men who considered Indians as only savages to be conquered or avoided.

"Your stories?"

"Something like that." She looked behind the boy but did not see Winona's dark braids anywhere in the yard. "Is your aunt with Reverend Thornton?"

Dakota nodded.

"I think it's too nice to stay inside, too, even if I still want to look at books." She closed her journal and patted the ground next to her. "Shall I tell you a story?"

He smiled and moved to join her under the tree. Even though she guessed he could understand not much more than half of her words, he still loved to hear stories as much as she loved to tell them.

She began to tell the Danish tale of Trillevip, the dwarf who helped a girl asked to spin twenty full spindles in a single night. Trillevip's price for his help was the hand of the spinning girl in marriage. Dakota knew what spinning was, for she could mime the actions. She was just getting to the part of the story where Trillevip would let the girl out of her bargain if only she could guess his name, when a shadow fell across the boy and herself.

"Trillevip's boasting reveals his name and he loses his bride." Clint's deep voice offered the next point in the plot. "She outsmarts him."

"Ah, but she is still in a fix," Katrine went on, "for the young man has chosen to marry her for how fast she spins, not knowing it is the dwarf who has made it happen." She looked up at Clint. "Did Lars tell you this one?"

The sheriff settled down on his haunches. "Not half as well as you do."

Katrine felt ill at ease continuing the story with Clint's dark eyes watching her. Stories of marriage and rescue and clever tricksters seemed somehow odd and wrong to tell in front of him, although she couldn't really say why.

"So Trillevip tells the maiden he will send three old crones to her wedding banquet, and she must call them mother, aunt and grandmother and be very kind to them."

"Our chief says we must always be kind to guests," Dakota offered. He was such a bright, considerate child.

"That's always true," Katrine agreed, "but Trillevip had a special reason for asking this of the maiden. The first crone showed up with horrid red eyes that drooped to her chin." Katrine looked up to see Clint making an awful face, pulling his cheeks into a clumsy droopy shape and crossing his eyes. Dakota erupted in giggles at Clint's theatrics. "She told the groom her ugly eyes had come from staying up late to spin too much yarn."

She mimed spinning and yawning, smiling herself when Dakota did the same.

"The next old woman was even uglier with a frightfully large mouth that stretched from ear to ear," Katrine went on, falling into more laughter as Clint spread his mouth with his fingers in a ridiculous face. "She told the groom her mouth had grown wide from licking her fingers to spin smooth yarn." Katrine watched as Clint made a grand show of licking his fingers. This was a side of him she had not seen—he was always so serious.

"The third old woman was the ugliest of all. She was bent up and old, barely able to walk even with two crutches to help her."

Sure enough, Clint leaped to his feet and began lurching around the tree, hunched over and dragging one foot. Dakota laughed so hard he nearly toppled over.

"This time the groom asked the old lady why she walked so, for he assumed all three of these old women were kin to the spinning girl. This old crone told the groom her bent legs were from treading the spinning wheel, and that no one should ever have to work as hard as she did or they would surely end up looking like her."

"What did the man do then?" Dakota asked.

"He told his new wife he never wanted to have her spin again," Clint offered, staring a moment too long at Katrine so that her cheeks felt hot, "for he wanted his wife to stay as young and beautiful as she was." His smile was warm and not at all for Dakota's amusement.

"And so it was," Katrine said after a moment, "that the spinning girl knew Trillevip had helped her one last time."

"Even though the clever little dwarf could not have the pretty young spinning girl as his wife, for now she belonged to another." Clint's words held just the slightest tinge of regret, making Katrine wonder who had just told what story to whom. "Trillevip could not have what he wanted." Katrine held Clint's pained eyes, even though it seemed unwise to do so, until Dakota's huff broke the moment.

"That is a silly story," the boy declared, evidently

far more amused by Clint's antics than Katrine's storytelling skills.

"The best ones are always silly," Clint said, putting his hat back on.

Not always, she thought to herself as she watched the lawman walk away. *The best ones leave everyone happy when they are done.* It always bothered her that the clever, loyal dwarf ended up alone.

Chapter Eleven

Clint was steeling his nerve later that day to go try to warn the Chaucer brothers when Gideon rode up beside him as he trotted down the main street. "Got a minute?" his brother asked, a concerned expression on his face.

"Sure." Clint turned his horse to the side of the road as Gideon did the same. "Everything all right?"

"Evelyn's fine, Walt's talking a mile a minute these days, and the horses are all well. But I have to say, that's exactly the question I meant to ask you." Gideon pushed up his hat and wiped the sweat from his brow with his sleeve. These days the sun seemed intent on showing just how hot an Oklahoma June could be. "Everything all right with you? I mean with Lars being so shortly gone and all…"

Clint knew he hadn't exactly been cordial lately, but he figured the ruse of grief ought to explain his sour mood enough for most folks. Still, Gideon's face showed a deeper concern. "What are you getting at?"

Gideon resettled his hat. "It's just that, well, Evelyn

and I both noticed the look on your face when Walt called you Uncle Clint the other day. We've told Walt he has two new uncles now, never figuring it would bother Lije or you to have him think that."

"It doesn't bother me." It didn't—at least not in the way Gideon thought. He'd enjoyed being an uncle before, had loved Gideon's daughter to distraction before God took her.

"It sure looked like it did. Look, I know Walt's not blood kin, but—"

"Walt's your son now, and that makes him kin enough to me. He's a fine boy." How could he explain to Gideon that these days Clint felt as if he were surrounded by babies, families, newlyweds and young'uns? It wasn't like they weren't there before—Brave Rock had only a few more families than it had had two weeks ago—it was just the confounded regularity with which home and hearth kept popping up into his once solitary life. His once solitary, nearly satisfactory life. An uncle was not a father, but Clint had found being an uncle was close enough to raising sons and daughters of his own. Up until lately, that is.

"But you left right after." Gideon could be like a dog gnawing a bone some days, relentless and without sense enough to quit.

"I'm fine, Gideon. I didn't mean anything by it, and I'm sorry if I caused you and Evelyn any worry." He didn't begrudge anyone their happiness. Even now looking at his brother it was clear Gideon was so hanged happy Clint couldn't be irritated with him. And Lije, well, he'd just spent an evening with Lije's happiness

on point-blank display, hadn't he? Both of his brothers
had found a love match weeks—even months—earlier
and Clint had tolerated the joviality just fine. Now, suddenly, all of it just set his teeth on edge and dragged his
imagination to places it ought not to go.

"Walt can call me Uncle any day of the week," he
went on, just to reassure Gideon his new family was
wholly welcome into the Thornton fold. If only the
Chaucers were as generous. "If anything, it may be his
other uncles that have a thing or two to say about it."

"You leave that to me," Gideon said, and by the look
in his eye Clint knew he meant it.

The brothers parted ways with a hearty handshake,
leaving Clint to darker thoughts as he turned his horse
toward the trio of spreads where the Chaucers had
staked their claims. *This might have been easier with
Gideon beside me,* Clint thought, feeling even more
alone. There were still miles of bad blood between the
Thorntons and the Chaucers, but even those men had to
accept that Gideon was now Evelyn's husband. No matter how those stubborn brothers chose to object, Gideon
was now kin to them, kin to their nephew. Maybe that
would be enough to get them to listen to his plan. Even
if they hadn't the decency to show up at their sister's
wedding, he hoped Theo, Reid and Brett Chaucer would
have the good sense to realize they needed to listen to
their brother-in-law and the town sheriff, even if he was
named Thornton.

Walt and Evelyn were, however, exactly why Clint
could not bring Gideon into this plan. This scheme was
Clint's and Clint's alone to see through; no one else

could shoulder this particular burden for Brave Rock. He just hoped it would go easy.

Any hopes for such dissolved as he spied Theo Chaucer inspecting the stretch of property fence that ran closest to town. Of the three Chaucer brothers, Theo would be by far the hardest to convince.

"Afternoon, Theo." The man was only a handful of years older than Clint, but the frown that planted itself on his features aged him a dozen more. "Fence holding up okay?" A Thornton making small talk with a Chaucer. Who'd have figured on that? He'd have to figure on a lot of "firsts" if this was ever going to work.

Theo pushed his hat back and squinted up at Clint. The man had sandy hair, dark eyes and a dark disposition to match. "Fine enough" was all he said. Kindly put, Evelyn was by far the friendliest of the Chaucer siblings. They'd given Gideon no end of grief before he'd taken up with Evelyn, and still hadn't warmed up to the idea of their baby sister tacking on the Thornton name.

At least try to be friendly-like, he told himself. Swinging down from his saddle, Clint took off his hat. "Good to hear. No troubles with it? No sudden breaks or suspicious-looking cuts?"

Theo planted the shovel he was holding in the ground and parked one elbow on the fencepost. "Now just what is that supposed to mean?" Word had undoubtedly reached Theo that at one time, Clint had suspected the Chaucers of being the men behind all of the trouble Brave Rock had seen lately. That wasn't exactly conducive to the partnership Clint needed now, but there was no help for that.

Clint tried to tone his words with friendly concern rather than suspicion as he took a step closer. "Chaucer, we need to talk."

"Not the way I see it. Besides, ain't that what we're doing now?"

A conversation Clint had categorized as "difficult" just slid into the "near impossible" column. "Someplace a bit more private, if you don't mind. With your brothers."

"If you want an invitation to tea or some such thing, that's Evelyn's department. As it is, I'm a bit busy for Friday social calls, Sheriff." Theo said the title with a nasty edge to it, a bite just short of disrespect.

Clint felt his lips press together and he made a conscious effort to unfurl his fingers. This was far more important than a family squabble. "As a matter of fact, I'm here on sheriff business. So no, I'm not expecting hospitality. But I do need you to hear me out."

Theo pulled the shovel from its place in the ground. "Say your piece, then. I'm listening."

Clint forced the exasperation from his voice, trying hard to sound reasonable. "Like I said, this ain't an outside conversation."

It took another ten minutes of persuasion before Theo tossed his shovel into the wagon and drove toward the Chaucer compound where the three men had situated their cabins. Clint kept his eyes open as he followed across the Chaucer land, trying to see it with McGraw's eyes. Where would they ride in from? What fence would be cut first? Which building could be set on fire without being seen? It soured his stomach to be thinking like a criminal, but second-guessing those of ill intent was part of his job and always had been.

Once the men had gathered, Clint didn't hesitate to give a straight-on account of what "certain suspicious parties" were planning. It wasn't yet time to reveal who was after them—Chaucers were a hotheaded clan, and if they went off straight to McGraw picking a fight, all this intrigue would be lost. A storm of proof-less accusations would only get him right back where he started from, and Clint wanted this over quickly.

"I think you're seeing things that aren't there." Brett Chaucer sat back in his chair with his arms folded across his chest. "I know the foreigner was your friend but ain't nobody had it out for him and ain't nobody have it out for us, neither. Especially if you can't even affix a name to these bandits you tell us are coming for our land."

Clint took a chance. "What if I was to tell you I have proof the Brinkerhoff fire was set deliberately to kill Lars? And that Gideon's fence didn't break, it was cut? And the Morrison well didn't fail all on its own? The Black Four are forcing good people out of rightful claims, and now it's clear they won't stop at murder to get what they want." Clint held Theo's eyes, hoping to appeal to him as the eldest brother. "They'll kill one of you as easily as they did Lars, if it suits them. You really want to take a chance that I'm wrong?"

"What I can't figure," Reid Chaucer cut in, "is why you'd bother to come out here with a wild story like this knowing we wouldn't fall for it? What's it to you if

Chaucers get run out of Brave Rock? It's not like we're all neighborly."

"We were," Clint felt compelled to point out. "Once." The families had indeed been close before the war between the states. Since then, the ravages of the South's reconstruction had driven a bitter wedge that had only soured with the years.

"Water long under the bridge, Sheriff." Brett's words had an air of finality.

"All right, then, think of it this way—I can't very well let innocent people fall prey to the likes of these bandits without trying to stop them. It's my duty to warn you of a threat, no matter what my last name is or whether or not we get along."

"I'd like to meet the man who thinks he can spook us off our land," Theo boasted. "Black bandana or no." It was exactly the kind of reaction Clint would have expected from the man.

"Monday night, I expect you'll get to do just that."

"Why can't you just arrest them now?" Brett asked.

Clint wiped his hands down his face, tamping down his growing frustration. "Because I need more proof, need to catch them red-handed. If things go as I hope they will, I'll be able to do that Monday night." He ignored the way the next words stuck in his craw. "But I need your help to do it. And I need to know you all are ready for whatever it is they've got planned."

Theo crossed one boot over the other, far too casual for Clint's taste. "Appreciate the warning, Sheriff, but I think we'll be just fine."

Clint put his hat on. This conversation was over,

whether he'd convinced them or not. "Just be on the watch. That's all I ask."

"Are you going to send up a smoke signal to warn us or some such thing?"

Warning them was a good idea. If they wouldn't be on guard the whole night, at least some sort of advance warning would take away McGraw's element of surprise. "I'll figure something out and get back to you."

Theo gave a placating laugh. "You do that."

Clint tipped his hat to the brothers, who looked as if they'd prefer to swat him out of their sight like an annoying fly. Being sheriff was a thankless enough job without being outright dismissed.

Some days foolish arrogance was as much a threat as any bullet ever fired.

Clint had been in sour spirits at Wednesday's dinner, leaving Katrine to fear that the sheriff was getting ready to put his plans into action. Tension pulled at his shoulders and clipped short his words. Twice since then, she'd caught him staring at her with a strange look on his face. It wasn't anything she could readily name, but it seemed to waffle back and forth between regret and determination. She couldn't help thinking he'd somehow settled for something—compromised or made do when that sort of tactic didn't seem to be in his nature at all. She'd find herself taken back by a battle-ready steeliness in his features, only to turn around and catch him with such a sad air of loss that she could nearly convince herself Lars was really gone.

Katrine watched the other folk from Brave Rock—

and even Clint's brothers—go about life as if they couldn't see what she saw. Was she truly the only one who could see the weight he bore on his shoulders? Could no one else recognize how he exiled himself to endure it alone? She seemed to see the force of it all pressing down on him harder with every day that passed, but she could not think of any way to ease his path. He would not tell her any more than the merest of details, and often shied away from conversations she would attempt to start.

And so it was that when Clint pulled the wagon up and insisted she come with him to the cabin site Saturday morning, Katrine didn't know what to think. Something had changed. Some part of his plans had clicked into place; she could see the certainty in his eyes. There was insistency in his eyes, too, and that set off a jolt of an alarm in her stomach. Whatever had happened, she couldn't tell if it was good or bad, only that it was important.

"Is everything all right?" she whispered as she allowed Clint to hand her up into the wagon.

"I was hoping you'd tell me after you see for yourself." Banter? From the serious Sheriff Thornton? Katrine met his offered smile with eyes narrowed in curiosity. "I didn't mean to give you a fright," he said as he turned the wagon out of town.

"It is not your fault. It's just when you rode up… I keep having an awful dream," she admitted. "You come to me and tell me Lars is really dead. You tell me McGraw found him and shot him. I wake up in tears."

"Now, when a woman says a man comes to her in

her dreams, tears are not the outcome he's looking for. A man yearns to be appreciated." He flushed suddenly, and looked out over the horizon, as if he'd not meant the words to come out quite the way they had. In truth, she could hardly believe such talk out of the man. He'd no doubt engaged in such teasing with his brothers, with Lars, even, but with her? The notion baffled her.

"I'd hate to think all I do is make you cry," he continued. "Lars would have my hide."

His loneliness was so plain to her. Maybe even more to her than to himself, she guessed. In these parts sheriff was in large part a thankless job. "All bad news and hard fear" Lars had called it once when he declined Clint's request to serve as deputy.

"I appreciate you," she blurted out. She did. She was not ready to think about the prospect of her feelings venturing far beyond appreciation, but when all this was over, she might have to do so. "And you do not make me cry."

There again was the sad look of loss, almost hidden behind an applied smile. "I don't know that I make you smile, neither, but I'm hoping today will change that."

His tone had definitely changed. Less gruff, less forced, but still with the reluctance she could not ignore. As if he was working hard to keep from saying certain things.

She could see that, mostly because she was trying not to say certain things herself. He did, in fact, make her smile. They were both swimming upstream against a river current neither one would admit was even there. And yet, as it did in the corners of his eyes just now, that current would rise up occasionally and take them a little distance. A little bit toward each other.

"What are you up to, Sheriff?" She chose not to hide her smile this time.

"Clint," he corrected, smiling back with a glint so surprising it nearly made her gasp. On any other man she might call such a look mischievous, but she could not imagine applying that word to Clint Thornton. "And you'll see soon enough."

It struck her not two seconds later: he was proud. Not a boastful, arrogant pride, but a pride of accomplishment. He'd done something he set out to do, something he now wanted to show her. Something *for* her. Maybe even just for her. Even though she had no idea what that something was, its power was already sprouting a glow of warmth inside her.

Of course, he already had done a great many things for her. "Look," she said, pointing to the hem of her skirt, wanting him to know he did not have to strive any further to win her gratitude. "A new skirt long enough and all my own." That had been his doing. Did he understand the power of that gesture? "Thank you."

"Just keeping the peace, ma'am." He actually grinned, and Katrine though maybe he really did grasp how much the new frocks had improved her outlook. "I can't have the men of Brave Rock leering after those fetching ankles or there'd be more chaos than there already is."

Fetching? While such words from Samuel McGraw would grow a knot in her stomach, Clint's words only made that earlier glow bloom farther up her chest to redden her cheeks. Such talk between them startled her. On the one hand, she welcomed the lightness and life of it. On the other hand, it felt like something that could become dangerous and uncontrollable. She knew that gentle river currents could swell out of control and sweep whole towns away—this felt just like such a current. Katrine told herself all this would disappear once Lars returned.

Still, it was enticing to let the river current carry her away for a short distance.

Preoccupied with her thoughts and fears, Katrine kept silent for the rest of the ride. She turned Lars's watch over and over in her hands, worrying it like a charm to keep the whirlwind of feelings Clint produced in her under some kind of control. When had it become both wonderful and awful to be with him?

"There." Clint touched her elbow and pointed to the nearly built cabin standing just to the west of where the old one had burned.

Katrine looked up to see sets of solid log walls—up to her chin all the way around, looking more and more like a home every day. It was even larger than the cabin that had burned.

But it was not the walls that made her breath catch.

It was the windows. Not one, but two lovely square windows, set perfectly within the eastern and western walls. Two windows. Escape for two souls. Which meant a home built to always house two. Without knowing he had done so, Clint had built her a house that promised she would never be alone. "Oh," she gasped, any suitable English word escaping her grasp. "Oh my."

Somehow, the sight of those two windows became the perfect antidote to the fear that Lars would one day no longer be there. It put to rest the constant twist of anxiety that had plagued her since the fire. Clint had restored her home before he'd even finished building her cabin. Katrine clasped her hands together over her pounding heart and began to cry.

"Now, wait a minute," Clint flustered, digging in his pocket for a bandana as she only cried harder. "I just got done saying…"

Katrine could not hope to stop herself from throwing her arms around his neck and hugging the dear man tightly. "Thank you," she whispered, "*Tak. Tak.* Thank you."

There was a wondrous moment where he hugged her back, and in that instant Katrine felt that powerful current sweep them far downriver. She felt something give way in the set of his shoulders, something melt off the stiffness of his fingers. For a brief second she imagined he inclined his head to rest on hers and thought she caught something powerful in the way he exhaled.

But just as quickly, she felt Clint's body pull back up into its stiffer countenance. When he pried her hands off his shoulders, she felt the loss like a hollow in her chest.

He shifted back on the bench. "So…so you like the windows," he said, his voice thick and gruff.

"They are wonderful." They were so much more than that.

"I set them askew a bit." He tugged at his vest and swung down off the wagon, as if stuffing facts into the moment would hide what had just happened. "I thought… I figured it might help to keep the wind from whipping in there once the cold comes."

"Yes," she said, not knowing how to respond. She should not have held him so, she knew that, but the moment was too much and she found she could not bring herself to regret it.

He walked over to the cabin, pointing to a pair of rectangular wood boxes that sat on the ground. "Window boxes," he said, lifting one up to show her where it would fit below the window once the cabin was finished. "First in Brave Rock, I reckon. One for each."

"Two windows." She walked toward the half-built cabin, dabbing at the running tears with Clint's bandana. The simple pair of square openings felt like an extravagance of riches, a gesture so deep and perfect it would never be matched in all her days. She wanted him to know. To realize what he'd done, even if he'd not done it intentionally. She waited until he stopped fiddling with the boxes and looked up at her. She let herself hold his eyes, not hiding what she felt even though it made her nearly shake to do so.

"For you," he said softly. Then, as she watched him pull away from her without taking a step, as she watched him hide what was in his eyes without closing them, he straightened and said, "For you and Lars."

He said it with such an air of pronouncement, such a tone of finality, that Katrine wondered how she could have ever thought he was going to say "For you and me."

It was as clear as the view through the widows that such a thought was now never to be, if it ever was at all.

Chapter Twelve

Katrine had spent all day and evening of Sunday writing today's letter to Lars. Between church and meals, it had taken four tries and many hours to find enough privacy to get it right, even in her native Danish. Still, the conversations she had with Winona had made it clear to her that Lars was struggling with matters of the heart as much as she, and she always did her best thinking on paper. Sitting next to Clint at Sunday service, it had become clear to Katrine that if Lars was beginning to think of a life out here with a family of his own, she owed it to him to let him know she had begun to do the same.

She could no longer deny it: when she'd spied those two windows, it wasn't she and Lars she saw sharing that house. It was she and Clint. Even if things never warmed between them—and right now she couldn't see how they ever would—the trip to the cabin had shown Katrine that the time had come to think about her life separate from Lars.

It wasn't as if they'd always expected to live together as brother and sister. They'd talked about raising families side by side, surrounded by bands of noisy cousins and big Sunday suppers. For all his denial, Clint was right about one thing—Lars worried a great deal about her, and she did not want to be the worry that stood between her brother and his future happiness.

So she had written to him. Hinted, in careful words that did not reveal who it was, that God may have shown her the man who would share her life. Nothing too detailed—mostly visions of their two families someday and how much she looked forward to such a life starting when he returned. She kept telling herself it was only to put Lars's mind at ease, but there was more. It was a declaration of independence of sorts. An opening to new possibilities. The storyteller in her sensed that by putting such tender notions down on paper, by telling them to the one other person who knew her best, she could settle her soul. Right now Katrine's soul felt far too jumbled to listen well to where God led next.

All of that had made great sense as she left the infirmary minutes ago. Now it seemed the most foolish idea in all of Oklahoma. She would be sending this letter with Clint, after all, since he would be the next to see Lars. At first she thought to wait and send it with Winona, but that was silly; Clint could not read Danish, and thereby not possibly know the contents of the message he carried. Still, she felt a wave of trepidation as she left the letter on top of Clint's desk in the sheriff's office Monday morning. Katrine was just turning the corner away from his office when she heard his voice.

"This is serious, young man, and I want you to pay attention." Clint's voice came dark and ominous from the side porch of Fairhaven's Mercantile across the street.

"Yes, sir, Sheriff Thornton." From where she stood, Katrine could see Martin Walters being walked across the street between Reverend Thornton and Clint. She ducked around the corner as the two men brought Martin toward the sheriff's office. The poor boy looked as though his fear would rise up and swallow him whole any second.

"The reverend tells me you saw young Luther Oswald take licorice from Fairhaven's on Saturday."

"I didn't mean to see," Martin said in a panicked voice. Katrine could feel for the lad. Clint's eyes could be a fearsome thing when the law was at stake. Half the boys in Brave Rock wanted to be Sheriff Thornton, the other half were sore afraid of the man. Clearly one to spout words when afraid, Martin launched into his side of the story. He packed the tale with so many details as they walked into the office that Reverend Thornton had to step in and cut them short.

"Why didn't you say something when you saw it?" the clergyman asked as Katrine edged back to the front of the building to peer cautiously into the window. Neither man saw her, focused on the boy as they were.

"Luther's big. I figured he'd clobber me for telling."

"That's likely true. Luther *is* big," Clint conceded, his commiseration with the boy bringing an amused smile to Katrine's face. While he would probably never admit it, Clint was very good with children. Walt had even told her he was his favorite of the boy's new uncles. Clint continued, "But he's also wrong for taking Felix Fairhaven's sweets without paying. You know that's stealing, I know you do. And while I know such things are hard to come by out here, that's no excuse for breaking the law like both of you did."

Katrine flinched at the word *both* at the same moment Martin did.

"Me?" Martin nearly squeaked. "I didn't take nothin'!"

"I know that to be true," Clint replied, looking as though he'd given this hours of consideration. "But you saw the crime and said nothing. Now, I know your mama and your papa to be fine folks. I'm sure they taught you right from wrong. So, Martin, I want you to look me square in the eye—man-to-man—and tell me if you knew telling would have been the right thing to do."

Telling would have been the right thing to do. Suddenly she was fourteen years old again, hearing her conscience shout the same thing to her night after night for months after she'd seen the murder. How many times had she walked past a police office back east, halting her steps in consideration, only to have the sinister look of the killer's eyes force her to run away?

Martin backed up against the reverend, but the clergyman's hand did not allow him to move. The boy looked duly terrified. His fist came up to his mouth, as if to hold in the words that would condemn him.

"I am the sheriff, Martin. Lying to me would be as bad as lying to Reverend Thornton. Maybe worse."

"Mama says that."

At that comment, Katrine watched Elijah and Clint exchange knowing glances. "And how's that?" Clint asked.

"She says I need to be extra good because she and pa are friendly with both of you. Being the sheriff and the preacher man, she says you both know everything about right and wrong and how little boys get punished."

"She's right," Clint offered. "But I expect she also told you that her friendship with Reverend Thornton and me would not get you any special ease should you break the laws. Neither God's nor Oklahoma's."

"Yes, she did. I remember," Martin said, the words coming faster and faster. "I sure do remember that."

"Which is why I am so vexed that you did what you did."

Martin scrunched up his face at the unfamiliar word.

"Why I am not at all pleased that you failed to come forward. In these parts, hiding a crime is nearly the same as committing one. In fact, it's my personal opinion that there is no difference between the man who did the crime and the man who failed to stop it."

There is no difference between the man who did the crime and the man who failed to stop it. Katrine pulled away from the window, her hand on her chest to stop the pounding heart underneath. She could not help the feeling she was hearing Clint lecture her fourteen-year-old self. No matter how she tried to argue, she could not take it as coincidence that she'd been party to this conversation. She could not ignore that not seconds after she'd braved the placement of her letter on his desk, she'd been witness to a lecture where Clint managed to give voice to every doubt that had plagued her over the years. Some horrible man was walking around free while someone's dear daughter lay unavenged in the ground, and all because she would not step forward.

You were a child. Only she wasn't. Not really. She and Lars had been on their own long enough that she could not claim innocence. And truly, could a woman who'd spent time as a barmaid—even if it was to keep her belly full—ever claim innocence?

You were threatened. Yes, she was, but so was Martin. For that matter, so was Lars, and look at all he was risking to ensure that justice was being served!

Surely he is being so strict to set an example. Perhaps, but no man would speak so harshly to a young boy unless he deeply believed what he said. She inched closer to the window with her back to the wall, straining to hear but afraid to show her face.

"What if in ten years Luther thinks that all he needs to do whatever he wants is to hold up a fist to a small fry like you? A man has to think about his future, his honor, when faced with a choice like yours."

Had that horrible man killed others, threatened other witnesses into silence as he had done with her? She'd never allowed herself to think about that, even when that one pale, lifeless face lying in the alley pushed its way into her nightmares. Now she kept her eyes wide open for fear a crowd of pale faces would shout accusations at her if she shut them. She was fourteen all over again, and no amount of logic would push back the rush of panic that seemed to pin her to the wall. Why was Lars not here? Faced with this panic, she might have been able to convince herself to finally tell him after all these years. Lars would know what to do. He might understand.

Or he might not. Katrine considered the very reason Lars was not here. He was hiding precisely because he was a witness to a crime and had been threatened. He had spoken out, done what she had failed to do. And Clint—Clint had spoken over and over about how he admired what Lars was doing, how Lars was willing to risk even his life to stop the wrongdoing he'd seen. After all, wasn't that what Clint did every day? The high calling he held himself to? How would a man with that kind of code view a person who'd kept silent about murder?

Not with the tender eyes she cherished when he looked at her. Not with the admiration he showed when speaking with Lars. Katrine flattened her palms against the office wall, begging her legs to move and carry her away, but they did not listen. The vision of that letter now sitting on Clint's desk imprisoned her as surely as if she were in the cells beyond that wall.

She tried to conjure up some excuse to walk in and snatch the letter back, but none would come. She could only gulp when the door to her left opened and out walked Reverend Thornton and Martin.

"I trust you learned your lesson here today, Martin?"

"Yes, Reverend." The words weren't much above a whisper. The boy stared at the ground and shuffled his feet.

"Grace has been extended to you this one time. Learn from it and make sure I never have to take you before Sheriff Thornton again. Be the man God intended you to be, and stand up for what you know is right." Katrine shut her eyes, willing herself invisible but knowing the foolishness of that.

"Miss Katrine? How are you today?" There was no hope. Reverend Thornton had spied her there, flattened ridiculously against the office wall. "Are you ill?"

She opened her eyes, to see Martin was gone. "Fine," she replied. Katrine was sure her voice was just as squeaky as Martin's had been earlier.

Katrine had been beyond careless, Clint thought, leaving a note in Danish out in the open on his desk like that. Only one other person in Brave Rock could read Danish, and that person was supposed to be dead. Had McGraw walked in here—and as a member of the Security Patrol, he had every right to do so—it might give him cause to wonder. Did Katrine realize the foolishness of what she'd done?

"You left a note on my desk, Miss Brinkerhoff," he said as he stepped outside his office and saw her with his brother. He didn't do a good job of reining in his annoyance, and the words came out more sharply than he would have liked.

"Yes." She looked at him with eyes as wide and panicked as Martin's had been. "I did." Was that regret in her eyes? She couldn't think to ask for the letter back in front of someone like Lije, not when there was Danish on the outside, for crying out loud.

He had to come up with something. "I'll take care of that list right away. Tonight, even." She ought to remember he was heading out to visit Lars tonight. Clint patted his shirt pocket to let her know he'd put her letter safely out of sight. "You remember you've got nothing to worry over. Not a thing." Her eyes showed the force of his words, and he wanted to kick himself for letting his anxiety get the better of his control. He took a step toward her, but it was as if she'd suddenly found use of her feet and she retreated from him. Hang it all, how could he make her see the importance of their secrecy without chastising her for her lapse?

"Fint, tak." She gave a forced-looking wave toward the mercantile as she translated, "I'm fine, thank you." Clint hoped no one else guessed that she resorted to Danish when she was nervous. "I was on my way to Fairhaven's for more thread."

"I'll be happy to walk you over there, Miss Brinkerhoff. You're looking a bit peaked." Lije was such a master of giving even common words a warm, caring tone. However, if Katrine's eyes were any indication, Clint was sure his words sounded more like a reprimand than a reassurance.

"No, thank you. I am quite fine. I need to go. Good morning."

Clint watched Katrine scurry into Fairhaven's as if a mountain lion were nipping at her heels. She'd stared at him with wide eyes, fisted hands hiding in her skirts. This ruse had gone on long enough—it was time to end it. He'd hoped to be able to keep her secure until Lars could return, but the look on her face just now told him even the combination of his support and Winona's hadn't been enough. Brave as she was trying to be, the passing days had strung her tight as a telegraph line. The best thing for Katrine was to get Lars home tonight. He'd be heading on over to the Chaucers one last time at sundown.

From beside him, he heard Lije push out an exasperated breath. "You shouldn't be so hard on her, Clint. She's not faring well." Of course, Lije would put her distress down to grief, but that just underscored Clint's urgency to put the whole scheme to rest.

"I know it's hard on her being alone."

"I wasn't thinking she was so much alone." Lije didn't have to say "because you've been spending so much time with her," for his eyes silently broadcast the thought. When Clint gave him a dark look, he said, "Come on, brother, even *you* have to have caught on that Katrine is a bit sweet on you."

Clint thought about arguing the point, but this was Lije—he was too smart about these kinds of things. While it made him a wonderful pastor, it made him an insufferable brother some days. "It don't matter none."

"It does."

Clint wanted to take his brother by the shoulders and yell, "Lars will be home soon and we can all go back to our peaceful lives!" But even as his mind held the thought, he knew it for the lie it was. Lars could come home a dozen times over and some things could never go back to being the way they were.

"How's Mrs. Murphy's ginger cake today?" Clint's attempt at changing the subject was as futile as it was ridiculous.

Lije sat back on one hip on the porch rail and narrowed his eyes at his brother. *Really?* his glare seemed to say. "I wouldn't know."

Clint put his hand on his office door, still open from the escapade with Martin. "Perhaps you should go bring some home to Alice." He waved a falsely cheerful good-bye. "She likes that sort of thing, don't she? It'd be a *husbandly* sort of thing to do." He gave the word a not-so-gentle emphasis that he hoped translated to *Perhaps you should clear off my office porch and not sermon me on how I handle my affairs.*

Just as he feared, Lije followed him back inside. "You know, Gideon just got through telling me his new black is the most stubborn soul in Brave Rock. I need to go on back there and tell him he's wrong. I think that honor goes to our esteemed sheriff."

"I'm just being realistic, Lije. I know that comes hard to your type, but—"

"You're being foolish. There. I said it. For a man who claims to be so observant, you can't see the truth when it's so close to your eyes it could bite you in the nose."

Oh, it bites, I tell you. Hard and sharp and right at the place under my ribs. Clint pointed a finger at his brother. "Lije, I'm only going to say this one more time…"

Lije surprised him by pointing a finger right back. "Don't you shut her out, Clint. Don't you be cold to her now when she's all alone like this. She needs you. Land sakes, you might even need her more, if you'd just be man enough to admit it." With that, Lije pushed through the door and slammed it shut behind him.

Clint stared at the door. Since the sheriff's office

had been built in Brave Rock, his own kin had never slammed the door at him like that. He didn't much care for the way it felt. Not one bit.

Chapter Thirteen

Katrine hadn't spoken to Clint since he'd barked at her outside his office this morning. He was right, of course. It had been a foolish risk to leave that note on his desk, but the truth was she had been relieved to find him out of the office. She lacked the courage to hand it to him face-to-face, even if he couldn't read the contents. *I should have waited and given it to Winona.* It seemed as if every ounce of patience she possessed had fled her lately.

Even her sewing irked her, going as slow as molasses. While the seams and waistband of her first new skirt whipped up quickly with the help of Evelyn's amazing stitching machine, the tedious yards of hemming on her blouse sleeves and second skirt seemed to try her strained nerves. Even outside, as she perched on a bench under the large tree that sat next to Elijah and Alice's house, the yards of fabric seemed to take too long to hand sew.

The bench had become her favorite place to be, for

sewing wasn't the only thing that tried her patience. Katrine had grown weary of her nights on the cot in the back of the clinic and her days in Reverend Thornton's home. Pleasant as the cozy space was, it had begun to feel confining. *Newlyweds ought to be left alone,* she thought to herself, *not playing host to homeless neighbors*.

Knotting off the end of another thread, Katrine looked up to see Clint walking toward her. He looked as weary as she felt. Their last encounter had clearly weighed as heavily on him as it had on her.

He sat down on a stump opposite the bench. "I apologize for being so short with you this morning. I was worried, but that was no reason to take it out on you."

"It was not wise to leave that note out as I did."

He took off his hat and pinched the bridge of his nose. "I can hardly expect you to think like a lawman, especially given the circumstances. You did no real harm. To make it up to you, I made sure Winona took the letter to him this afternoon."

The letter was in Lars's hands. He knew now. The fact set off a storm of butterflies in her stomach and she hid her eyes in her sewing rather than look at Clint. No one knew what she felt for him, of course, not even Lars—but yet she felt exposed and fragile.

Clint picked up on her reaction. "You still look upset. Missing home?"

She sighed and dropped the stitching to her lap. "I try not to think of it, but some days I feel lost. Homeless." Her hand went to Lars's watch where it hung around her neck. "They are…were just things, but…"

"All this is about to be over, Katrine. You'll not have to bear up much longer, I promise you that."

There was a seriousness in his voice. "Over?"

"Tonight, actually. It's why I was so short with you. I've got a lot on my mind. And a fair bit to do before sundown."

She dared a look into his eyes, sure there was something he was not telling her. "And this means…?"

He stepped closer, leaning in toward her so as to speak softly and not be overheard. Heavens, but it made her skittish to have him so close. He'd not been so near since she'd written that letter, and it made her heart gallop just to have him nearby. Even though they were not spoken to him, her words in that letter had been a declaration of sorts. They had changed everything, without changing anything.

Clint looked at her for a long moment before speaking, and she knew he was deciding how much to tell her. His looks could steal her breath lately. She could read these things in his eyes now, see his doubts, his worries and the things that pleased him more than he would say aloud. "It means," he said as he picked his words carefully, "that tonight I will arrest Samuel McGraw. All the Black Four, actually."

She licked her lips, her mouth suddenly going dry. Tonight. Tonight would bring Lars home. "That is a good thing, *ja?* That is what we have been waiting for."

"Katrine." The expression in his eyes was half tender, half pained. The deep sound of his voice saying her name made her clutch at the cloth in her hands. "I don't expect these men to go quietly. It might not…go smooth."

"There are dangers." She'd known that all along, but they seemed all too real just now. It had always been about justice, but now it was about putting people she cared about in harm's way.

"They're going after Chaucer land tonight, and the Chaucers aren't taking the warning as serious as I'd hoped."

He saw that as a failure—she could read the regret clearly in his eyes. "You tried to warn them."

"And I'll try again. But even that won't change the fact that there'll be a fight. If I succeed, not much of one. But if I don't…well, it could get nasty."

"I know." She said the words, but she didn't really mean them. She didn't have any real idea what these men were capable of. She only knew how much she wanted all this to end. How much she wanted Lars to come home and all this watching and worrying to go away.

Clint shifted his weight the way he did when saying something he didn't care to say. "Katrine, you ought to know that I'm going to tell the Chaucers that Lars is alive and that he will come out of hiding tonight. It's the only way I can see to end this. We're out of time. I want to think those Chaucer men are smart enough to heed my warning when they see Lars coming, but it also means Lars will be in the thick of it."

"You must do whatever it takes," she said, seeing the frustration in his eyes. "You are the sheriff." She wondered for a split second if somehow Lars had guessed her heart and said something to Clint. Did he know? Was that why he'd come to tell her these things? The thought made her feel twice as pinned by his powerful eyes, every feeling she'd written to Lars roaring up stronger than ever.

Clint could be killed tonight. The startling thought grabbed her like a hand around her throat. If he didn't know how she felt, he could die without ever knowing. For that matter, Lars could be killed tonight. "I will pray all day and night that justice is done tonight and good men are not harmed."

She could not go so far as to say she'd pray for him, and that felt cowardly. Here Clint was risking his life for the sake of justice, for the sake of peace in Brave Rock, and she could not risk her heart in what might be his final hours. The admission made her feel small and damaged, a mistake of justice rather than its champion as Clint was. She had no claim on this honorable lawman, nor could she. There was one thing she could do, though, one thing that absolutely could not go unsaid. She reached out and touched his arm. "Thank you, Clint. For everything." She meant so much more than those measly words, but her fright and his nearness tangled her tongue.

Something that might have been regret darkened his eyes. "I was just doing my job."

"No, it was more than that. You were…you are… being a good friend to Lars." Somewhere down deep she found enough courage to say, "And to me."

"I'd like to think we're friends, Katrine." His words were lovely and awful at the same time. Her head told her she could grow to think of Clint as a loyal friend, but her heart had already raced well beyond that. If Lars had guessed anything—or if Clint had known with or without Lars's response—the result was clear. Clint's declarative use of the term *friend* spoke what he could not openly say.

Like Trillevip and the spinning girl, they could not share a future. She had resigned herself to an acceptance of that when he asked softly, "Are we? Friends?"

Katrine was sure her heart stopped altogether. "Yes, of course." The answer gushed out of her in a rush of breath. She was sure her face was pink, and her hand flew up to her chest as if to tamp down the pounding she felt there. Was he confirming her last statement that he'd been a good friend? Or was he asking the much more dangerous question if she thought of him as more? All her resolve fled. "Of course," Katrine repeated, flustered.

"Well then," he said, breaking the closeness with his own withdrawal. The moment, if it had ever truly been there, was gone. The tender look in his eyes vanished, and Katrine could practically watch him become the hardened lawman preparing for battle. Something fierce settled behind his eyes—something like determination, but much deeper. "I'll be glad to know my *friend* Katrine is praying for my safety and for Lars's. Tonight we'll need all the help we can get. I do believe the Almighty might be the only force to get through to those Chaucers." He tried to force a laugh—to make light of what she knew he considered a very serious situation—but it failed.

Panic filled Katrine, and she reached out to grip Clint's hands. "Be safe, Clint." She squeezed the hands that had pulled her to safety, the hands that had wrapped his coat around her for protection that horrible night, the hands that had begun to rebuild her home. Her heart stilled when he responded by wrapping her hands in his. They were so warm and so very strong. She sputtered out, "Both of you," just to put some safe words into the very dangerous-feeling air between them. "Bring my brother home."

He held her eyes for a moment that seemed to stretch out forever. He started to say something, but never spoke. Nodding very slowly, he released her hands as he stood up and turned back down the path.

All the sensible thinking in the world could not change the fact that when the sheriff walked away, he took her heart with him.

It had begun.

After tonight, Brave Rock might either be free to grow in peace, or several men might lie dead. Perhaps both. Either way, Clint was more than ready to put this burden down and make some kind of peace with the storm that had jangled his insides for the past two weeks.

It was Brett Chaucer's condescending smirk that he saw when he knocked on the man's door come suppertime Monday evening. The Chaucers had arranged their adjacent claims so that while their land stretched out in three directions, their cabins were close and shared some outbuildings to form a family compound. This only made McGraw's job easier.

Clint was already hot and tired, having backtracked and then circled far south out of his way in the blazing late-afternoon heat so that neither McGraw nor his men had the chance to see him arrive on Chaucer land. *When I think of all the energy I'm spending trying to save their hides,* he thought darkly to himself. Still, they were citizens of Brave Rock—exasperating, thankless citizens, but citizens just the same. As such, even though they didn't offer even a hint of the warm gratitude Katrine had shown him earlier, he owed them his protection.

"Evening, Brett."

"Evening, Sheriff." Brett bowed in exaggerated solicitude. "Won't you come on in?"

Clint ignored the mockery in Brett's voice and walked inside. The cabin was well-appointed with food and supplies, but clearly the spartan home of a bachelor. There wasn't a "homey" touch in sight, which made him wonder how much time Evelyn spent with her brothers anymore. Still, Clint was relieved to find that Theo had honored his request and gathered his two other brothers. This was going to be hard enough to tell once, much less have to repeat.

"Theo. Reid." Clint tipped his hat to the other men in greeting. "Hope you don't mind me asking if you all are alone?" It sounded overdramatic, but tonight's situation called for every precaution.

"Just us." Theo spread his hands around the room with the indignant grin Clint tried not to let get under his skin. "Not a bandit in sight. Sit on down and tell us why we ought to be boarding up our windows and loading our rifles, why don't you?"

Clint sat down, doing his best to ignore the jab. *Don't let them get to you. You can't expect decades of bad blood to dissolve overnight.* He folded his hands on the table and gave a serious look to each of the three brothers as he filled in every detail of the siege that was about to take place. "Late tonight, five men on horseback with black bandanas over their faces will ride onto your property from the northern side. Two men will stay behind and cut your northern fence so as to drive some of your cattle across the river on their way out. The other three will head south to each of your barns where they plan to set fire to your grain stores and any outbuildings that look like they might burn quickly. Make sure your horses and other animals are elsewhere—these men can't be bothered to be careful."

"You're serious. You've somehow come by the advance information that the Black Four are raiding here, tonight." Clint dearly hoped Reid's shock was the beginnings of belief, rather than open ridicule.

"I do."

Theo crossed his arms over his chest. "How?"

"I'll get to that in a moment. Right now you need to—*I need you* to listen." Clint longed to snap at them to quit their grousing for once and do the right thing, but that wouldn't help matters at all.

Reid let out a low whistle. "You really believe this is happening."

Clint chose to take that as acceptance and kept going, hoping the other brothers would follow. "Store up water buckets, blankets and move as much of your grain and hay elsewhere. Set two men with rifles to guard the house, and a third on the southwest corner of your land so that he'll see my messenger."

Theo actually laughed. "Your messenger?"

"I've gotten myself in with the Black Four. They think I'm one of them now. That means I'll be riding with them onto your land. I can't very well duck out and warn you, so I'm sending someone else. Someone you can't help but notice."

"Well, who would that be?" Brett planted one elbow on the table in mock interest.

"Lars Brinkerhoff."

Theo laughed harder. "You're sending *a ghost* to warn us?"

"I'm sending you a flesh and blood live man who escaped murder by Samuel McGraw and his fellow cavalrymen of the Security Patrol—who are the Black Four—by letting them think he was dead."

"Wait just a minute!" Reid nearly shouted. "You expect us to believe it's McGraw who's coming after us tonight? And they're the ones who set fire to Brinkerhoff's land?" He pushed back from the table with such force his chair nearly toppled over. "The Black Four is Sam McGraw and the Security Patrol? And Brinkerhoff's not dead?"

Clint had to admit, it did sound outlandish put that way. Tonight required a leap of faith that would be hard to ask of a good friend, much less a longtime family enemy. "McGraw and his cronies have a middleman set up in the next county. Since the government forbids them to buy the land, McGraw simply spooks you off yours, tips off his crony to buy it cheap, then he'll buy it back right after his commission expires. All four get prime land dirt cheap and no one's the wiser."

"But it's our stakes, our land," Reid countered.

"Not if they can clear you off it like they did the Thompsons." Clint hesitated before adding, "Or kill you. They figure you've got prime land, and without any widows or heirs to worry about, things don't get complicated if one of you happens to die. Or all of you."

"But Brinkerhoff's sister still has their land," Brett pointed out.

"They didn't want Brinkerhoff's *land,* they wanted his *silence.* He saw what they did to the Thompsons. He knows enough to connect McGraw to the Black Four. We were hatching a plan for me to get in with McGraw and bring them down from the inside, only they took things up a notch and decided murder was just a short hop from vandalism. McGraw set the fire to the Brinkerhoff cabin with the direct intent to kill Lars." He looked Reid directly in the eye. "They nailed the only door shut before they set a torch to the place."

Even now, it still sent a chill down Clint's back to speak of it. It was sinister, what McGraw had thought he was doing, and only the grace of God kept him from succeeding.

"Only they didn't know Lars wasn't inside," Clint went on, glad to see the men were listening at last. "It was best for everyone—Katrine included—if they thought Lars was out of the way." Clint glared at the eldest brother. "These men *kill,* Theo, and easily. You're next. Whether you believe me or not, you can't ignore the possibility. You've got to be ready for tonight."

"I think you're plum out of your mind," Theo balked. "Dead men bringing warnings and cavalrymen riding like bandits. It's crazy talk."

Clint had known this wouldn't be an easy persuasion, but he'd counted on the Chaucer brothers having more sense than this. Then again, what about any of this made sense? Would he have believed a Chaucer, if roles had been reversed and *they* had come to *him* with so wild a story? He took a deep breath and tried again, surprised to find a prayer of *Let them believe me, Lord* silently appearing in his mind. Well, now, Clint could count himself as officially desperate enough to resort to prayer. "I know this ain't easy to swallow, but think about it—what possible reason could I have for making this up?"

"Who knows why a Thornton does anything?" Brett's voice sounded too much like the sour echoes of his father, who'd taught the boys to hate their former neighbors. War and its devastating aftermath had made enemies of these two families. The bitterness had fermented for years, and even Evelyn's affections hadn't softened the sting. One night of cooperation—even against a common enemy—wouldn't undo so deep-seated a hatred.

Clint caught each man's eyes in turn, looking for any sign that he'd been successful. Their expressions remained hard and dark. "I'll warn you one last time. Make yourselves ready. When you see Lars coming to your gate, you'll know I'm telling the truth and Mc-

Graw and the Black Four are on their way. But you won't have much time and you need to get ready *now*. Lars will help you defend your land when he gets here. When the time is right, I will, too."

"You'll help us defend our land?" Theo scowled. "Now I know you're soft in the head. Thorntons are the reason we lost our plantation. I've no mind to believe you are gonna lift a single finger to save our land now. You got a lotta nerve coming here with a cockamamie story like this and expecting us to bar up windows and load up guns."

There was nothing more to be done. Clint was out of both time and arguments to change their minds. "I've said my piece. What you choose to do with it can't be helped. I'll see you tonight."

"I doubt that," Brett replied.

Clint had one sorrowful thought as he rose from the table and left the cabin: *you may die for that doubt*.

Chapter Fourteen

Winona worried the fringe at her sleeve as she had for the past hour. "The sun sets on slow feet tonight."

"Indeed," Katrine replied. The two of them stood on the newly built church steps, looking west toward town. Tonight, Winona would stand watch on the small hill just east of town. Clint would tack a red bandana to the back wall of the blacksmith's shop as he rode to join McGraw, which would be Winona's signal to ride out to Lars's hiding place and send him on to the Chaucers' lands. How she wanted him to come here first, to hug her and tell her things would be all right before riding off on such a dangerous mission.

Winona had explained the plan in simple enough terms. She believed in Clint and the wisdom of any plan he put together. Still, such faith couldn't stop the endless list Katrine's brain concocted of things that could go wrong.

"You worry for Lars, don't you?" she said to the Cheyenne woman when her dark brows knit together for the hundredth time that hour.

At first she only nodded in reply, then she added, "I have been praying. To Christ, as Reverend Thornton has taught me to do."

Katrine offered a sigh. "What else can we do right now but pray for His will and protection?"

"I know Reverend Thornton tells me I should pray for God's will to be done in my life. I should want that God's will is done tonight, but my own heart is strong in what it wants. What if they are not the same? What if that blocks the way of my prayers?"

Katrine could easily understand those feelings. Hadn't centuries of believers felt the rift between human wants and Divine Sovereignty? "I believe God knows our hearts, weak or strong. It is a fool thing to hide your own feelings from Him." Her own words made her wonder if she'd attempted to hide her feelings for Clint from God. She'd poured her heart out to Lars, but she had never really taken the matter to prayer, had she? She pushed out a sigh, hoping Winona's fear of "blocked prayers" could not be true. "If God heard our prayers only by what our hearts wanted, we'd go no end of wrong, *ja?* I believe it is the Holy Spirit's job to change feelings that pull us from God's purposes." *Holy Spirit, You have much work to do tonight.*

Katrine tried to meet Winona's eyes with kindness and peace rather than worry and fear, but she suspected the wise young native saw right through her ruse. "We cannot help but fear tonight, but we also know God holds the outcome. So," she said as she squared her shoulders and folded her hands in her lap, "I shall try to set aside the fear and pray in trust."

Winona considered the words for a moment, then spoke softly. "Have you set aside what you feel for the sheriff?"

Katrine took a breath to start a flurry of denials, but then realized how useless an attempt that was. In the end, she merely shook her head.

"Hearts wander in foolishness." After a second, Winona added, "Or perhaps they are the wiser than our heads in what matters most."

Katrine ran one hand along the newly painted church rail, thinking of the new square windowsill Clint had built for her. "I don't think that is true. My heart feels very foolish right now."

"My heart began to see Lars far before my spirit looked to your God. I saw how God made Lars who he is. How his faith shapes him as a man. At first there seemed to be so much between us, so many differences. Now I see that much of that is of no matter to God or hearts."

If Lars felt for Winona the way the Cheyenne woman felt for him, then Katrine couldn't help but think Lars's heart had chosen very wisely indeed. "It would be lovely if that were true."

Winona caught Katrine's arm. "What do you believe stands between you and Sheriff Thornton?"

There seemed no simple way to put it. Then again, maybe it was as simple as the answer that came to her. "Things that cannot be changed."

"Reverend Thornton would say God is more powerful than anything man can do, yes?"

"Yes. Only some things cannot be undone. Even

God's forgiveness cannot change a past deed." *A woman is still dead,* Katrine thought. *A murderer still roams free.*

"There is a deed on your soul?"

The simplicity of Winona's words did not come close to describing the tangled route Katrine and Lars had had to take on their difficult way across the nation to be here in Oklahoma. And yet, that's exactly how she felt. As if there was a dark spot staining her life that could not be removed, even if it was forgiven ten times over. "Yes."

Winona narrowed her eyes. "The sheriff does not know of this deed?"

"No." The word hung in the darkening air, final and sad.

"And you do not tell him because you fear it would change his heart against you."

His heart against you. The choice of words stung, and Katrine swallowed hard.

Winona's gaze seemed to take stock of Katrine's sagging shoulders and dismiss them. "And so you decide his heart for him by not telling him."

"Do you know the word *compromise?*"

Winona shook her head but guessed. "Something between two people?"

Again, so simple. Perhaps that was why the Cheyenne always looked so serene—there seemed to be no complexity or compromise in their world. "Often it's more than that. It can be…bending to agree to something, or it can be doing what you must when you would rather do something else. Like a mistake, only different."

"So you have made a mistake, a…compromise that

you think would drive Sheriff Thornton from you if he knew."

"Sheriff Thornton is not a man who compromises. Not when it comes to the law."

Winona folded her hands together. "That is true. But this compromise, it is not the same as a crime, yes?"

Katrine felt her sigh to the bottom of her shoes. "It depends on your point of view." That really was the crux of it, wasn't it?

"Do you regret whatever it is you have done?"

Did she regret doing what it took to keep that man from hurting her? Katrine was never sure of the answer to that question. On her worst days, she was angry at the world for forcing such a choice on her at that age. On her best days, she knew the person she was now had very little to do with the frightened girl who pretended not to see that woman in her pool of blood on that street so many years ago. That act, she could sometimes forgive. The many other poor choices the torment of that act had fostered—well, those were filled with regrets. "I wish I had not let it harm me so."

"You told me once you felt you were given another life when you were pulled from the fire. Can you not choose to leave all that behind you?" She met Katrine's eyes with a powerful dark gaze. "Can you not let Sheriff Thornton choose if he would want to leave that behind, instead of choosing for him? It seems to me this is also about the fear and trust you just mentioned."

Winona, for all her simplicity, was right; Katrine was allowing fear to deny Clint his own choice about her past. She was taking away from him the chance to choose, in the fear his choice would be to end their friendship.

Only their goodbye this afternoon had already ended that friendship. Not because she didn't want his company, but because she wanted it more than ever. She wanted more than a friendship from him. Mere friendship with Clint, genuine as it may be, would never be enough. "Yes," she whispered to Winona, "it is about fear."

She feared she would be like Trillevip, surrendering her loved one to another's heart. *Dear Father, can You make me brave enough tonight to risk what I have for what I want most?*

As if it knew what deeds McGraw planned, the moon hid its face tonight. McGraw was delighted to have such cover of darkness, but Clint could argue the inky night both helped and hindered his plans. Shots fired in the night could easily go off target, one man could easily be mistaken for another. There was just so much that could go wrong.

Not to mention his own concentration. Something had shifted between Katrine and himself this afternoon. Neither one had admitted their feelings to the other—in fact, their words declared the opposite—but the denials rang hollow and Clint was sure they both knew it. The clarity of her eyes made her a poor liar— they spoke so much more loudly than her words. That woman had so much love to give the world, and yet she held back, often hiding behind Lars's outgoing nature. She needed a family to love and to love her. Watching her with Dakota and Walt—and every other child in Brave Rock who thought of her as The Story Lady—showed that clear as day.

Which made his path clear as day as well: he'd have to tell her he could never give her a family. Outright, in the clearest—and maybe cruelest—possible words. He'd tried to tell himself differently, that all her pretty dreams about happy homes and big families didn't involve him. Still, he couldn't deny what he saw; even as she spoke the word *friends* he knew that wasn't the half of it. Glory, but when she touched his arm it was easy to forget there was a near decade between them. When she spoke his name he could make himself dismiss how they were from different worlds.

This entire week—and what was about to happen tonight—had shown him things he'd tried not to see. Katrine was sweet and pure, she'd surprised him by how brave she could be. But none of that could deny the hard truth that Katrine was not suited to live the risks of a lawman's wife. Especially not if she wanted all those young ones. He, like every Thornton, knew the pain of growing up without a father. Children needed a father they could be sure was coming home safe and sound. As sheriff, that wasn't part of what he could bring to a woman's home. No, he wouldn't risk such a constant threat of loss for any wife of his.

"Thornton!" McGraw pulled his horse up beside Clint and cuffed him on the shoulder. "Where's your head at, son? If you want to stay alive you'd best keep your mind on your business tonight. We're riding out. Where's your bandana?"

Clint held up a red one, and watched McGraw scowl, glad his scheme to get it up onto the blacksmith's wall was already in play. "What in blazes is that thing? I told you to get yourself a black one." He peered at Clint, doubt narrowing his eyes. "You getting cold feet?"

"Not one bit," Clint shot back, inserting confidence in his voice. "Just didn't think of the details." He shrugged as if he didn't think it was that important but would go along with commands, then cocked his head back in the direction of the smithy's. He'd hung a black one off the back wall earlier today. "I saw a black one hanging off the blacksmith shop. I'll go swap it out."

"Hurry it up." McGraw turned his horse away, muttering something about fools and lawmen.

As he galloped up to the back of the blacksmith shop and pulled the black bandana from its nail on a back door post, Clint felt a clumsy prayer gush from his heart. *Let Winona see. Keep Lars safe. Spare lives tonight. I'm more than ready to be done with this.* With a final glance in the direction of the hill where he knew Winona would be watching, Clint turned his horse toward the end of town where Bryson Reeves waited.

He and the private veered north out of town, following the Cimarron River until they came to the side of the Chaucer property that jutted up against its banks. Full dark was settling in fast. An owl hooted over Clint's shoulder, a pair of dogs barked at each other from back toward town. The quiet night sounds of Brave Rock would not stay quiet for long tonight.

Reeves swung down off his saddle and pulled a heavy set of wire shears from his saddlebag. "Bend the wire back," Clint advised when Reeves began snipping random wires to make a hole big enough for cattle.

"There's hardly time for that," Reeves balked. "We don't want it to look obvious." Obvious was exactly what tonight was.

McGraw really was the brains of the outfit, Clint realized. That was clear enough. "Well," he countered, "there's hardly a point to risking scrapes on cattle we might be able to sell later." Just because the private gave him a blank look, Clint couldn't help but add, "Anyways, won't it be obvious once we start shooting?"

Reeves shrugged and kept snipping until Clint swung down off his own horse and began pushing the sharp wire back on itself to make a safe exit. So many things could go amiss here. The further he got into this, the more it was going to take an act of God to come out of this with no men dead.

A shout and burst of light to his left told him the other three had ridden onto Chaucer property and a barn fire had taken hold. Now was the time to make his move.

Keeping his voice casual, Clint pulled his black bandana back up and said, "Time to get going." As if it were all part of the plan, Clint got on his horse and pulled out his rifle.

Only it wasn't, and Reeves hollered, "What are you doing?" They were supposed to begin driving the cattle across the river, only heading over to the houses if the signal of two gunshots had been given.

Clint turned his horse in the direction of the three cabins.

Reeves at least had the good sense to look puzzled. "I didn't hear no gunshots."

Clint reverted to the oldest trick in the book. "You didn't hear that?"

Reeves eyed him suspiciously. "I didn't hear nothin'."

Clint wasn't interested in lingering for a debate. "Time to go, Reeves."

"I'm telling you, I didn't hear no guns."

If Clint made it to the cabins in time, there might be no guns to hear. It was a long shot if ever there was one, but tonight was a night for slim chances to succeed. "Suit yourself," he called over his shoulder as he galloped toward the house.

The familiarity of the scene was like a punch to the gut; Clint found himself barreling through the night toward a fire with lives at stake. If the Chaucers had any sense at all, the barns had been emptied of people and animals, but he couldn't count on that. He couldn't count on anything except himself tonight—and maybe a little Divine assistance—and the weight of it pressed down on his lungs with a fierceness that hadn't ever left since the night of Katrine's fire.

It had become "Katrine's fire" in his mind. Not Lars's fire, or the fire, but a personal event. Over the course of the past two weeks, this had become not just about Brave Rock's future, but hers. He admitted to himself that he was not rebuilding a cabin for Lars, but for Katrine. It was as if he could not help himself from fixing everything in her life that he could reach, deeply aware of the parts he was helpless to restore. Or ever to bring into being. Today had shown him she'd come to mean more to him than ever was wise. He'd fight tonight to bring McGraw down so the scoundrel could never hurt Katrine again. He'd fight tonight to make Brave Rock a place where Katrine Brinkerhoff could safely raise a family with whatever husband God had in mind for her.

The fact that it couldn't be him would just have to fester as the wound that it was.

McGraw, Strafford and Wellington—nearly unrecognizable in dark clothes and black bandanas—were circling around the eldest brother's barn, touching torches to any parts that hadn't yet caught fire. McGraw had somehow seen fit to dismount his horse and commandeer the Chaucers' wagon, now filled with tools and items clearly pulled from the barn. So McGraw had decided open thievery suited his tastes as well as scare tactics, had he? Really, was it hard to believe a man capable of burning Lars in his own bed would stop at any crime? Clint could tell by the way McGraw's head kept turning toward the cabins that if the private felt the barn fire failed to give the Chaucers enough incentive to clear out, one if not all of the homes would be next. Theft, fire, destruction—it was only a matter of time before someone would start shooting.

The thought slid into Clint's head as easily as he raised his weapon. *Might as well be me.*

Clint had thought the moment he actually turned on McGraw would feel huge. Momentous and dangerous, like jumping off some kind of a cliff. It didn't. It felt more like pushing out of a dense forest into a field where the straight path in front of him opened up into clarity. Without a word, without so much as a hitch of breath, Clint kept his horse at its current speed and rode right through the line, sending three bullets into the wagon's front wheel.

The sharp sound filled the night sky, followed by shouts, a cascade of splintering wood and the whinny of the horse as the wagon crashed off its wheel and pulled everything down. The confusion gave Clint just enough time to yank off his bandana and hat so that his face could be seen, and head full tilt toward the cabins, hoping Chaucer eyes would find him before Chaucer bullets.

Chapter Fifteen

Katrine stared at the spot on the hill where Winona no longer stood watch, feeling as void as the bare landscape. Winona had ridden to Lars, giving the signal to set the drastic events of the night into motion. Everyone Katrine cared about was galloping headlong into danger, and she felt as trapped out here under the open sky as she had inside the burning cabin.

You can pray. You must pray. She knew these truths, but her hands refused to fold and her head would not bow. She paced the grass in front of the church, stared back at the yellow light of the windows, then paced more. Somewhere to her west in the direction of the Chaucer lands, where she could now see a menacing yellow glow begin to flicker over the ridge, a trio of gunshots rang out, and Katrine's whole body flinched.

Tell someone. The thought shook her to action, as far from her youthful need to keep quiet as Katrine could ever imagine. It was as though she had no choice—this time, staying silent would not, *could* not stand. Without a shred of hesitation, Katrine ran into Elijah and Alice's house, banging open the door without so much as a knock.

"Katrine?" Elijah looked up from his chair.

"Guns! At the Chaucer lands. Clint is there, and Lars will be soon."

"What?" Elijah dropped the book he was holding.

Katrine squinted her eyes shut, her English failing her at a time when she must explain so much so quickly. The sound of two more gunshots filled the air through the open door—a more convincing alarm than Katrine's words could achieve.

Sending up a wordless burst of prayer for clarity, Katrine tried again. "Lars is not dead. McGraw tried to kill him when he burned our cabin. He's been hiding because Lars knows McGraw and the other privates are the Black Four."

Alice rose off her chair. "McGraw? The Security Patrol?"

"Yes." Katrine tried not to shout, but her heart begged him to hurry with every beat. "It was those four who trapped me in my house and set it on fire. They thought Lars was inside." Elijah's eyes widened, and Katrine's throat tightened in frustration. It was too many details to make sense. She hardly understood it herself. How could she convince Elijah and Alice to lay aside the deception and offer their help? "They are horrible men and Clint is riding with them right now to trap them. Winona went to tell Lars to help the Chaucers before McGraw takes their land and—"

The sound of more gunshots stole whatever words

remained, leaving her only to cry "Help!" and clutch the watch that hung from her neck in desperation.

Elijah was already off his chair and reaching for the holster that hung on a peg by the door. "Clint had you keep this from me?"

"If too many knew, it would be more dangerous for Lars."

"Gracious!" Alice's hand went to her chest. "Lars is *alive?*"

The exclamation seemed to feed Katrine's sense of dread. What good was Lars alive if he was heading into a gun battle at this very moment? What if he and Clint both lay dying at the hands of that terrible Sam McGraw? Her eyes went to the reverend. "We must do something!"

Elijah's eyes took on a hardened quality Katrine had never seen the man display. "Alice, gather a basket of medical supplies. I'm going to get Gideon. Evelyn can stay here with Katrine while we sort this out." For one brief second he stilled, his eyes boring straight at Katrine. "McGraw. You're sure? Clint is certain?"

More shots rang out and someone in the distance shouted, "Fire over west!"

Sure enough, Katrine's next breath nearly choked at the faint scent of smoke. "Yes!"

Elijah finished the buckle on his holster and grabbed his wife's hand. "Then Heaven help us all tonight. Alice, bring the wagon as soon as Evelyn arrives, but stay back behind the pond. I'll send injured folks to you or send a messenger if it's safe to come onto the Chaucer land."

Katrine and Alice stood staring at the open doorway

as Elijah raced out, mounted his horse and galloped into the darkness.

Alice's fingers trembled as she grabbed Katrine's elbow. "Samuel McGraw and his men are the Black Four? How could they do such things?"

All the fear and anger Katrine had been struggling to hold in check seemed to roar out of control, licking at her like the fire that had devoured her house. "Because he is an awful, terrible, heartless man!" She put a hand to her forehead, ashamed of her own outburst but beyond being able to control it. "And he is shooting at Lars and Clint while we are standing here doing nothing!"

An efficiency settled behind Alice's eyes. "We will not sit here and do nothing. We have medical supplies to pull together and Evelyn will be here any moment. Your ordeal ends tonight, Katrine. God willing, our men will put a stop to the Black Four for good." She put her hands on both of Katrine's shoulders. "And Lars lives! I shall pinch Clint Thornton's ear until he hollers for putting us all through that—right after I hug him for saving so many lives." She undid the apron around her waist and picked up a lantern, heading for the infirmary. "Come now, let's go. We can pray while we stock my bags."

They had barely gotten the wagon hitched and the infirmary lanterns lit when Evelyn's voice came from the yard. Katrine rushed to the window in the vain hope that either Lars or Clint had come as well, despite the foolishness of that idea. "In here!" she called to Evelyn, waving her away from the cabin and into the infirmary.

Evelyn burst through the door, eyes wide and out of breath. "McGraw? The other cavalrymen? It can't be true, can it?" Her hand went to Katrine's. "And Lars is alive? I can barely take it in."

"My brother has come out of hiding to help save yours," Katrine said, grasping Evelyn's hand tightly. "These are dangerous men. I am worried for all of them."

"Our men are brave and strong and in the right," Alice declared as if the very words sent protection to Gideon, Elijah, Clint and Lars. "God defends the faithful. He is on the side of justice. That's what we must try to remember." Alice selected three bottles from the shelf and packed them alongside the bandages. She handed canteens to Katrine. "Here, fill these with the water from that jug over there and cap them off as tightly as you can."

Katrine was grateful to have a task. As she ladled the water from the large jug into the set of small flasks, she begged God to keep Lars and Clint from harm. *I will tell Clint how I feel and what I've done,* she told her Lord. *I will tell Lars what happened that night. I will trust in the truth and in You. Only give me the chance.* She wiped a tear from her cheek with the back of her hand, pushing away the thought that such a chance might never come. *"Gud nade,"* she prayed, aloud, falling into Danish. *"Gud nade."*

Evelyn raised a dark eyebrow, more in tender curiosity than any kind of judgment. It was the first time Katrine noticed that Evelyn's eyelashes were wet also. All of her brothers were in danger as well as her husband.

"God have mercy," Katrine translated, tightening the last cap with resolve. "God have mercy on them all."

"Amen to that," Alice replied, taking the last flask from Katrine and closing her bag. "Keep on praying and don't stop. If we are very fortunate, no lives will be taken tonight and we'll have much to celebrate in the morning." She ducked out the door and deposited her bag in the wagon bed. "I'll try to make sure word reaches you as soon as I can. Tend to each other now, and boil some water so we're ready to treat the wounded here."

"I pray we won't need it," Evelyn said, looking toward the western ridge and the ominous orange glow that burned through the dark sky.

"You never know—someone might want to boil Samuel McGraw before the night is over." Alice settled herself in the wagon seat and snapped the reins. "To think how much we all trusted them to be keeping the peace, not stealing it."

"Gud nade," Katrine called as Alice rumbled off toward the chaos.

"God have mercy," Evelyn repeated, the tears finally winning over whatever calm she had left.

"Where have all those guns come from?" Reid Chaucer yelled as he reloaded his pistol with his back to the wall. The orange glow of the barn fire cast the cabin in long, flickering shadows.

"They have government supplies stocked up all over the territory," Clint called back, his memory cataloguing every place he'd met the cavalrymen and how Lars had come across crates of ammunition. The more he uncovered the depths of these men's evil, the more astonished he grew that Lars and Katrine were still alive.

Lars had not died. Katrine had not died. The marvel in that stuck to his soul, an antidote to some of the dark corners that had stolen his faith in recent years. All Clint had to do now was live through the next few hours.

That, and fight back the four varmints who currently had him and the Chaucer brothers outgunned, cornered and close to burning down. *Anytime You'd like to show that Mighty Hand of Yours, Lord, I'd be obliged.*

The volley of bullets died down for a moment as the Black Four—it made no sense to call them soldiers anymore, they were a bandit gang if not far worse—reloaded or moved closer. Clint peered through the window opening and found a shadowy target. Just before his finger pulled the trigger, a yell and Lars's whistle signal broke the temporary quiet. Strafford cried out, clutched his leg and tumbled from his horse.

Clint's jaw dropped as not only did Lars's tall frame appear out of the smoke, but Gideon's and Elijah's, as well. As the gang whirled in surprise to meet the attack from behind, Theo Chaucer slipped out of the woodshed to pull Bryson Reeves down off his mount and knock the private out cold. As Clint pushed out the door, Gideon pointed to the side of the house in just enough time for Clint to send the butt of his rifle into Jesse Wellington's chest. Half a minute more, and Wellington might have breeched the cabin door and killed both Clint and Reid with the pair of pistols he flaunted in his hands. Clint looked up toward the Heavens, sent up a silent *Thank You kindly,* and pulled a length of rope from his belt to tie Wellington's hands behind his back before he got even a bit of his wind back.

Reid stormed up to Wellington from behind Clint, his hand drawn back for a solid punch. Clint caught the fist midair. "Hold on there, fella. There'll be time enough for pleasantries later. Right now we've got a fire and animals to deal with. Drag him onto the porch and line him up with McGraw." Thankfully, it hadn't been hard to nab McGraw once one of the splintered wagon spokes had gashed his leg wide open. "No need to be gentle, but keep your temper in check for now."

Looking up, Clint whistled through his teeth. "Gideon! They're driving the cattle over toward the river. They've cut the fence."

Always the best Thornton with animals, Gideon didn't need any further instruction. "On it!" He wheeled his mount around and headed off in the direction of the riverbank.

Turning back toward the porch, Clint found Reid and Theo knotting off the ropes that bound McGraw's feet. "We ought to send 'em into the barn to fight the fire!" Reid sneered, clearly hoping the barn would come down on these foes.

The darker part of Clint welcomed the visual of McGraw trapped in smoke just as he'd done to poor Katrine, but sense prevailed. "Not a smart idea," he counseled, realizing his left hand was covered in blood. Somehow in the battle he'd reopened the gash he'd received pulling Katrine to safety. "Can't risk these sneaky louts running off in the confusion." Clint paused and gave

McGraw his meanest scowl. "They'll get what's coming to them, I promise you that."

"Look out!" came a cry as the east side of the barn gave way with a hideous groan. Sparks flew everywhere, and the next minutes were lost in a fury of water buckets, beating blankets and smoke. Lars and Clint fought back the fire side by side, their only greeting a quick, sweat-streaked smile between buckets of tossed water.

After an hour's chaos, the furious noises of the night finally died down to spurts of shouting, the hissing of wet wood, and the forlorn quiet of a finished battle. Clint hadn't even realized Alice was on the scene until he found her picking glass out of Lars's bloody hair. She was weary, dirty, but smiling.

"You're the first dead man I've had the honor of stitching up," she said to Lars. She caught Clint's gaze with a narrowed-eyed smirk. "Of course, you weren't ever really dead, so I doubt it truly counts." Those eyes softened into something all-too-knowing when she said without moving her stare from Clint, "Lars, your sister will be beyond relieved to know you and Clint have not been harmed. I've sent word up to the house, but I don't think she and Evelyn will stay put for long so you'd best get along up there."

There was nothing Clint would have liked better than to see the relief that would be in Katrine's eyes. She'd been so brave for so long, never letting her sweet spirit descend into the bitterness of having been caught in McGraw's vicious crosshairs.

That sweet spirit had become the light of his life.

Sometime between her goodbye this afternoon and the moment when Lars had appeared out of the darkness, he'd fixed his life to hers and could never hope to take it back. Even if she chose not to make a life with him—which she very well might, once she knew everything about him—he couldn't cease to love her any more than he could cease to breathe. If Lars couldn't see it, Clint would argue with him until he could.

Lars would see it, however, for the look in the Dane's face when Winona came running up the path toward him said it all. Lars pulled himself from under Alice's hand, the bandage still untied and trailing from his head as he ran toward Winona, circling the Cheyenne woman in his arms and holding her there.

"Now wait just a cotton-pickin' minute," Theo said, coming up to stand next to Clint. "Lemme get all this straight. They were the Black Four," he said, nodding toward the quartet of bound soldiers slumped on the other cabin's porch. "He's not dead," he continued, pointing to Lars, who was still clinging to Winona, "and he's with her." Theo cast his eyes on Gideon, Elijah and Clint. "And y'all risked your lives to save us."

Clint didn't really have an answer to that astonishing list. He was too busy thinking about his own startling revelation—one that had nothing to do with Chaucers or Thorntons but everything to do with a stunning blonde woman who probably was wringing her hands with worry back at the infirmary. And not just for her brother.

"I'd say that about sums it up." Elijah shrugged.

Turning toward his friend, Clint saw a flood of happiness and relief in Lars's eyes. Their ordeal was over. It was time to build the lives each of them had come to Brave Rock to create, and Clint found himself ready to take the night's biggest risk.

He extended a hand. "Hello, friend, good to have you back."

Lars looked at the hand, then at Clint, then side-stepped the handshake to clasp him in his arms. "It is very good to be back." The Dane's eyes wandered over to the dark eyes of the Cheyenne woman beside him. "Very good indeed." They began walking toward the cabin where Reid, Alice and Elijah were packing things up. "You and I have much to discuss, *ja?*"

Clint stopped walking and returned his hand to Lars's shoulder. "Far more than you know."

Chapter Sixteen

A while later, Clint and Elijah stood on the remains of a Chaucer front porch and surveyed the damage. Nearly every window was broken, the front door was in splinters and debris covered most of the yard. For all the Chaucer brothers' work to raise up decent homesteads, the compound looked more like a battlefield. Still, Clint felt grateful no lives had been lost tonight—or was it already this morning? It had to be well past midnight, probably closer to dawn.

Reid, scraped up and covered in soot, walked up to them after conversing with Gideon. "We got back most of the herd. There are a dozen head of cattle still unaccounted for. I expect we'll find them somewhere on the other side of the river once the sun comes up." He took off his hat to wipe his brow as he stared at the one remaining barn wall left standing, now a skeleton of charred beams. "We'd have lost the horses for sure if we hadn't moved them out of the barn."

"You still have your land, and those scoundrels are

done putting others off theirs." Elijah placed a hand on the man's shoulder.

Theo came out from the house, wiggling his fingers inside a thick white bandage. "I'm still shaking my head. If you'd have told me the Black Four was Sam McGraw and the rest of those men—"

"Actually," Clint couldn't help but cut in, "that's *exactly* what I told you." Elijah shot him a "behave yourself" look only an older brother could muster.

Theo conceded the point with a nod. "If I hadn't seen it with my own eyes…"

"If I hadn't seen *you* with my own eyes," Elijah echoed as he turned to Lars and offered him a hearty handshake. "I am glad beyond words to know you're safe and sound." He pinched the bridge of his nose with his free hand. "Although I have to say, I don't quite know how to take back a funeral. I reckon Sunday's sermon may be my most interesting one ever."

Clint was glad to discover he could still laugh. It was all over now—most of it anyway. There were still some dicey parts to go. And then there was the business of Katrine…

"I am very sorry to put you all through this," Lars said, catching Elijah's and Gideon's eyes in turn. "We were sure it was the only way. It was hard on Clint and Katrine, but they were strong."

"So you hid Lars from your own family, but pulled him out of hiding to save ours?" Reid looked as if he couldn't quite pull those facts together.

Clint leaned against a porch post, the adrenaline of the battle giving way to a wave of exhaustion. His hand stung where his gash had broken open again, not to mention the other scrapes and bruises starting to make themselves known. "The Black Four had gone beyond scaring weak or foolish folk out of their claims. They started getting greedy enough to feel like no law bound them at all. The fire they set to Lars's cabin was meant to be murder, no doubt about it."

Brett Chaucer walked up, looking as tired and bedraggled as his brothers. "They're the worst kind of men, those four. Black-hearted schemers down to the last man."

"I knew once they'd succeeded there, they'd do it again," Clint went on, glad to know Brave Rock would finally see those men for the crooks they were. "And with more ease every time. No land would ever be enough. If Brave Rock was to know any peace, they had to be stopped—at any cost."

Brett Chaucer put his finger through a nasty gash in his hat. A bullet had missed his head by inches. "Cost us a pretty penny, I'd say."

Reid shot his brother a dark look. "Didn't cost us our lives nor our land."

"It will be a long while before I stop giving thanks to God for that mercy," Elijah added. "If ever."

"And thanks to the Thorntons," Reid continued, scratching his chin. "Peculiar as that seems."

"Only a fool would fail to say thanks for what you've done here tonight," Theo conceded with slow words. "And I'm no fool."

"It weren't thanks I was looking for," Clint said, holding Theo's gaze, "but I've never taken you for a fool man, Chaucer. You were only believing what your pa told you."

Elijah extended his hand to Theo. "Perhaps it is time to lay old grudges down and let tonight be the start of true peace for these parts."

For a second, Clint couldn't be sure Theo would take the olive branch Lije offered. He found himself shooting up a single, wordless plea to Heaven that tonight would indeed bridge the gap between these two families. Brave Rock would never be big enough to hold feuding Chaucers and Thorntons. Glory, but knowing his brothers and the Chaucer men, all of Oklahoma wouldn't be big enough. Gideon's new family deserved better, now that he was kin to the Chaucers. When he saw Theo begin to extend his hand, Clint held out his good hand to Reid. Gideon followed suit, shaking hands with Brett. Chaucers were shaking hands with Thorntons. It was a sight Clint never thought he'd see in all his days.

"Go home to my sister," Reid said to Gideon. "Tell Evelyn her new husband has my thanks."

"I'll gladly do that, but you'd best have some help fencing in those cattle for the night or you may lose more across the river. I can have Lars send word of my safety when he shows up alive and well to Katrine."

"I'll take the help," Reid said.

Alice came out from inside the damaged cabin, wiping her hands on her nursing apron. "Clint and Lars, why don't you two head on back? I'm sure Katrine will be more than glad to see that both of you made it through unharmed." She nodded her head toward the gash still bleeding through the bandages she'd put on

Clint's hand half an hour ago. "Well, mostly unharmed." She looked toward the porch of the second cabin where McGraw and his men were tied up and slumped in varying degrees of injury. "It doesn't pain me to say it was those four who ended up the worst of the night."

Clint felt like every rib had been kicked out of place; he heard every joint calling for peace and rest. It seemed a week since he had exhaled or let his guard down. "I'll be glad to see them behind bars."

"Bars or no bars, I doubt those swine are going anywhere tonight," Gideon said. "Most of 'em look as if they couldn't make it off the porch at gunpoint."

"You go on now," Reid said to Clint. "We'll see to those boys for the evening."

"No," Clint argued, even though he felt as though he could lie down right where he was and sleep for a week. "They need to be in the jail now."

"Let's let that wait 'til morning," Reid said with a sideways grin. "I kind of like the idea of them trussed up on my porch for the night like the animals they are."

Duty insisted he not leave such a task to someone else, but Clint was too tired—and too eager to talk to both Lars and Katrine—to argue the cause of duty tonight. He'd just given nearly all of himself in the service of Brave Rock, and he knew he needed to see the relief in Katrine's eyes. "Just give me a pair of hours to take care of a few things and gather handcuffs and shackles from the office. I'll be back by dawn."

"Oh, no, you take your time," Theo said, his voice full of menace.

Clint raised an eyebrow and pointed a finger at Theo.

"No harm, you understand? I'm not calling for hospitality, but I do expect to come collect four live men when I return." If justice was to prevail in Brave Rock, it had better start right here. Even the worst of Brave Rock's criminals needed to receive due process. He needed to know the Chaucers would be men of the law and of their word, even when sorely tempted otherwise.

"Fair enough," Reid reluctantly conceded, holding up both hands.

When all three Chaucers and all three Thorntons shook hands one final time, Clint found his weariness replaced with a sensation he hadn't felt in far too long: hope.

The sounds had been awful. Every shot had felt like it pelted through Katrine's chest, every whiff of smoke had sent her pulse racing in fear. She had heard people talk of the war in the most dreadful terms, seen those who carried wounds or lost kin, but never seen actual battles. Tonight, it felt as if a very war had broken out right here in Brave Rock. Lars was there. Clint was there. Those bloodthirsty soldiers were there.

And now she was here, staring at a pot of water that stubbornly refused to boil. Katrine tossed the dish towel on the infirmary table in frustration. "Now that it has quieted, I want to go there. I feel so helpless here."

Evelyn, who seemed to be having no better success with setting out rolls of bandages, put her hands on her hips. "I know. There has to be something else we can do other than just sitting here, waiting for news. Surely others from town have already gone to help—

why shouldn't we?" Katrine trusted Clint with her life, and he must have had some reason to set things up the way he had. Still, doubts plagued her. Clint's plot required some kind of secrecy, but those men were too dangerous to face alone or even with Lars's help. Had she helped Clint by telling Elijah? Or had she hampered him? She turned to Evelyn, desperate for some affirmation that she hadn't placed Clint in further danger. "I have done the right thing, haven't I?"

Evelyn's brows furrowed. "In what?"

"Clint would have asked for help if he needed it. I know he had a plan. But I could not stay silent when I heard the guns. I wish I could know that telling Elijah helped Clint, not harmed his plan."

Evelyn drew closer. "How could Clint not need all the help he could get?"

Katrine did her best to quickly explain how Clint had been pretending to be on McGraw's side. Telling the plan again, even now, only seemed to make it feel more dangerous. It all had hung on so thin a thread. Katrine couldn't help worrying that Lars's fake death might already be all too true. Why wasn't he here yet? "I am trying to rely on God's providence, but I am too frightened."

Evelyn blinked back tears. "I am frightened, too." After all, her Gideon had been on that "battlefield," as well. Her new husband, the man who now stood as a father to her precious son, Walt, might still be risking his life to secure Brave Rock's future. "And I am glad you came to Elijah." She took in a deep breath, dabbing at her eyes with one of the bandages she held. "Sometimes a good man is too stubborn to ask for help, don't you think?" She squinted her eyes shut against a new wave of tears. "When I think of my brothers facing those bandits…"

Katrine put a hand on her arm. "Your brothers had warning. Clint went to them and told them McGraw was coming. But," she hated to add, "they were not quick to believe him."

"Oh, I can see how that would happen. They have been fed too many years of false stories against the Thorntons. I doubt they'd believe Clint on the color of the sky as they stared at it, much less this." The temporary quiet was broken by a loud crash from the end of town where the Chaucers lived, causing Evelyn to flinch and grab Katrine's hand. "I am glad you sent help," Evelyn declared, squeezing Katrine's fingers. "I am. And I believe that help has saved my brothers." After a second, her dark eyes widened. "And yours. Your brother is there. And alive. Surely God can't have spared his life only to take it tonight."

And here everyone had thought the highest stakes had played out on the rush for land. Once the wooden stake hit the ground, the future was secured—wasn't that how everyone in Boomer Town viewed the promise of the rush? Who would have believed so many would be fighting to keep that land mere weeks after setting up homesteads? All Katrine's hopes seemed to burn up, just as her cabin had. She covered her eyes with her hands, picturing the two logs Clint had built into the new cabin's walls. Hope was not burned, merely scarred. She could believe what Evelyn had said. "I want to believe I did the right thing." *I want God to grant life to Clint as well,* her heart cried. *I want God to grant me a chance at a future with him.*

She felt Evelyn tug slightly on her hand. "There's more, isn't there? Katrine, what aren't you saying?"

Katrine felt she would burst if she did not speak the words aloud to someone. Silence had been the enemy for too much of her life. "I worry for Clint."

"Of course, we all worry for Sheriff—" Realization halted her words. "Oh." Evelyn put her hand on Katrine's shoulder. "Yes, of course you do." A warm smile replaced her tears. "I suspect he…worries for you, as well."

Katrine felt heat warm her cheeks. "I believe he does. But it is not simple, *ja?*"

"It never is, is it?" The understanding in Evelyn's eyes came from experience. To be with Gideon she had overcome a storm of obstacles—not the least of which was the disapproval of the very brothers under fire tonight. She sighed. "It ought to be, but it never is."

Together they stared at the frustratingly quiet water, worry filling the room as much as the steam beginning to rise from the pot. "I don't know if it will ever be simple," Katrine said. She dared a look into Evelyn's eyes. "But I would like the chance to try."

"Then we shall pray you get that chance." As another alarming crash sounded across the night air, a few hopeful bubbles slowly began to rise in the deep pot.

Finally, Katrine felt like she'd accomplished one thing in this night of helpless waiting. Boiling water was not much of a victory, but she would take it as a start. She would take this friendship with Evelyn as a start, too, and hold firm to the hope that tonight would be a new beginning and not a disaster. "Everyone in Brave Rock deserves a chance to be happy."

Evelyn set the lid back on the big metal pot with a declarative clink. "That's what they're all fighting for over there. That's why you did the right thing."

Chapter Seventeen

As they headed back to town in the wee hours of Tuesday morning, Lars and Clint rode in weary, thoughtful silence. Lars was surely pondering how a dead man rode back into the town that had mourned his passing. As for Clint, he was trying to figure out how to broach the subject of Katrine with Lars—and all she had come to mean to him.

"I... Your sister..." Clint tried to begin, but he couldn't seem to get any more words out than that. He'd just faced down a torrent of gunfire and found himself terrified of this? This heart business was a fearsome thing. No wonder Elijah and Gideon always walked around with such fool looks on their faces.

"*Sorgfult* Katrine." Lars shook his head and sighed with one hand on his chest as if the heartache for his sister's anguish was a physical ailment. He didn't have to translate. If the way Clint's heart felt right now was any indication—half lit firecracker, half leaden stone—maybe that gesture wasn't so far off.

The sun was coming up and they were both beyond exhausted and eager at the same time. Clint would have preferred to gallop, to get to Katrine as fast as possible, but there was a part of him that needed this settled with Lars first. That part somehow recognized that once he saw Katrine, it would all be lost. He'd be unable to stay away no matter whether Lars gave his blessing or not. Maybe that's what made him so skittish now—he wanted to go into that moment with Katrine knowing that if she returned his feelings, there was no obstacle.

If. And that was a mighty big if.

"Katrine," Clint began again, watching Lars's eyebrow rise. Until now he'd been careful to refer to Katrine as *your sister* or *Miss Brinkerhoff* in company. He cleared his throat and repeated, "Well, Katrine…" Hang it, he had no idea how to have this conversation. It couldn't wait, but now seemed like the worst possible time.

"Katrine and you," Lars said after a pause that pressed on Clint's chest, "have had much to bear." When Lars added "…together" in a tone Clint couldn't hope to decipher, the night air seemed thick enough to choke a man.

"She's strong. And she was brave." That truth was an easy admission.

"Katrine has great faith." Lars fished for something in his pocket as they rode, and Clint was grateful the Dane had someplace else to focus his piercing blue eyes. "And a very big heart."

"Yes. It was hard for her to watch good folk grieve over you. Your sister loves you very much." *Which is why I'll be sunk if you can't see your way clear to us being together,* his mind finished. If it were any other woman, Clint was enough of his own man to disregard what other people thought, but this was Katrine, and this was Lars. He could never be a wedge between these two, ever.

"Broderkaerlighed."

"Huh?"

"Broderkaerlighed," Lars repeated. "The word for what a brother feels for a sister, and such. For what is between you and Elijah and Gideon. Family." The Dane tapped his heart with his open hand. "What I feel for Katrine."

What I feel for Katrine. It'd be hard to find words that didn't prick sharper than that. Clint only nodded, unable to come up with any other response.

Lars pulled a folded sheet of paper from his pocket. "Only that is not the word Katrine used."

"She's such a fine writer, she's probably got handfuls of words to use." They were getting closer to the church. Clint was going to have to turn this conversation away from vocabulary, and quickly at that, if he was going to gain Lars's approval before he saw Katrine.

"Katrine writes stories, but she also writes truth. That is a good thing." Lars pulled his horse to a halt and held the paper out to Clint, pointing. "See the words here?"

"Those?"

"These words mean *to lose one's heart to another.*"

Clint stared at the soft, flowing letters, absorbing

their meaning. He felt Lars's hand come to his shoulder as their horses stood side by side.

"In English you would say *fall in love.* Only in our language it is closer to *are too in love.* I like that better than *falling,* but now I know why you use that word." A wide smile crinkled the corners of Lars's eyes. "And now *you* use that word as well, *ja?*"

Clint was beyond wide awake now, and not the least bit tired. "She wrote you? She said she…?" He couldn't even manage to choke the word out, just pointed to the Danish words on the paper.

"Winona brought it to me two days ago. It is the letter you say you found on your desk. She does not use your name, but Winona told me she had seen Katrine's heart turn toward you long before I realized it. A brother does not always see these things, *ja?* But Winona is wise that way. So you see?" His hand gave Clint's shoulder a jovial squeeze. "We *both* fall."

Clint felt a mile-wide smile spread across his face. "You and Winona."

"We are very different, but then again not so much. God is fond of surprises, don't you think?"

Clint actually laughed. "I think God is mighty fond of big surprises. I'm glad God is mighty patient with the likes of me, too."

Lars started his horse to walking, with Clint echoing his movement. "I am glad to see your soul has found its way home. I would not see Katrine wed to a man who is not right with God."

"Wed?" Clint hadn't quite gotten that far in his thinking—at least not that he was ready to let on to Lars.

"It is what men in love do, is it not?"

Clint's head was spinning faster than his heart was pounding. "I suppose it is." A life with Katrine. He hadn't allowed himself that splendid of a daydream.

"I was thinking how wonderful it would be to erase my false funeral with a true wedding. How much more joy with two!"

Clint stopped his horse again. "I haven't told her, Lars."

Lars stopped his horse and met Clint's gaze. "You will tell her how you feel."

"No, not just that. I mean I know she wants a family and…I haven't told her. I can't give her that." In all the conversations he'd had with Lars, Clint had hinted at the fact that he felt he'd always be alone, but he'd never revealed his inability to father children.

Lars was silent for long moments after Clint explained the problem now, and while the pause was difficult, Clint found himself glad the Dane gave the admission the thought it deserved. Finally, he looked up at Clint with understanding in his bright blue eyes. "I am not Dakota's father. But he has become a son to me. Yes, Katrine will be sad, but she has a big heart and a strong spirit. And God is fond of surprises."

"Lars…" Clint didn't know how to ask this final question.

"What, my friend?"

"What if…" He stared at the blood that had seeped through the bandage on his hand, remembering the helplessness he felt the night of the Brinkerhoff fire. Nothing, not even his brothers, had come to mean so much to him as Katrine. Doubt that he could ensure her happiness uncurled under his ribs. "What if I am not enough?"

Lars's brows furrowed for a moment, a shadow of understanding coming over his pale features. He was a man who had made his way halfway across the world with no more family than a single sister. He knew the truth Clint lived every day; a man who loved was a man who could lose. "No man is ever enough. God must fill the rest."

And there it was. The final truth Clint had slammed up against tonight, the one he'd been pushing toward for years now in his quest to be good enough, strong enough, vigilant enough, man enough. "Yes."

The smile returned to Lars's eyes. "Let us hope that is what *she* says."

"Has Winona already given you her yes?"

Lars's smile widened. "She has. For a dead man, I have an excellent life ahead of me."

Clint adjusted the set of his hat and nudged his horse into a trot. "A fine life indeed. Give me an hour and I hope to say the same."

It was nearing four in the morning and Evelyn's grace and optimism had long since run out. Now she simply paced the room. "It has been too long. Something must have happened."

Katrine was trying to keep such thoughts at bay. "No," she said, more to herself than to Evelyn. "They must have won the battle or someone would have come by now. The delay means good things." She didn't really believe that, but she could not allow her worries to gain words. Not now. Not with Lars and Clint still out there.

"What if there were more than four? Gideon said whoever was behind all this had lots of guns. There is good land to be stolen here. Maybe they have more bandits coming."

"There are only four," Katrine declared.

Evelyn turned toward Katrine. "How do you know?"

Katrine put her hand to her forehead. She was beyond weary. Too much time had passed and she and Evelyn had switched composures—now she was the one quietly hoping for the best and Evelyn had given in to a rising panic. "I don't. But I am trying to tell myself the story that will keep me most calm."

"What story is that?"

"A story where good men turn back evil, and peace comes to Brave Rock. A happy ending."

"I doubt words can save our men."

"Only hours ago, you thought my brother was dead. He is alive because he and Clint are smarter than those men. I choose to hope and tell myself stories that do the same."

Evelyn returned her gaze to the window. "I will not bury a second husband. I will not find Gideon only to lose him to the likes of Sam McGraw."

Katrine sighed. "Those are hopeful words. Keep to those." She checked the pot, which had already boiled down several inches. She tried to take her own advice. "I will see Lars again. We will celebrate his return home." *I will tell Clint what my heart feels for him. I did the right thing by not staying silent. I will not be that frightened girl in the alley anymore.*

With a gasp, Evelyn pressed her hands to the windowsill. "Horses!"

Elijah and Alice would be in the wagon—horses had to mean Clint and Gideon or even Lars. "They are back!" Katrine felt the relief spark her tired body to life. The past several hours had felt a thousand years long, filled with sounds and sights and endless worries. She understood now why Clint gave everything in the service of justice—the threat of just a few evil men could take so much from Brave Rock.

Katrine pulled open the door and rushed out onto the porch, ready to greet Clint and Lars and give thanks that they were home safe and sound. Instead, she backed against the infirmary wall in dread as the bloody image of Samuel McGraw staggered down off his horse. His gun was drawn and aimed at her even though it wavered a bit, and his face gleamed with sweat. "I let you get away once," he sneered, limping toward her, "I don't aim to let it happen again."

Evelyn gave a small yelp from behind her. Katrine tried to shut the door, but a second man already had her by the arm. "Looky here, Sam, there's one for each of us."

"The men will be here in a moment." Katrine tried to make her voice hold Clint's confidence, but she failed. If McGraw was free, did that mean Clint and the others had come to harm? Or might even be dead? The way McGraw looked at her turned what little hope she was holding into thin, brittle ice.

"Don't matter much if we got here first." He took another step toward Katrine, wiping his dirty mustache with the black bandana that hung loose around his neck. "Tie 'em up, Wellington. But nice and careful-like. We don't want to be taking home damaged goods."

Wellington gave an ugly laugh as he pulled Katrine's hands together and she felt the harsh bite of a rope on her wrists. Evelyn tried to cry out, only to have Wellington yank the bandana from his own neck and wedge it into her mouth. Even though she kept silent, Katrine grimaced when McGraw did the same. She hated that the cloth had been near his mouth, felt nearly sick at the foulness of it all.

The men were quick despite their injuries. It seemed only seconds before Private Wellington was hoisting her up onto a horse in front of McGraw. Katrine turned her face toward the barely lightening sky, willing Clint and Lars—or anyone—to come over the ridge and save them. *Send him to save me again, Lord!* The smell of soot and blood radiated off McGraw as he turned the horse away from town.

There was no log to kick now, no exit of her own to make in time to grab Clint's saving hands. Katrine tried to throw herself from the horse, thinking whatever injury the ground could give would be far better than the wounds McGraw had in mind.

The private only tightened his arm around her and pulled her closer. "Hang on there, Katie darlin'," he sputtered through labored breaths that felt as if they were crawling down Katrine's back, "we've a hard ride and I can't have you fallin' off."

Katrine managed to find Evelyn's wide eyes in the dark chaos. She looked just as frightened as she rode on Private Wellington's horse. Now that they had been exposed, McGraw and his gang had nothing left to lose and only vengeance on their minds. "Did you know your brother was alive, missy?" McGraw hissed in her ear as they rode away from Brave Rock. "Have you known the whole time?"

Katrine was glad to hear McGraw confirm that Lars—and hopefully Clint—was alive. Still, even if the private pulled the gag from her mouth, Katrine would not give him the satisfaction of an answer.

"I don't take kindly to being played the fool. Neither by your brother nor by that sheriff who thinks he can outsmart the likes of me."

Clint is alive. Katrine gave silent thanks.

"Hey, McGraw," Wellington called, "what are we gonna do with these little fillies anyway?" Out of the corner of her eye, Katrine saw Private Wellington finger a lock of Evelyn's dark hair with fascination until she yanked her head away.

"A hostage is fine leverage against your enemy," McGraw declared in a superior tone. "When it's a pretty one, well, I always find that just makes the time a little easier to pass. Veer down by the river for a spell so we can hide our tracks. Then head over to that hut past the river bend. We'll be fine holed up in there for the day." He shifted in his saddle. "Need to rest my leg a spell anyways."

"How bad you hurt?" Wellington asked.

"Don't you worry none about my leg," McGraw replied, but Katrine noticed the strain in his voice. "Nothing a little nursing by a pretty lady can't fix up."

"How will those Chaucer boys and that foreign fellow know we've got their sisters? Don't they think we're back with Reeves and Strafford?"

"Wellington, some days you don't show a lick of sense. They've long figured out we're gone. When they come to find their women gone, they'll know who took 'em." He gave a dark laugh. "They just won't know *where.*" His hand reached around to finger the lace at Katrine's cuff. "Maybe we'll send them a hint or two, just to keep things interesting."

Katrine yanked her hand away from McGraw's grasp, only to have him hold her more tightly against him. One thought settled quietly in her brain, dark and still as a graveyard: *He tried to kill me once. He'll do it again. Father God, do not let him succeed.*

Chapter Eighteen

"Clint! Lars!" Gideon's voice rose above a thunder of hooves sounding behind them. "Hold up!"

"Changed your mind about needing to see Evelyn?" Clint teased, only to drop his smile when he saw the panic on Gideon's face.

"It's McGraw. And Wellington. They're gone."

"I didn't figure they were wounded that badly." McGraw had a pretty bad gash in his leg, but it didn't look like the kind of thing to kill him. Alice had tended to the wound, besides.

"No, they're *gone!* One minute the four of them were slumped together, out cold, the next time I turned around Reid was running around yelling. I don't know how that pair of snakes did it, but those two made off." He gave the next two words the gravity they deserved: "With horses."

For one leaden moment, silence filled the air while each of the three men envisioned the possible outcomes of McGraw's escape. Then, as if all of them had come to the same conclusion, they set off at a gallop toward Elijah's cabin and the infirmary.

Clint knew it was too late before he was even onto the property. The infirmary door swung open in the night wind, a chair lay toppled over just outside the door. Lars said something in Danish that needed no translation—his tone matched the slam of dread in Clint's chest.

"He's got her." The very thing he'd tried so hard to prevent.

"And Evelyn," Gideon added with alarm. "Evelyn was with Katrine."

"I don't think he'll hurt them," Clint said with a certainty he didn't truly feel. His mind recalled the lecherous way McGraw had eyed Katrine. The private was smart enough to know possession of the two women gave him enormous leverage. He'd play that to the hilt, given his fondness for cat-and-mouse games. Still, he didn't need their deaths to take his revenge—a man of his moral lack could harm good women in other ways. Clint battled to keep the rage boiling in his chest under enough control to let him think clearly. He stared at the open door. They'd taken no care to cover their tracks. "He wants us to know he has them."

"If he so much as touches one hair on Evelyn's head…" Gideon ground out through his teeth as they swung down off their horses to survey the scene.

Clint dreaded the question, but it had to be asked. "Lars, do you know where Winona is?"

Relief flooded the Dane's blue eyes. "She told me she would gather Dakota and wait for me at the Gilberts'."

Clint ran his hands down his face, calculating who was where and could offer what help. "That's good."

"McGraw does not know her…" Lars struggled for the right way to say it "…value to me. She may be useful."

Gideon looked a bit puzzled, but now was certainly not the time to go into specifics of that nature. "No," Clint replied, "best keep her safe and out of this. Elijah and Alice are a bit behind us, right?"

Gideon began reloading his rifle, his tinderbox of a temper about to get the best of him. But Clint knew dealing with McGraw—especially now that the stakes were so high—would take strategy, not gunpowder. If he was heading anywhere close to an ammunition stash the size of one Lars had seen, McGraw could not be outgunned. He had to be out-thought. "Hold on there, Gideon."

"That lout's got Evelyn!" Gideon nearly shouted.

Clint could empathize—his insides were shouting for Katrine with every slam of his pulse. "I know. I know. But *think,* Gideon. We've got to try to think ahead of him. We've got to try to figure out where he's taking her." He turned to Lars, who had already begun to scan the scene like the master tracker Clint knew him to be. "What do you see?"

Lars had grabbed the lantern still burning in the infirmary and was inspecting the ground beside the building's front porch. "Two horses." He went a few steps farther. "Blood."

"Blood?" Gideon surged forward to the dark splatters illuminated by the lantern.

Clint came up behind his brother and steadied him with a hand on his shoulder. "That's good news. Mc-Graw was injured, remember? If he's still bleeding, he's in bad shape." *Don't let it be Katrine's,* Clint found himself praying, feeling as if no one but God Himself could keep her safe for the next hour. *Or Evelyn's blood, either. Think, Thornton. Be a sheriff.*

Casting his eyes through the open door into the infirmary, Clint saw that the room was still in an orderly state. "They didn't think to take supplies from the infirmary, so they'll need food, water and medicine. Lars, you discovered some of their caches. Which ones are closest?"

Lars closed his eyes in thought, and Clint turned to see Elijah on horseback and Alice in the wagon coming up the way. They were expecting a joyful reunion, not another dose of trouble. It took Lije all of three seconds to read his brothers' expressions. "No." His word was almost a moan as he swung down off his saddle.

"McGraw's got Katrine and Evelyn," Gideon snarled. "Somehow that snake slithered right out from under those Chaucer noses and he's got them. Him and Wellington."

"But they were both injured. McGraw especially." Alice came down off the wagon to grasp her husband's arm. "I'm sorry I stitched him up at all. But it was a bad wound, Clint. If he's running off like that, the stitches will never hold."

"He's still bleeding," Lars said, pointing to the red spots on the ground. "And badly enough to not venture far. I think they would go to the shack downriver from

Gideon's. Or the cave up over the ridge to the southwest beyond where our cabin was."

"Where your cabin will *still be,*" Clint corrected, although it didn't seem a detail worth worrying about at the moment. Still, the thought of those windows without Katrine's face peering out of them made him want to pummel McGraw with his bare hands.

"Why are we standing here?" Gideon growled, pacing. "Every moment we wait they get farther away!"

Lars gave Clint a steady look. "It must be one of those places. The others have only ammunition, not food and shelter, right?"

"Only ammunition?" Gideon cut in. "You said they were well armed. They're going to where they've got *more?*"

Clint grabbed Gideon's shoulder. "Look at me." He held his brother's gaze until the wild rage steeled to a hard, determined focus. "Do you care how many guns they have?"

"No," Gideon said.

Clint would have ridden straight into a cavalry with a dozen cannons to save Katrine. "Neither do I. We *will* get them back. We will." He felt his resolve settle down into that rock-solid place that made him the lawman he was. It was now an indisputable fact: the sun would not go down on this day until he gazed into the blue of Katrine's eyes.

"Lije, you ride southwest with Lars. Gideon, you and I will take the spot downstream." He handed Alice the keys to his sheriff's office. "Alice, run into town and wake Daniel O'Grady. Send him over to the Chaucers with the handcuffs from my office. I want those last two locked up in a cell as fast as we can. Tell Dan to scare them up a bit on the way—maybe they'll rat out their partners who left them to hang."

"We'll need more than the four of us," Elijah cautioned. "If they're desperate enough to try this, they'll be desperate enough to try anything."

"What are you saying?" Clint's impatience was starting to match Gideon's.

"The Chaucers will help you. Evelyn's their kin."

"The Chaucers are the ones who let McGraw get away in the first place!" Gideon barked.

"You don't know that," Elijah argued.

Clint had to admit Lije was right. "Even if it's so, that'll make them all the more willing to hunt McGraw and Wellington down. Swing by the Chaucer place and fill them in. Take one with you and send the other two downstream to us."

"Chaucers and Thorntons working together," Alice said as Elijah helped her up into the wagon. "Never thought I'd see the day."

"Well, God is mighty fond of surprises," Clint replied, bringing a stunned stare from Lije. "I hope He's mighty fond of justice, too. Let's go!"

"There now," Private Wellington said with a civility Katrine did not at all feel. "Ain't that homey?" He had spread a thin blanket across a pallet on the floor of the ramshackle structure and handed a tin of canned meat each to Katrine and Evelyn.

Evelyn frowned at the *Property of the United States*

Cavalry stamp on the tin. "You steal food from the government?"

"Those rations are necessary provisions for our well-being," McGraw said as he took another healthy swig from a whiskey bottle Katrine also imagined he would classify as "necessary for his well-being." He'd broken into the crate of liquor first thing upon pushing into the shack and hadn't let up yet. It didn't take Alice's nursing skills to see he was in a great deal of pain. He grimaced with every movement and a sheen of sweat covered his face and arms. A wet blotch of purple stained his dark blue pants.

McGraw followed her gaze, and subsequently nodded at Evelyn. "You finish off that ham and then you'll tend to my leg."

Evelyn's chin rose. "I'll do no such thing."

McGraw slammed the bottle down on the table where he sat with his leg propped on one rickety chair. "I'd advise you to drop your contentious Chaucer ways if you have a mind to live until sundown."

"I'm no nurse." Evelyn's reply was more defiant than Katrine thought wise. *Clint, come save us! He will only grow more mean as the pain goes on. Lars, find us!*

"You got a boy, don't you? I ain't never met a mother didn't know how to bind up a wound. That box over there has a medical kit inside, and if you know what's good for you you'll put it to good use."

Wellington, as if it would help matters, turned the little tin key that peeled the top off the tin of ham and handed it to Evelyn. He'd done the same for Katrine, and terrible as the rations tasted, she was too hungry to refuse what might be her last meal for hours if not days. Wellington waited a minute or two as Katrine choked down the last of the awful, salty ham. "You," he said, pointing to Katrine, "come with me to fetch some water from the river."

"Don't leave me alone with him," Evelyn cried out.

Her alarm only brought a snicker from McGraw. "Don't you worry your little head over that, missy. I've no eye for dark eyes and hair." He turned to Katrine, and she saw McGraw eye her with the same barely concealed appetite she'd seen at the mercantile that one day. "I like 'em with yellow locks."

His gaze was so hungry that Katrine gladly followed Private Wellington out of the shack just to be away from it. She had always thought that the murderer from her younger years was the most evil man she had ever met, but McGraw was more awful still. Grabbing a pair of buckets, Wellington led them down a small path toward an offshoot of the Cimarron River. At least she hoped it was the Cimarron River—she'd lost all sense of direction in the wild ride to this camp.

Katrine looked up at the thin pale sky, trying to find the sun behind a blanket of gray clouds. She prayed that God would stave off the rain so as not to wash away the tracks, as Lars had always said. It had become clear that their only hope of safety was if Lars or Clint were able to track them to wherever it was McGraw had taken them.

Where am I? She peered at the tree line as she walked, scanned the landscape for anything that looked familiar. She hadn't even the sun to work out the direction they'd ridden. Nothing she could see proved any help at all. Katrine tried to not let her rising panic get the best of her wits, for they seemed to be all she had to help herself now. *Find the drafty corner and start kicking.* She could almost hear Clint whisper the words in her ear.

Wellington let out a groan of pain as he leaned into the river to fill his bucket. He seemed less evil than McGraw—a soft man merely following orders. Perhaps he was the weak corner in all this danger and she could make some headway with him.

"You are hurt?" she asked, pointing to where the private clutched his side.

"Don't you worry about that. I'll be fine."

He clearly wasn't, but she was unsure how far to push the subject. She tried to imagine how Clint had talked the soldiers away from her cabin. "Getting alongside them," he'd called it. Could she get alongside Wellington? "Why do you follow him?" Katrine kept her voice light as she bent over to fill her own bucket.

"What kind of fool question is that?"

"He has no honor, no loyalty. Not to you. Not to anyone." With the hand that wasn't holding the bucket, Katrine worked the pale blue ribbon from her braid, bunching it up in one fist.

"You just shut your yappin', missy. I'm of my own mind here. I know where my reward is and where it isn't."

"I do not see reward here." Behind her back, Katrine began winding the ribbon around a branch at the top of a nearby bush.

When Wellington slammed his bucket down, spilling water over his feet, Katrine startled, but kept herself between Wellington and her ribbon so he could not see. "You hush up!" he barked, and she knew she'd hit a nerve. "Look what you made me do! Now, you go refill that bucket for me, you loudmouthed foreigner woman." He tugged a second black kerchief from his pocket, using it to mop up his wet boots. Katrine went down to the water's edge and, as she filled the bucket, piled three small stones one on top of the other. It was the way Lars marked his trails. Katrine held a vision of Lars and Clint riding through the growing light, working their way toward her, guns drawn and eyes relentless in their search for clues. *Find me,* she called out in her mind, not caring how futile the gesture was. *I'm kicking. Come save me.*

"I said hurry up there!" Wellington's tone was becoming an all-too-close copy of McGraw's nasty commands. Katrine began to worry she'd pushed too hard, angering the private instead of getting on whatever good side he might still have left under all that greed.

As they worked their way back up to the shack, Katrine's eyes cast about the clearing. No clue of their location came to her. She could now guess they'd ridden east, but that was all. East by the river. It was something, but useless if she could not find a way to get the information to Clint or Lars.

Back inside the shack, Evelyn was gathering discarded strips of bloody bandages to toss into the small fire. McGraw's pant leg had been cut away, showing angry red skin covered in new bandages. Katrine poured some of the water from her bucket into a bowl so that Evelyn could wash her hands.

"I left my ribbon by the riverbank," she whispered as she handed Evelyn the cake of soap. "Lars might recognize it. He tracks well."

"We rode for hours," Evelyn sighed. "Heaven knows where we are." She stopped and held one hand to her waist, closing her eyes. "Heaven *does* know where we are. I need to remember that." She shook her head. "Poor Walt. He must know by now that I'm missing. My poor boy."

"I'm sure Gideon has given him as much reassurance as he can. And all of them are out looking for us. They must be."

"Unlessen you want your gags back on those pretty little mouths, you'd best shut them now," McGraw called from his chair in the corner. "Jesse, tie them back up."

"No, please," Katrine pleaded, her wrists still raw from their last binding.

"You needn't do that," Evelyn added, backing away.

Jesse sneered at Katrine, then looked back to McGraw. "Why do we have them with us anyways? They're bothersome."

"We need 'em. They're leverage."

"I'm tired of looking at 'em, and them staring at me. Let's just leave 'em and get out of here."

"No!" McGraw growled, rising out of his chair.

"Well, I'm lockin' them up in the next room." Jesse pointed to the small shed attached to the cabin through a makeshift doorway. "At least I won't have to look at 'em, that way."

"You want them waltzing away on us?" McGraw called back.

"Where would we go?" Evelyn flung her hand wide. "We have no idea which way town is and you have our only food."

"This room here has a lock and no windows. A bar over the door and they're as good as tied up." He eyed Katrine. "I need me some shut-eye. We been up all night."

The shed didn't look too comfortable, but Katrine prayed McGraw would concede. Anything was better than being in his company.

McGraw flicked his hand in the direction of the shed. "Well, go on then, lock 'em up."

Chapter Nineteen

Evelyn dusted off her skirt and pushed her hair back off her forehead. "It's filthy, but it's a far sight better than being in there with them."

Katrine was grateful that the privacy of the shed allowed her to undo her collar buttons and roll up her shirtsleeves. "I wish we had asked for water. It is hot in here." She leaned against the wall. To be in a small, hot room with no windows made her pulse pound from memories of the fire.

Evelyn caught her reaction. "Are you all right? You seem ill."

She was sweating and short of breath, but it wasn't from illness. "It feels…" she groped for the words, English always failing her for such emotional subjects "…too much like the fire."

"Such an awful thing." She looked back toward where the men were. "To know he did that to you. To think we all trusted them to be the law and order here."

"I am glad we have Clint as our law and order."

Evelyn's eyes warmed. "He is a good man. He saved you."

Katrine's mind cast back to the moment where her flailing hands found the strength of his. "Yes," she said quietly, the memory still able to overcome her at a moment's notice. "I am safe because of him."

"Only we're not safe. Not yet, at least." Evelyn worried her hands in her skirts. "They could choose to kill us at any moment." She looked at Katrine. "I've never seen anyone shot in cold blood like that, have you?"

Poor Evelyn, she had no idea the terrible weight of the question she had just asked. Katrine felt her answer claw its way up and out of her chest. "I have," she nearly whispered. "Once." She didn't think she possessed the energy to hold up any deception in this close, stifled place. It wasn't the whole of the story anyhow. "I was younger. It was terrible." Even those facts felt a step too far, although some small part of her was amazed that she had admitted even that much and not fallen to pieces. Katrine rushed to change the subject. "Think of Walt. He is safe from all of this, and Gideon is so fond of him. And now he has two more uncles to dote on him."

"I've spent so many years hearing of the evils of the Thornton family. It seems a terrible waste, doesn't it? Clint's warnings undoubtedly fell on deaf ears. My brothers weren't likely to believe such tales from a Thornton." She put her hand to her forehead. "But if Clint and Lars were able to get through and warn them…"

"Yes," Katrine encouraged. "We must hope."

"*Thou art my hope in the day of evil*. It's from Jeremiah, I think."

"This is a day of evil, to be sure. Those are terrible men. But I do not think they mean to kill us now, or they would have done so. We are—what is the word?—hostages."

"Yes, hostages." Evelyn sat down on the blanket, the shed wall groaning as she leaned her back against it.

Katrine thought about the drafty corner, wondering if she would be forced to kick her way out of this tomb, as well. *Come quickly, Clint. Save me again.* She sat down beside Evelyn. "We shall choose to hope, yes? Hope in Clint and Lars and Gideon, and all your brothers?"

"They are strong, smart men, but God holds our futures more than they, don't you think?"

Katrine let her head fall back against the wall, watching the dust float lazily through the air as though it hadn't a care in the world. "Such trust is not easy for me."

"I've seen you in service. I've heard Lars talking to Winona about faith. Surely you believe in God's sovereignty?"

Katrine felt her sigh come up through her every bone. "I believe the world is a broken place that needs God's mercy very much."

Evelyn pulled back to look at her. "But you speak as if all that mercy is for someone else. Now I am sure Clint is sweet on you—you sound just like him."

Katrine's mouth fell open to hear such an assurance. "Truly?"

Evelyn managed the only smile Katrine had seen

from her all day. "Now that I look back, it is easy to see. And when I think of it, I believe Gideon knows, as well. He said something about Clint softening up to a certain kind of sunshine the other day, and I didn't catch his meaning. Now I do." She rested a hand on Katrine's wrist. "You suit each other well, I think."

"He is older," Katrine offered.

Evelyn furrowed her brow. "I don't see how that matters, especially out here."

"He is so serious." Katrine had a dozen reasons why they might never be happy.

"Maybe he wasn't always. Maybe you and your stories will be good for him."

"I do not think he wants a great big family like I do."

Evelyn's amused face darkened completely at this fact. Katrine was glad—some part of her knew she could keep listing small reasons, but the big reason of her past would come out if she kept going. "He does." Her tone was very strange.

"He wants a large family?" Katrine had never seen anything to make her think this. She'd seen him go out of his way to avoid children. And yet, he was patient and tender with Walt and Dakota. Clint could be so kind if he thought no one was looking.

"I think Clint would like very much to have the big, full family he never had." Evelyn's face became very peculiar when she added, "But wanting is not the same thing as having."

"He has never married, yes?"

Evelyn tightened her hand around Katrine's wrist. "Katrine, I'm not so sure this is mine to tell, but maybe

God's made it so you can know. I think Clint has a heart big enough for an enormous family, but he…can't."

"Can't?"

"Clint had the fever when they were children in Pennsylvania. He was off helping some poor family down the street and they took sick. Clint brought that sickness home to the rest of the boys but he got it much worse than Gideon and Elijah. Nearly died, to hear Gideon tell it. And, well…it's an awful story, really. Clint cannot be a father. Worse yet, their cousin Obadiah used it against Clint. Told him it was a curse, that he'd been denied the chance to be a father because he'd brought illness home to the family. Can you imagine? It's tragic enough already, but to make a young boy think he'd brought such a thing upon himself?"

"Clint cannot have a family." Though she repeated the statement, she couldn't make the thought seem real. In her weakest moments, she'd allowed herself to daydream about the big, noisy family they could have together. Brown-eyed boys boasting *My pa's the sherriff!* in the schoolyard. A doting Clint standing wildly overprotective over little girls in braids. She hadn't even realized until just this moment how clear the whole dream had become in her heart. Without consciously deciding it, she'd dreamed up a version of the life he'd saved—her life—lived beside him even though she never had reason to think he'd want that life with someone like her. Too many truths—whether secret or not—stood in the way of that dream. How could it be that while she knew that fantasy was never possible, it now seemed twice as impossible? How could it hurt so deeply? It stunned

Katrine that she could grieve so fiercely for something she could never truly have had in the first place.

"You didn't know, did you?" Evelyn said the obvious with such tenderness.

Katrine had no words. She only shook her head and slumped against the wall.

"Seems a sorrowful waste, don't you think? He'd make a fine father. He, Gideon, Elijah—they've all become fine men despite the difficult lives they've had. God's grace can heal all, and all of their lives show it, even if my bull-headed brothers can't quite get their heads around the idea." She sighed. "Maybe all that nonsense is done with after today. Maybe God's got better things in store."

She went on, filling the empty time and worry with words, but Katrine didn't hear most of them. She turned her face away, wanting to hide her pain from Evelyn. Winona's words last night—had it really just been last night?—had cracked open her hope, let out the dream that somehow Clint might see beyond her past. Now it hurt terribly to know should that obstacle be surmounted, it couldn't all end happily. No family? After all that waiting and hoping and dreaming? Having gone so long without a mother, knowing all the pain that had brought her, Katrine's dearest hopes centered around loving children of her own. Now she loved a man who could not share that dream. It felt so cruel and pointless. *Why would God send my heart to him?*

"There has to be a reason," Evelyn consoled.

Katrine hadn't even realized she'd spoken the question aloud. "I cannot see any reason at all."

* * *

It was the night of the fire all over again. Every minute that passed seemed to place Katrine in more danger. Clint knew McGraw had no honor, no code, and that made him unpredictable and lethal. Worse yet, now that he was exposed, he had nothing left to lose, which made him dangerous and desperate. Clint was grateful Brett, Reid and Gideon had little need for talk as they rode. He'd spent the ride down toward the river trying to get into the head of a man like McGraw, to second-guess his tactics and whatever it was he thought he could now get.

It didn't work. Instead, his brain clouded with thoughts of Katrine in pain, Katrine fighting back fear. McGraw hadn't been subtle in his amusement with her, and she of all people knew how low that lout was capable of stooping. He hated that she would be fully aware of the threats against her. She was smart that way, reading people and their intentions. It was one of the things he liked most about her, and it killed him that it would now be what made her wait for his rescue all the more terrifying.

She was waiting for his rescue. That was the only way he could think about today. Today would be the day he saved her again. The alternative was too awful to swallow.

A smudge in the riverbank caught his eye. A hoof-print in the dirt just beyond that rock. Fresh, from the looks of it, still wet in the deepest parts. "There!" Clint pulled his horse up short and pointed to a place where the grass on the bank looked disturbed. "Look there!"

Gideon knew horses like no one else in Brave Rock. He swung down off his saddle and looked at the track. "McGraw rides a Morgan, don't he?" Gideon shook his head, his hands fisted in frustration. "It's deep enough for a horse carrying extra weight, but it's too small for that horse."

"They switched horses for the raid. He might not be on his horse." Clint scanned the scene before him for any detail, any clue that they were close to McGraw's hideout and the women.

"Looks enough like one of ours," Reid said, crouching down over the track. "There's another, and it's headed in the right direction."

Come on, Katrine, kick on a log. Send me something. Lead me to you. Clint felt the desperate ache like heat spreading out from a lamp. Could that connection, that pull he'd felt between them since the fire, extend far enough to let her feel him finding her? Let him sense her near? His mind went to the surprisingly natural extension of that thought. *Lead me to her, Lord. You see us both. You see us all. You can't want McGraw to win this. I can't believe You saved her only to have it end this way.*

The thought startled him. *You saved her. Not me. I was there, but it was Your doing. I am the law in Brave Rock, but our lives are Yours.* He'd taken the whole thing on his shoulders, nearly buckling under the strain of keeping lives safe against an endless stream of threats. The shift from *I have to find her* to *Lead me to her* held power. So much power. This had to be the power of prayer Lije was always going on about, that thing Clint believed in once, when he was young and hadn't yet seen all the pain the world could dish out. He felt his desperation settle into a quiet, tingly focus.

"What is it?" Brett pulled up alongside Clint.

"Huh?"

"You started going faster. What do you see?"

Clint didn't quite know how to answer that. "I got a hunch."

"A hunch?" Brett didn't seem to find that particularly comforting. "A *hunch?*"

Gideon came up beside the two of them, catching Brett's arm. "This is what he does. Let him do it."

Brett wasn't satisfied. "I'm not leaving Evelyn to some hunch in—"

"Evelyn's *my wife*. I want her back as much as you."

They rode on in tense silence. Clint could feel Brett's and Reid's frustration prickling behind him, feel Gideon's trust stretching thin as fear wore down everyone's resolve. It wasn't supposed to take this long to find them, and that was nothing but bad news. *Send me. Guide me. Keep him away from her. Help me.* Blurts of desperate prayers seemed to leak out of Clint with every passing minute.

"I hate feeling this helpless," Gideon ground out through his teeth, and Clint could sympathize. The only thing keeping him from boiling over himself was the chance that if they weren't on the right track, Lije and Lars were.

"Over there!" Brett pointed to a bush by a spot where the riverbank had clearly been disturbed. "Is that anything?"

A sky-blue ribbon fluttered in the hot wind. With a surge of relief Clint noticed that the ribbon had been wound around a branch, not just tangled. Someone had put it there. Evelyn wore her hair up but Katrine always wore her hair in a thick braid down her back—tied with a colored ribbon. It was the reason Sam McGraw had tried to buy her some ribbon at Fairhaven's back in town. He scanned the scene for some other clue, audibly gasping when he saw three small rocks piled up on each other. Lars's trail mark. They were here. Bless her, she'd found a way to kick a log free. He reached down and pulled the ribbon loose, thankful to be touching some part of that extraordinary woman and to know she was still alive.

"It's Katrine's," he called through the surge of admiration and affection that gripped his throat tight. "They're here and they're alive."

"A path!" Reid surged forward to where Clint could see a small trodden path up away from the river. It curved around a crop of scrubby trees, just the sort of path that would be worn by carrying water up to a hiding spot.

It curved blindly around the trees. Clint held his hand to stop Gideon from following Reid and was taking a breath to yell a warning when the shot rang out.

Chapter Twenty

"Looks like we found 'em!" Gideon cried out as he reared his horse around to pull back behind a copse of trees.

"Reid!" Clint called, crouching down himself and scanning the clearing for the best possible position. "You okay?"

In answer, Reid came sliding back down the small incline. "Fine. But I saw the building. Tiny cabin of a thing with a shed alongside. One window, a pair of horses tied up outside."

"They know we're here," Gideon said just before a second rifle shot rang out overhead through the trees.

"The last thing we need is a gunfight." Clint cast his eyes back and forth between the two men beside him. "We're all good shots, but there are women in there. We can't just storm the place." Clint pinched the bridge of his nose, weighing the options. "Reid, could you make out where Katrine and Evelyn might be?"

"Looks like a one-room cabin with some sort of

shack attached," Reid replied, checking his pistol. "They've got to be in there."

"Then we've got to draw them out. As long as they're in there, they've got the upper hand."

"Can't say I wouldn't welcome the chance to smoke them out if it weren't for Evelyn and Katrine. Those boys ought to get a taste of their own medicine." Gideon looked over his shoulder in the direction of the cabin. "I tell you, if he's so much as laid one greasy hand on my Evelyn..."

Clint put a hand on Gideon's arm. He was a boiling pot of anger himself, but anger wouldn't get Katrine and Evelyn home safely. "Steady, brother. We're smarter than those two and don't you forget it." After a second's pondering, Clint had an idea. "So let's find out what they've done. Gideon, yell to your wife. Whether or not she answers could tell us a lot."

Gideon closed his eyes for a second, and Clint found himself praying, as well. God's intervention seemed the only way to come out of this whole mess alive, seeing as those bandits had become so unpredictable. When Gideon opened his eyes, Clint met his gaze and nodded.

"Evelyn!"

Katrine could hardly believe she had dozed off, even though they had been up all night. Still, the sound of Evelyn's name shot both of them wide awake as they sat slumped against the shed wall.

She looked at Evelyn's wide eyes, still not yet sure she hadn't dreamed the sound.

"Evelyn!"

"Gideon!" Evelyn said it in an astonished whisper, her hands flying first to her chest in surprise, and then to the floor to push herself upright. "Gideon!" she shouted back. "Gideon!"

The shed door banged open, Private Wellington and his cocked pistol pushing through the doorway. "That's enough of that!"

Evelyn, clearly emboldened by how close her husband now was, took in a breath to continue shouting just as the private pulled back to hit her with the handle of his gun. Katrine pulled Evelyn down just in time to miss the blow. Monsters. These men were monsters.

"Y'all hush it in there!" came McGraw's voice as he limped into the shed. Katrine drew in a breath of shock at his appearance. They had not been kept that long in the shed, but the man looked far worse for the passage of time. The bandage Evelyn had applied earlier was now soaked through, mottled brown and red. He could barely put weight on the leg, and his blotchy face was both flushed and ghostly pale. Katrine watched him waver a bit before slumping against the doorjamb, the flimsy shack groaning under his weight.

"McGraw!" Katrine's entire body reacted to the sound of Clint's fearsome roar. "Samuel McGraw!"

"Jesse Wellington!" a third voice called out. Two more distinct voices repeated each of the men's names.

That meant four men were now surrounding the shack. Katrine grabbed Evelyn's hand.

"I heard Reid's voice!" Evelyn said on a rush of breath. "Our prayers have been answered. They're here to rescue us."

"Stop that nonsense. Ain't no rescue going on—this here's a trap." McGraw used the tip of his gun to lift Katrine's long braid off her shoulder. "And you're the bait." Katrine's skin shivered where the metal of the gun had skimmed her shoulder.

"Evelyn!" Gideon's call came through the trees again. Evelyn began to inch toward the sound as if drawn, even though it placed her closer to McGraw.

McGraw lifted his rifle and used the stock to knock out a corner of the shed's flimsy wall closest to Gideon's voice. Then, without even aiming, he shot a round into the air. Katrine and Evelyn both flinched at the blast, covering their ears and crouching back down against the far wall.

"Next one goes through your little missy here!" McGraw called into the trees.

"No one said nothing about killing them!" Wellington hissed to McGraw.

"Don't kill us," Katrine found her voice, pleading to Wellington with her eyes, as well. "We've done nothing to you."

"Nothing's right," McGraw growled, spinning to face Katrine and Evelyn. "Most of you don't pay us no mind. Men of the U.S. Cavalry. Used to be that counted for something." He pointed his rifle at Katrine, and she felt her blood halt in her veins. "Only you pay that misguided sheriff more mind than you do me."

Katrine decided every second McGraw was talking to her was a second he was not shooting at Clint, so she engaged him. "You have the respect that comes with your uniform. You need not kill to get more."

"I got more men out here than you have in there, McGraw," came Clint's commanding voice. "End this before anyone gets hurt."

"Listen to him," Evelyn pleaded.

"I don't take orders from the likes of you!" McGraw snarled.

Wellington peered through the hole McGraw had knocked in the wall. "How many you reckon he's got out there?"

"He's bluffin'," McGraw answered, wiping his brow with his grimy sleeve. The thick, coppery scent of blood combined with the sour order of sweat to fill the room and turn Katrine's stomach. "He's got two. Three at the most."

"I dunno, Sam. I counted at least four." Wellington was beginning to look worried.

"You!" McGraw barked, pointing at Katrine with an unsteady hand. "Up!"

Evelyn grabbed Katrine's hand. "Don't."

"I said *up!*" McGraw's voice was beyond mean.

Without a word, Katrine rose slowly to her feet.

"Jesse, tie her hands and hobble her feet so's she can't run. Enough to walk, though. Just a few steps."

As Wellington began to do as he was told, Katrine forced herself to stand tall, nearly eye to eye with Mc-Graw. "You burned down my house." The words were thin as paper, but something hardened in her spine as she forced them out. "You tried to kill Lars." If she was going to be paraded out onto the soil to die, Katrine was going to speak McGraw's crimes to his face.

"No news to me, missy. You done yet?" he snapped

at Wellington, who was tying off the line he'd lashed around Katrine's boots. "Hurry it up."

Katrine was not done. "All the accidents. The fences, the cattle, the wells…they were you."

"That's enough!" With a shove rough enough to send Katrine nearly tumbling to the floor, McGraw pushed her through the shed and into the larger cabin. Limping ahead of her, he pushed open the cabin door and motioned with his rifle. "Walk out there nice and slow. Make sure Thornton gets a good look at ya. Just remember, if you even look like you're tryin' to run, I'll shoot you down sure as we stand here."

Slowly, Katrine shuffled to the door as McGraw stood out of sight beside it. The bright sunlight hurt her eyes, trapped for so many hours in the dim shed as they had been. She had no idea what time it was or where they were, only prayed as she hobbled out into the clearing that this sunshine wouldn't be her last.

"Katrine?" Clint's voice was tight and sharp from beyond the trees where she strained to see him but could not. "You hurt?"

"Not yet she ain't!" McGraw's voice came from behind Katrine. "But I got a clear shot and like you said, you already seen how I treat my enemies."

Branches ahead of her shifted and Clint appeared from behind a copse of trees. He placed his rifle down on the ground and walked slowly.

The sight of him brought such a flood of relief to her body that Katrine felt herself wobble a bit. His eyes held hers for a moment, then looked over her shoulder. His face tightened into a dark, focused expression and she knew he was doing what he did so well—gathering details, plotting tactics, assessing danger. How he managed to look so calm and still while his mind worked that fast, she could not guess, but the effect of his control gave her courage.

She wanted him to come closer, but he stopped several yards away. He seemed deliberate in his choice of spot, but she had no idea of his plan. "Trust me, I know what I'm doing," his eyes said, even though he simply repeated his earlier question. "Are you hurt?"

Katrine shook her head. She was many things—terrified, tired, assured, confused—but not hurt.

Clint pointed up to his face as if to say, "Keep your eyes on me." It wasn't hard to comply with his silent request. Katrine felt if she didn't keep her eyes on Clint she might very well fall over. Her pulse galloped in her ears as it was.

"This has gone far enough, McGraw. I got nothing you want, and these women will only slow you down if you escape." Clint's voice was remarkably steady despite his current position as a clear target out in the open. Then again, so was she. Katrine felt her head spin again. She did not want to end her life shot in the back by the likes of Sam McGraw.

"Got you here, didn't it?"

Katrine watched Clint's hand move behind his back, a small, almost imperceptible gesture. Clint raised an eyebrow—just a tiny bit—and his head fell a fraction of an inch. "Let 'em go, Sam. This is between you and me, anyways." She watched his eyes dart back and forth between her and the cabin behind her. He had positioned himself, she guessed, so that her stance blocked part of his body from McGraw. When his fingers flicked, Katrine caught movement in the bushes far to her left.

"I came for her, not for you. I'd love to hunt you down like the weasel you are, but right now I'd just as soon never see you again."

I came for her. The words sank themselves deep into Katrine's fear, giving her something to hold on to. He was reaching for her even now, just the same as when he pulled her out from the fire.

"As if I'd believe the likes of you would just stand there while I waltzed away."

"Let her go, let Evelyn go, and I may surprise you."

A twig snapped far to Katrine's right, and she fought the urge to swing her head around toward the noise. Clint's eyes told her not to move, and she heard the command as clearly as if he'd spoken.

"You telling me you got eyes for this one?" McGraw ground out. "What makes you think I don't already know that? What makes you think that ain't exactly why I took her? Why I might not just keep her for myself just to spite you?"

While Sam was talking, Clint cast his eyes down toward his left hand, his fingers spread flat against the leg of his pants. When she looked back up again, it took her a second to realize he was mouthing something to her, but she could not make it out. She gave Clint a puzzled look.

"'Cause even you're not that much of a snake, Mc-Graw," Clint went on, his eyes continuing to dart between her and what she could only assume was the rifle-ready stance of Sam McGraw behind her. "Or do you want to prove me wrong?" Clint said. His face was taut and fierce, yet somehow he managed to keep his words casual, almost like children daring each other in the schoolyard.

He cast his glance down to his hand again, which now had four fingers flat against his pant leg. When she looked up again, it only took Katrine a second to realize he was mouthing the word *fire—four* in Danish.

He was counting down. Counting down to do something—but what?

Chapter Twenty-One

McGraw could fire on him at any moment. Clint knew that, but he also knew somewhere in his gut that McGraw would not. He kept it up, baiting McGraw into conversation, waiting for Katrine to realize he was signaling her to get ready.

The middle of an armed standoff was not an ideal place to declare his affection for Katrine, but he needed distraction and this was the biggest surprise he could conjure up with a gun aimed at his heart. Funny, that was half how the words came out—if McGraw was going to shoot him down in the open, part of him wanted to make sure the words were spoken before he took a bullet. *I came for her.* An odd peace told him that if he was going to go, staring into Katrine's blue eyes seemed like a good way to meet his Maker.

Only Clint Thornton had no plans to meet that Maker anytime soon. He was going to let McGraw think he had the upper hand only long enough to get the man surrounded. Keep him distracted long enough to have

Gideon in position to ensure Evelyn made it out alive, as well. Her shouts had confirmed what Clint suspected—that McGraw had locked the women in the little shed off the cabin.

Slowly, Clint curled his ring finger into his fist so that three fingers now lay flat against his pant leg. "Where's your buddy Wellington?" he called. "Did you promise him prime stakes of land? Pocketfuls of money? Evelyn?" He knew he'd succeeded in antagonizing McGraw, and that increased the chances the man would tire of the game and start shooting, but Clint knew his job and knew how to take a desperate man down. He mouthed *tre—three*—to Katrine, and she gave a barely perceptible nod.

"Two claims of my own!" Jesse shouted from out of a hole McGraw had knocked in the shed wall earlier. Clint calculated what Gideon would already guess—Wellington was in the front of the shed and Evelyn would be frightened enough to stay back as far as she could. "I don't want no momma with a sniveling young'un."

"You sure you can take a man like McGraw at his word, Wellington? I wouldn't be, not after what I've seen. After all, where are the other two of the Black Four? What's to say he won't leave you behind as easily as he did them?" He curled his middle finger into his fist so that only two fingers lay against his pant leg, no longer needing the Danish numerals Lars had taught him one afternoon to pass the time on a long ride.

Suddenly, a shriek came from the direction of the shack as a shot rang out from the shed. A ball of fire exploded in Clint's left shoulder, knocking him a step backward. Katrine screamed and ran toward him. Despite the pain racing through his arm, Clint yelled his planned final command, *"Komme ned!"*—"Get down!"—and pushed her toward his feet as he reached behind with his good arm to grab and then fire the pistol he'd slipped in his waistband. He figured he might have the chance of two revolver shots to take down McGraw and his rifle; he prayed God granted him aim enough to do it in one.

He watched the wood of the doorway explode in splinters from his first shot as his vision began to blacken around the edges. Thrusting Katrine behind him, he sank to one knee and fired again, more by instinct than any true sense of aim. Behind and in front of him the other men shouted and fired rifles and pistols; the battle seemed to be waging in every direction. He strained through the noise to hear Evelyn, knowing her cries were from fear, not injury. Clint threw his body over Katrine's just as Wellington hollered in pain. As he raised his head, a rifle shot from McGraw's direction sent a bullet whizzing inches from his temple. He covered Katrine's head with his bad arm, even though the resulting pain made his ears ring and his head spin. The crashing and yelling seemed to go on for hours, although it could hardly have been a handful of minutes before the only sound he could hear was Katrine's terrified whimpers underneath him.

Clint rolled off her, falling flat on his back in the soil with enough strength left to turn his head in the direction of the cabin where he saw Gideon, Evelyn clinging to his side, standing over the limp body of Sam McGraw facedown in the dirt. He turned back toward Katrine and gasped in fright at her closed eyes and bloody cheek. He rolled to his side toward her, sliding his wounded arm up to lay a bloodied hand against that red-streaked cheek, only to crumble in relief as those blue eyes opened wide to meet his gaze.

"Are you alive?" He had to ask. He had to hear her voice the words.

"Ja," she whispered. "But you are shot. Clint, you are shot!" She began to cry. "So much blood." He noticed the red pool on her blouse, panicking until he realized it was from where he had lain on top of her.

"Help!" she cried, scrambling to her knees and frantically undoing her apron to hold it to the wound as Alice must have taught her. It stung like a hundred bees but Clint was so happy to see her unwounded he couldn't bring himself to mind.

Theo Chaucer was over him then, blocking out the sunlight and extending a hand. "Can you sit up?"

Clint managed to maneuver himself upright with Theo's help, even though the world spun fast around him and his pulse thundered in his ears. His sleeve was warm and wet; sparks of burning fire were shooting down his arm all the way to his fingers. He felt Katrine's arms around his neck, helping to hold him upright. They were soft and cool, soothing the burning sensation now creeping out in every direction from his shoulder.

"I see a hole in your back where the bullet went clean through," Theo said. "I reckon if we can get this bleeding stopped, you'll live to tell the tale."

"There's bandages and ointment inside where we were tending to McGraw." Evelyn's tearful voice came from somewhere to his left. "Bring him in there."

Clint angled his feet underneath him, feeling Theo's grip pull him to his feet. Katrine's tender hands wrapped his good arm around her neck. His last thought, before the world went black and spun him down the rabbit hole, was that she proved his earlier prediction right: she did fit perfectly under his arm.

Katrine wiped the last of the blood from her hands and sat down beside the rickety cot where Clint had been laid. When he'd tumbled over in the clearing, it had taken both Theo Chaucer and Gideon to hoist him into the cabin so his wounds could be tended. It was gruesome to step over McGraw's lifeless body, and she was glad the men tended to McGraw's and Wellington's corpses while she and Evelyn worked to clean and dress Clint's shoulder.

He was alive—she knew that by the half-conscious grunts and groans he made when Evelyn applied the stinging whiskey and pressed on the wound. Still, they could not seem to slow the bleeding down enough, and Clint had made his presence known with a loud yell when Gideon pressed a glowing knife to his wound to burn it shut. How ironic that fire—which had tried to take her life—ended up saving his. Much as she wanted to get back to Brave Rock and Lars this very minute, Gideon had suggested giving Clint a stretch of time to heal and settle before they attempted the trip.

She spent most of that time sitting beside him, staring at his jaw, his hairline, the set of his shoulders. Every detail seemed new and precious, even the things she'd noticed about him long before now. They'd been in close proximity many times since the fire, but not close like this. This was altogether different.

Katrine reached out and placed his hand in her palm. It was warm—not fever warm, thankfully, but a solid, strong kind of warm. These hands had come to mean so much to her. The pads of his fingers and the heel of his palm were calloused from hard work, and the back of his hand still held the reddened scar from where he'd scraped himself in the fire. They'd stripped his bloody shirt off to treat the gunshot wound, revealing strong arms and muscled shoulders. It was not just physical strength she could see, but the inner force of a man who accepted his calling to protect others. The strength of these arms had protected her not once, but twice.

Now, staring at Clint, Katrine knew she wanted more than protection from these arms; she wanted their embrace. She knew for sure now what she'd begun to realize last night—she was ready to risk telling him of her past. Wasn't it the only way to ensure that whatever future they had—if God was kind enough to grant them a future—could be built on truth? Katrine was done with secrets and wanted none between her and Clint. Not this morning, not ever.

Lifting the hand on Clint's good side, she raised it to her cheek and kissed the back of his palm. His eyes fluttered open, at first lost in the haze of his injury, then leaping to life when he caught sight of her face.

"You're all right." He said it with such a genuine relief, his eyes falling back shut for a moment, that Katrine felt the lump in her throat rise back up and threaten more tears.

"Yes," she whispered softly, "I am fine, thanks to you." She kept his hand to her cheek, even while he awoke fully. It felt like a bold declaration, and then again the most natural thing in all the world.

He stiffened for a moment as his awareness returned. "McGraw?"

Of course Clint's first thoughts would be of securing safety. She felt herself smile and nod, even as she waited for him to recognize that she was holding his hand. "Dead. Wellington, too. You saved Evelyn and me—you and Gideon and the others."

Clint winced. "He shot me, the dishonorable varmint. Thought I was unarmed and shot me anyway." His words were a little slurred and unchecked. She'd not heard Clint resort to name-calling ever, and she found such a peek into his unguarded feelings tender and amusing. The vigilant lawman with his guard down. It doubled her affection for him even as he'd yet to realize he was touching her.

Still, his hand rested against her cheek with an instinctive ease that made Katrine's breath sparkle in her chest and made her want to laugh. "I am very glad Wellington is a poor shot. Theo says the bullet missed your heart. It went clean through and your shoulder will heal."

Clint grunted. "Theo ought to know what my shoulder feels like before he makes such claims. Everything burns."

Katrine moved her hand to wipe Clint's furrowed brow. "We will get you to Alice as soon as we can, but for now you must stay put."

His fingers moved softly against her cheek even as his eyes fell shut again. "You're all right. He didn't hurt you?"

She smiled at his repeated questions. He did care. She'd known it on some level long before today, but today his clear and unguarded affection settled warmly in her heart. "I am fine." She brushed a lock of dark hair off his forehead, glad to feel it cool and free of fever.

The intimate gesture seemed to waken him. It was a glorious thing to watch, to see his dark eyes glow with warmth as he realized how his hand lay against her cheek, how she touched him. There was a second of panic—the old Clint standing guard over his feelings—but it quickly fell away to a relief that made her want to cry.

"You came for me." It said everything and nothing all at once.

The smile that started at the corners of his mouth seemed to ignite his eyes. With a wince he rolled his head slowly so he could look her fully in the face. "I came right out and said that, didn't I?"

Words fled out of reach, and Katrine could only nod, still pressing his good hand to her cheek. She felt his fingers spread against her skin, as if verifying she was solid and real, not some pain-induced hallucination.

"Didn't plan on that. Just sort of jumped out while I was staring at your eyes. Your eyes are so blue." His voice began to fade a bit. "Not seen anything else so blue in all my days." His eyes fell shut for a moment, then reopened. "You're not hurt?"

"No, silly," she reassured him, filled with such affection that she leaned down and kissed his cheek. She'd meant it to be a quick, gentle kiss, but found herself staying softly pressed against his stubbled skin for a lingering, blissful stretch of time.

His sigh at first was deep and contented, until awareness caused his eyes to open wide. "What's that for?"

Now she laughed. "What are any kisses for?"

He stared at her, the full realization finally hitting him. She'd never seen anything so delightful. "So," he fumbled, looking half his weathered years, "you…are too in?"

When she raised an eyebrow, he continued, "Lars told me it's not *falling* in Danish, it's more like *are too.*"

Katrine wondered if Clint had lost more blood than they realized. "I don't understand."

Clint closed his eyes, his brows knitting together in concentration. "The Danish phrase for being sweet on someone. In English we say *falling in love* but Lars said the Danish is more like *are too in love.*"

Katrine had to think about it for a moment, but in a direct translation, Lars was right. "Yes. *Jeg elsker dig.*"

Clint was wide awake now, managing a big, if slightly slanted smile. Truly, Katrine felt as if she'd watched a completely new man emerge from the shell of the old one. Would anyone believe such a glint could inhabit the sheriff's eyes? "I sure hope that means what I think it means." His voice held hope and joy.

There was only one way to respond. Katrine leaned

over and brushed his lips with hers. "It means my heart is yours," she whispered.

Clint moved his good hand from her cheek to slide around her neck and pull her close. His kiss was tender and full of life. While it was a small kiss, it was more than she'd imagined, and full of so much relief she thought she'd cry again right there on the spot.

He brushed her hair back from her forehead. "We have loads to work out. There are things you need to know."

Katrine put her finger to his lips. "Shh. I know what I need to know. And we will have time enough for that later."

He ventured a look around him, wincing as he tried unsuccessfully to rise. "Don't think I'm going anywhere anytime soon. So we got time for this." With that, he pulled her close and proved to Katrine that a man does not need the use of his shoulder to show a woman his heart.

Chapter Twenty-Two

The ride back to Brave Rock felt a hundred miles long. Clint had been shot before—wounded far worse, near as he could remember—but Wellington's bullet seemed to light fire to every nerve up and down his left side. The bleeding had finally stopped; he could give thanks for that.

He could give thanks for lots of things today.

Except one. "You *looking* for the bumps up there?" he called through gritted teeth as he sat in the payload of the wagon Lije had brought. "Or are they just finding you?" Every jolt of the wagon reminded him that whatever Alice had given him for the pain wasn't near enough.

"I'm actually being careful," Lije called over his shoulder. "Try to be glad we could get the wagon up here at all." McGraw had chosen his hiding spot well— that shack had been out in the middle of nowhere— and in the vast Oklahoma territory, that was saying something. The wagon took another vicious jolt and Clint hissed through his teeth. "Sorry!" Lije offered. "That was a big one."

"They're *all* big ones," Clint muttered. Katrine squeezed his good hand, and he distracted himself in the stunning blue of her eyes. "I'll try to remember I hurt 'cause I'm alive."

Alice leaned over the backboard. "Is he bleeding, Katrine?"

Tender hands inspected his bandages. "No, no bleeding." Katrine needed no encouragement to fuss over Clint. If it weren't so pleasant to have her fawning over him like this, he might be annoyed. As it was, he couldn't contain his wonder at the nearness of her. Clint couldn't be sure if it was the pain medicine or the intoxicating smell of her hair that made him woozy. He was surprised to discover he didn't care. He was going home to a free and peaceful Brave Rock, and that's all that mattered.

"I'm going to be fine," he assured her worried eyes. "Soon enough."

Katrine smiled. He'd been fascinated by her smile before, but now that she smiled *for him,* it unwound his common sense. He could conjure up a list of twenty reasons why they shouldn't be together, and in one look she could whisk them away like weeds in a dust storm. "I am glad to hear it," she said, checking his bandage yet again. "I have done enough worrying for ten years, *ja?*"

Enough worrying. He certainly had done his share over the Black Four. Now, two of the awful gang were locked up in the Brave Rock jail while the other two lay dead under burlap sacks in the wagon Lars and Gideon drove a few yards behind them. The Chaucer men had gone on ahead, having much rebuilding work ahead of them after the battle waged on their property. Clint gave Katrine's hand a reassuring squeeze and brought it to his lips. "Enough worrying. Today we lay that burden down. We lay all of them down."

"Yes, all of them." They'd talked a long stretch at the cabin, peeling off the layers of history and doubt between them. He was sure he'd split in two from regret as he told her all he could not give her, astounded to discover she already knew. She *knew,* and wanted him anyway. It didn't seem possible.

And Katrine had cried as she told him of the terrible burden she'd carried since that night in that alley. Oh, how he'd wanted to hunt that man down and throttle him for hefting such a burden on a young girl. To think he'd ever given her reason to think he'd hold something like that against her. The law in Brave Rock would be about justice and mercy, not the kind of condemnation that had given Katrine such deep wounds.

"You are a good woman, Katrine." He gave her hand another kiss, just because he could and just because it felt so wonderful to do so. "More kind and caring than I deserve." The words felt like they were coming from some other man—some poetic, lofty gentleman like Lije rather than the ragged soul he knew himself to be. Still, he felt compelled to tell her—over and over—that her past held no sway with him. When she pressed it further, telling him of the sordid jobs she'd taken at saloons and the like over the years to keep her and Lars fed, his admiration for her only grew. She'd done what she had to, made sacrifices far beyond any he'd made in battle or law. She survived. Katrine Brinkerhoff was far braver and stronger than he'd ever suspected.

The wagon gave another nasty lurch, knocking him against her shoulder, and he allowed himself to rest his head there. He, Clint Thornton, allowed himself to rest against her. The day might never hold a greater wonder than that. All this time he'd been striving to protect her, never realizing the perfect partner, the exquisite help-mate, she could be to him.

"Tak Gud," he whispered into the yellow bliss of her hair. For some reason, the Danish words had become his personal prayer rather than the English ones. God had returned His presence to Clint's life. Of course, that wasn't really true—it was never God who left but only Clint's admission of Him that wavered. Still, *tak Gud* had become like a heartbeat, pulsing over and over through his weary chest.

"Tak Gud we are almost to town?" she mused aloud, her voice so close to him he could feel it hum against his cheek.

How had he managed to keep such a distance from this beauty for so long when now it seemed as if an ache began every time she left his side? He turned to look up at her. "That," he said, starstruck for the hundredth time by the color of her eyes, "and much more."

He watched the pink come to her cheeks, feeling something so close to delight he wanted to laugh. He must have, for Katrine shushed him with a gentle finger against his lips. "Alice's medicine has clouded your head."

That wasn't it. Clint felt as if he saw the world clearly for the first time in years. It was yellow and blue, bright as sunshine and clean as wind—as clean as the wind that would blow through the two windows in the cabin he'd built.

He knew, now, that he'd not built that cabin for Lars and Katrine. Without knowing it, he had built it for Katrine and himself. When she'd told him what the pair of windows had meant to her, Clint recognized it could not be any other way. There were lots of details to work out—a man couldn't rightly toss his newly resurrected best friend out into the night with no place to stay— but Lars and Winona would need to carve a future of their own, as well.

There would be time enough to work all that out. Clint had his whole future to work out a life with Katrine in Brave Rock. For now, the perfection of her shoulder was a fine place to rest.

It took Katrine a second or two to recognize the sound. At first she thought it a trick of the wind, but as the distance closed, she heard the shouts and cheers for what they were. Turning the last corner into Brave Rock, she peered over the wagon's front bench to see a crowd gathered all along the main street. It was like a tiny parade as the wagon pulled into town. Molly Murphy cried into her handkerchief, shouting offers of free meals and ginger cake delivered every night from the café until Clint was on his feet again. Dakota ran alongside the wagon, waving wildly until Katrine lifted her hand to wave back. The Gilberts stood waving as well, shouting "Thank you!" and "Get well!" with such enthusiasm that Clint managed a laugh or two. When Felix Fairhaven rushed out of his store with a pair of new shirts tied up in twine, Clint fingered the "Heard you needed these" note with an expression of stunned disbelief. Two loaves of bread followed a few feet down the road, hoisted onto the cart by one of the Ferguson sisters. Half a minute later Maureen Walters, Martin's mother, slid a whole pie onto the wagon bed.

He'd never done his job with the expectation of thanks; that was not who Clint Thornton was. He simply, quietly, fulfilled his calling. Katrine felt her heart swell for the gift of this wild, noisy outpouring and what it would do to Clint's spirits. She knew he felt the weight of all the damage the Black Four had been able to do before he could bring them to justice. He took it as a personal failing that he had not been able to prevent their slew of crimes before good people had abandoned their hope of a future in Brave Rock. The law had always been deeply personal to him; it always would be. It had been one of the reasons she'd been afraid her past could stand between them. The man fed his life on justice the way she'd fed her life on story and faith. She'd hoped now that their future could be a story of how justice and faith wove together to create hope and grace.

Hope and grace, however, had to wait until this lawman's shoulder healed.

"I said I wanted to go home," he muttered as the wagon turned toward the infirmary. For all his new lightness, Clint's stubborn streak had not lapsed.

"You know Alice won't hear of it. She's insisting

you stay in the infirmary at least two nights until she's satisfied the wound won't open again."

"One night," Clint grumbled, wincing when the wagon hit another ditch. "No more. Besides, where will you sleep?"

"Oh, I will be just fine." Katrine had hoped to save that for later, knowing once she revealed her news it would take both his brothers to hold Clint down on the infirmary cot.

"You can't stay there with me in the infirmary. It'd be improper." He was still watching out for her. His protection wrapped around her like a soft shawl, banishing the worries that had pressed down her shoulders for weeks.

"Of course not." She smiled at him. She was beginning to wonder if she would ever stop smiling at him. "But I am settled for now, so there is no worry."

Clint eyed her as the cart came to a stop. "Where?" He'd needed to know where she was every moment since he'd woken. Not out of control, but out of a craving to keep her near. It made her feel beautiful in a new and splendid way.

"With Alice and Elijah, of course. Close enough to keep an eye on you," she teased. How long had it been since she could feel such laughter in her voice?

"Close enough for *me* to keep an eye on *you,* you mean." His good hand tightened around hers. More than one person had noticed how close they were sitting in the wagon payload, and part of her worried about being on display, as they rode into town. Still, Katrine was delighted to see smiles from friends, and even nods of approval as she could see their eyes register how Clint's hand was wrapped around hers, or the way she could not help but look into his eyes. Goodness, could everyone know already? She could not bring herself to care—this happiness was too dear to squelch even one little bit.

"Besides," Clint went on, "I thought you said Lije and Alice were a bit too lovesick to be around any longer."

She smiled at Clint and squeezed his hand. "It is not so hard to see now, *ja?*"

Clint said nothing, merely ran his thumb along the back of her hand in a way that made Katrine's breath hitch. He looked different. She felt different. People looked at her differently. Did the inner change—which felt like it had washed through her with the power of a flood—show on the outside with the same force?

"Not much longer, you two," Alice called from the wagon bench. There was a warm teasing tone to her voice, too.

"Alice knows," Katrine whispered.

Clint laughed. "No kidding?" he teased, for Alice had been anything but subtle in how she cooed over Katrine and Clint. "Oh, believe me," Clint moaned, "Elijah does, too. He was giving me all kinds of brotherly grief while he got my shirt back on. Actually, from the looks of things, I think all of Brave Rock knows. Where's Gideon? I half expected him to join in on the fun."

"He'll be along, I am sure." Katrine knew exactly where Gideon was, and what he was doing, but this was to be a happy secret for now.

The wagon bumped to a stop, and Clint let out a sigh. "I could have ridden. It would have hurt less."

"And miss your grand return to town?" Katrine motioned to the back of the wagon, which had filled with gifts of good wishes as much as Alice's table had filled with gifts of comfort the morning after the fire. Everything was coming full circle, healing, as if God were going out of His way to spread her joyful new life out before her. Before both of them.

Clint shifted his weight to rise, grimacing. "Well, yes, that was kind of the idea."

He wasn't fooling anyone. For all his grousing, Katrine could see the satisfaction in Clint's eyes at the town's gratitude. By now, they all knew what lengths he and Lars had gone to in their efforts to protect Brave Rock. Why deny these good people the chance to show their gratitude?

As Katrine moved the many gifts aside to let herself and Clint climb down off the wagon bed, her eyes met those of her brother. Lars stood smiling on the infirmary steps, looking as happy as she felt. He held Winona's hand. Looking up at Lars with obvious affection, Winona clasped Lars's hand in both of hers. Katrine recognized the impulse to clutch these heroes close.

Gazing at the happiness washing over her brother's face, Katrine had her answer: yes, love did show on the outside. It radiated from Lars and Winona like summer sunshine.

Clint must have seen it as well, for he gave a groan and tapped Katrine's hand. "We don't look like that, do we?"

"Ja," Katrine laughed softly, "I am sure we do."

Chapter Twenty-Three

Clint had spent Tuesday night drifting in between pain and sleep, waking many times to see both Katrine and Alice dozing on chairs in the infirmary. Most things were hazy, but he knew he was home. Well, close to home, if everyone would just stop their fussing and let him get on back to his quiet cabin.

Nothing doing. By midday Alice had poked at his wound too many times and an endless stream of nosy visitors came to wish him well. Each time he thought he'd gotten a chance at a few moments alone with Katrine, Alice would return with new torments.

"You'll have a nasty scar," she tsked as she dabbed anew at his wound with something that smelled awful and stung worse.

"Won't be the first," he said through gritted teeth. This morning, Clint felt as if he'd been hurriedly stuffed into someone else's body—one that was tight, battered and tossed downstream. He'd spent so many hours giving recounts of yesterday's battle that he felt more like the town storyteller than the town sheriff. He flexed his arm despite the jolt of pain, just to show Alice that it was working fine and needed no more of whatever that vile bottle held. "I'm fine."

She narrowed one eye. "So you keep saying. You're still staying here."

"Lije?" Clint appealed to his brother when he appeared with lunch. "Call her off. Aren't you the head of this household?"

Elijah laughed and tossed his head in the direction of his cabin. "I am the head of *that* household. She is the head of *this* infirmary. If she says you stay another day, I'll sit on you myself if required."

"Where's Gideon? He'll spring me."

"Only for an hour," came his middle brother's voice from behind Alice. "I have some important business with the sheriff."

"Anything to get me away from this." Clint reached for Katrine's hand, though, just to let Gideon know he wasn't quite ready to let Katrine out of his sight.

"You will have to come back," Katrine chided. "Today you can only go out for a short visit."

"Anywhere but here," Clint grumbled, then added, "No offense," when Alice raised her eyebrow.

"It won't be all that bad." Gideon laughed. "I've borrowed a carriage for the occasion. Less bumpy."

Once out in the sunshine, Clint felt some of his energy return. He was tired, but one look at the blue of Katrine's eyes seemed to pull his spirits back to life. Would it always be that way, or was that just the wonder of new love?

He stared at her the whole carriage ride, not caring the destination, only glad to be nearly alone with her someplace halfway quiet. *I love her.* The thought settled in his chest with ease as he watched the breeze lift tendrils of her blond hair. *I've loved her for a while.* "*Tak Gud,*" he whispered into her ear as she sat next to him on the carriage seat.

"Yes," she whispered back but then pointed through the carriage window, "but thank them, as well."

Clint hadn't bothered to notice where the carriage had brought them. Before his eyes stood Katrine's cabin, finished right down to the blue gingham curtains fluttering in its double windows. Evelyn and Walt were standing on the grass outside the cabin, as were Elijah and Alice and a host of other Brave Rock citizens.

Clint tried to form a word—any word—but ended up with his mouth just hanging open in shock. Every ounce of pain and fatigue left his body, along with all the air in his lungs. If he'd have been standing, Clint couldn't rightly say he wouldn't have fallen over.

"Welcome home, brother," Gideon's voice called from the front of the carriage. Walt broke free from his mother's hand and rushed up to the carriage, jumping up a few times to catch the door latch and swing it open.

"Uncle Clint! Uncle Clint!"

This time the words did not sting at all. They felt warm and welcoming. "Hi there, Walt."

"Uncle Clint? Will you be the baby's goodfather?"

Clint's head started to spin. "The *what?*"

Gideon's sheepish face peered around the carriage door. "Walt, you were supposed to wait on that."

"Wait on *what?*" Clint grabbed Gideon's arm as he eased himself down out of the carriage. He did not let go of his brother. "Wait on what, exactly?"

Evelyn came up to take Walt's arm. "Walt was supposed to ask you if you would be the baby's godfather. *Tomorrow.*"

Clint tightened his grip on Gideon. "Do you mean…?"

Gideon grinned. "Just after Christmas, near as we can tell."

Katrine threw her arms around Evelyn. "A baby! *Tillykke!* Congratulations! Oh, you must have been so worried before!"

Evelyn's hand went to her waist. "Yes, I was very frightened. But I am fine. And all this was supposed to be for tomorrow, not today." She gestured toward the cabin behind her. "Today was for you."

Clint shook Gideon's hand heartily, amazed at how easy it was to be happy for his brother. "That's wonderful. Really."

"I didn't want to steal your day, brother, but we could hardly wait to tell you."

"Of course I'll be the baby's 'goodfather.'" Clint winked at Gideon and ruffled Walt's hair.

"Come take a look." Gideon gestured toward the tidy homestead. "Everyone pitched in, just like they did for me."

Clint walked toward the completed cabin, taking in the thousand tiny details people had managed to finish. "It's done."

"Well, mostly." Gideon shrugged. "There's a bit more

to do before you can move in. But we ought to be done by the time Alice lets you out of her clutches."

"Which isn't for another day yet," Alice cut in, her sharp orders undone by her wide smile. He hadn't even noticed that she and Lije had come up behind him.

Clint gaped at Katrine. "This is where *you* live."

"No," Katrine said, "this is where *we* will live."

That was the way he'd always seen it, hadn't he? The notion that wouldn't leave his heart no matter how he lectured himself on the impossibility?

Katrine squeezed his hand. "We will get married and live here, *ja?*"

Clint was pretty sure the ground just lurched under his feet. "Aren't…" He blinked, trying to make his tongue work properly. "Aren't I supposed to ask you proper first?"

Katrine began to laugh. "You did. Four times last night. I do not know about the proper, but I did say yes every time."

"I heard it," Alice offered. "Well, one of them, at least. I was worried you were going to send me off to fetch my husband to do the honors right there and then."

"You'll marry me?" Clint could hardly believe the words were coming from his mouth. He didn't think there was this much happiness in the whole world, much less one piece of Oklahoma.

"Very much so. And we will live here. With two windows—one for each of us."

Clint wrapped his arms around his soon-to-be bride. "One for each of us." He rested his forehead against hers. "That will be enough?"

She nodded, tightening her hands around his neck. "It is more than enough."

He kissed her, right there and then, right long and hard, not minding who saw or who cared. "I love you."

She smiled against his cheek, laughing softly. "You said that many times, too. But I do not think I will ever tire of hearing it."

He already knew the answer. "Did you say it back?"

"Every time. But here is one more just so you are sure. *Jeg elsker dig.* I love you."

Clint kissed her again. *"Tak Gud."*

Epilogue

September 1889

This was worse than any gunshot. Clint looked at the window of the Healing Hearts Clinic and felt his stomach tumble toward his boots. He hated the thought of Katrine being ill. They only had each other—even the slightest hint of losing her made his heart freeze into sharp splinters. He'd made such a scene in the infirmary that Alice had been forced to shoo him outside.

Clint stared at the church, now finished, and thought about the morning he wed her under that very steeple. *I can't lose her, Lord. I'll die. It's that plain and simple.*

Lije came out of the clinic door, a serious look on his face. Clint knew that look. Nothing good came from that look. He'd never tell Lije he called it The Pastor Bad News Face, but Clint could see his brother steeling himself for a difficult conversation as clear as if there were a sign around Lije's neck. *No.* Three months ago, he'd have classified himself as a man never given to hysteria. Clint was pretty sure he was on the verge of hysteria now.

"How is she?" he blurted out, remembering the sallow look on Katrine's face, how the energy seemed to be seeping out of her with every day. "She's lost too much weight, hasn't she?"

Lije came up and put a hand on Clint's shoulder. It felt like Lije handed him a shovel and told him to pick out a pretty spot for a headstone. He cleared his throat. "Clint…"

"That bad?" Katrine could not, *would not* be Brave Rock's first true funeral.

"I need to have a…difficult conversation with you."

How would you like to bury your wife?

"You were…alone a long while before you met Katrine."

You'll know what to do when you are alone again.

Lije cleared his throat again. Glory, how bad was it? Was she gone already? They wouldn't leave him out here in the yard while his wife drew her last breaths, would they? "In all that time, Clint, did you ever… have you ever…"

"Ever what?"

"I'm trying to get to that, little brother. I want you to know we'd do our best to look past a straying of that sort given how…"

"Exactly what are you askin' me, Lije?"

Lije ran his hands down his face. "Have you ever been with a…"

The nature of Lije's question hit Clint like a cannonball. "Have I ever…?" He stomped, pulling his hat off to slap it against Lije's shoulder. "What kind of man do you take me for? No! No, I have never…what you're suggesting…before my wife. Hang it, Lije, what kind of question is that?"

Lije pinched the bridge of his nose. "So we've never really known for sure, then."

Clint was near his boiling point. "Known what?"

Lije shrugged and held Clint's eyes with a glare that said, *you're not going to make me say it, are you?* After a ridiculously long pause Lije chose his next words with pastoral delicacy. "What if Cousin Obadiah was wrong?"

What did long-dead Cousin Obadiah have to do with— Clint felt his world grind to a halt. He wasn't even sure he could spit the next words out. "Wrong about…"

"Clint, Alice thinks Katrine might be pregnant."

Clint felt his knees buckle underneath him. He had to grab on to Lije to keep from keening over. He looked up at his brother with his mouth open, but couldn't get even the start of a word past the firecrackers going off in his chest.

"Actually," Lije said with a smile that was quickly dissolving into full-blown laughter, "Alice is almost certain Katrine is pregnant."

Clint grabbed Lije's face in his hands, staring into his brother's eyes. He had to be sure that's what he heard. "Katrine. A baby."

"Yes."

"Katrine is having a baby." He shook Lije's face as

the firecrackers inside nearly consumed him. The world spun too fast all of a sudden. "We're having a baby."

Lije steadied Clint's shoulders. "So it would seem."

For a long, crazy moment, Clint stared in disbelief at his brother. He wouldn't lie, not about something like this. Not with that look of flat-out wonder and joy in his eyes. Then it struck him; why on earth was he staring at Lije's eyes when he should be inside, staring into Katrine's eyes? "What am I doing out here?"

With a wide grin, Lije stepped aside and made a sweeping gesture toward the open infirmary door. Clint took the yard in a matter of seconds, flying over the threshold in something far too close to a leap, skidding into the room to see Katrine sitting up on an infirmary cot with glistening eyes. She looked frail and radiant and weary and beautiful, all at once. He went to pull his hat off his head, only to realize he'd dropped it somewhere along the way.

"What is it you always say?" Katrine said through the tears that made her eyes shine like stars. "God is mighty fond of surprises?"

He knelt down on one knee beside her on the bed, feeling like all the air had just gone out of the room. "Really?" It seemed far too much to hope for, more happiness than he knew how to bear.

Katrine nodded, another precious sob of joy shaking her dear slim body. He touched her hands, her shoulders, her wet cheeks in an attempt to convince himself he was wide awake. Katrine took his hand and moved it to her belly, and Clint thought he'd up and die of joy. Never, in every lonesome day since leaving Pennsylvania, did he dare to think Obadiah could be wrong about something so terribly serious. He'd memorized every inch of Katrine's tall and slender build, but now Clint felt just the slightest hint of a curve under his hand. He closed his eyes for a moment, overcome at the thought of the child under his palm. His child. Their child, the family he and Katrine had worked so hard to do without.

Alice's voice came soft over his shoulder. In truth, Clint had forgotten there was anyone else in the whole world right now. "She'll need to be careful, feeling so sick and all, but these things tend to pass later. I expect she'll be just fine and about April…"

"April," Clint repeated.

"A spring baby," Katrine said, meeting Clint's eyes which were now filled with tears. "Just think. Brave Rock was born in April this year, and our baby could be born on Brave Rock's first birthday. It fits, don't you think?"

"It fits perfectly," came Lije's voice from behind him. Clint looked back to see his brother holding Alice's hand as she wiped away tears of her own.

Suddenly Gideon's frame filled the doorway, concern in his eyes. "Walt told me you brought Katrine in sickly. Is everything all right?"

"More than that," Clint said, bringing Katrine's pale hand to his lips and planting a kiss there. "Way beyond, in fact."

Gideon shifted his weight. "Someone want to tell me what's going on here?"

Lije lifted an eyebrow at Clint. "He ought to be the next to know, don't you think?"

Clint turned and stood to face his brothers. "We're having a baby."

Gideon's eyes popped big as saucers. "A baby? But I thought—"

"We all thought. It's what Cousin Obadiah always told me. Never occurred to me not to believe him." Clint wiped his hands down his face and took another long, wonderful gaze at his wife. "I ain't never been so glad to have thought wrong in all my life."

Suddenly the room was filled with shouts and hand-clasps and enough happiness to fill the entire territory. Clint came back to the cot and swept Katrine up carefully in his arms. When she rested her head against his shoulder, it was as if the world slid perfectly into place and the future opened up wide and wonderful before him.

"Well," he said into the sun-yellow of her hair, feeling like it would take a dozen years for the smile to leave his face, "at least we know one thing."

Katrine raised her head to stare into his eyes. Glory, he hoped the child got her stunning, sky-blue eyes. "What's that?"

"That baby's going to be one strong kicker."

Katrine laughed and threw her arms around his neck to hold him tight. She was brave and beautiful, his wife, and he never dreamed he could love her more than he already did.

Well, God was fond of surprises, wasn't He?

* * * * *

Dear Reader,

Too often we strive and strain when life hands us burdens—and life is very good at handing us burdens. I'm far too guilty of thinking I must hold everything up on my own, be strong and have it all together. The truth—if we'd only see it—would hand us so much peace: it is God who does the holding. He has already turned the corner we fear, and none of life's corners ever come as a surprise to Him.

I hope you've enjoyed your visit to Brave Rock and its charming citizens. They've become dear to me, as I hope they have to you, as well. If this is your first visit to Brave Rock, I hope you'll find the two prior books in the Bridegroom Brothers series and share Elijah and Alice's story as well as Gideon and Evelyn's.

As always, I love to hear from readers. Visit my website at www.alliepleiter.com, email me at allie@alliepleiter.com, or write me at P.O. Box 7026, Villa Park, IL 60181.

Blessings,

Questions for Discussion

1. Family feuds aren't just in history books. Where has a rift developed in your family and what damage has it caused?

2. Would you have taken part in the Land Rush if you were alive at that time? Why or why not?

3. What do you think of Clint's plan to hide Lars? Did he have another option?

4. Katrine and Evelyn both say how grief is exhausting. Who in your world is grieving and how can you offer help and encouragement?

5. Would you keep the burned logs if you were Katrine? Why or why not?

6. Winona says, "Hearts wander in foolishness. Or perhaps they are the wiser than our heads in what matters most." Why is that a good thing? When does it cause trouble?

7. Do you agree or disagree with Clint that "there is no difference between the man who did the crime and the man who failed to stop it"?

8. Love can cross many cultural barriers. Where has this been true in your life? In the life of someone you know?

9. Katrine lets a past mistake define a great deal of her future. Where have you done this? How can faith redeem a situation like that?

10. Elijah tells Clint "the strongest people make peace with their scars." Where has this been true in your life?

A HERO IN THE MAKING
Brides of Simpson Creek
by Laurie Kingery

Opening a little restaurant of her own—that's Ella Justiss's dream. She never factored in Nate Bohannan or the chaos he'd bring to her life. Though getting to know the handsome drifter may lead her to find unexpected happiness with this unlikely hero.

GROOM BY DESIGN
The Dressmaker's Daughters
by Christine Johnson

Ruth Fox is desperate to keep her father's dressmaking shop afloat while he's ill. She finds herself falling for Sam Rothenburg, but doesn't realize his secret new business could spell doom for hers.

SECOND CHANCE CINDERELLA
by Carla Capshaw

When a maid comes face-to-face with the man she loved long ago, who is now a self-made London gentleman, will her secret keep them apart or reunite them?

THE WARRIOR'S VOW
by Christina Rich

Outside Jerusalem, a hidden princess must put her life in the hands of the warrior who is on a mission to overthrow her mother the queen.

REQUEST YOUR FREE BOOKS!

2 FREE INSPIRATIONAL NOVELS
PLUS 2
FREE
MYSTERY GIFTS

Love Inspired.
HISTORICAL
INSPIRATIONAL HISTORICAL ROMANCE

YES! Please send me 2 FREE Love Inspired® Historical novels and my 2 FREE mystery gifts (gifts are worth about $10). After receiving them, if I don't wish to receive any more books, I can return the shipping statement marked "cancel." If I don't cancel, I will receive 4 brand-new novels every month and be billed just $4.74 per book in the U.S. or $5.24 per book in Canada. That's a saving of at least 21% off the cover price. It's quite a bargain! Shipping and handling is just 50¢ per book in the U.S. and 75¢ per book in Canada.* I understand that accepting the 2 free books and gifts places me under no obligation to buy anything. I can always return a shipment and cancel at any time. Even if I never buy another book, the two free books and gifts are mine to keep forever.

102/302 IDN F5CN

Name	(PLEASE PRINT)	
Address		Apt. #
City	State/Prov.	Zip/Postal Code

Signature (if under 18, a parent or guardian must sign)

Mail to the **Harlequin® Reader Service:**
IN U.S.A.: P.O. Box 1867, Buffalo, NY 14240-1867
IN CANADA: P.O. Box 609, Fort Erie, Ontario L2A 5X3

Want to try two free books from another series?
Call 1-800-873-8635 or visit www.ReaderService.com.

* Terms and prices subject to change without notice. Prices do not include applicable taxes. Sales tax applicable in N.Y. Canadian residents will be charged applicable taxes. Offer not valid in Quebec. This offer is limited to one order per household. Not valid for current subscribers to Love Inspired Historical books. All orders subject to credit approval. Credit or debit balances in a customer's account(s) may be offset by any other outstanding balance owed by or to the customer. Please allow 4 to 6 weeks for delivery. Offer available while quantities last.

LIH13R

For the first time in longer than Ryan Travers could recall, he was having trouble keeping his mind on his work.
He couldn't have cared less about Jasper Gulch's missing
time capsule; it was pretty Julie Shaw who occupied his
thoughts.

"That's not good," he muttered as he stood on a metal
rung of the narrow bucking chute. This rangy pinto mare
wasn't called Widow-maker for nothing. He could not only
picture Julie Shaw as if she were standing right there next to
the chute gates, he could imagine her light, uplifting laughter.

Actually, he realized with a start, that *was* what he was
hearing. He started to glance over his shoulder, intending to
scan the nearby crowd and, hopefully, locate her.

"Clock's ticking, Travers," the chute boss grumbled.
"You gonna ride that horse or just look at her?"

Rather than answer with words, Ryan stepped across
the top of the chute, raised his free hand over his head and
leaned way back. Then he nodded to the gateman.

The latch clicked.

The mare leaped.

Ryan didn't attempt to do anything but ride until he heard
the horn blast announcing his success. Then he straightened

as best he could and worked his fingers loose with his free hand while pickup men maneuvered close enough to help him dismount.

To Ryan's delight, Julie Shaw and a few others he recognized from before were watching. They had parked a flatbed farm truck near the fence beside the grandstand and were watching from secure perches in its bed.

Julie had both arms raised and was still cheering so wildly she almost knocked her hat off. "Woo-hoo! Good ride, cowboy!"

Ryan's "Thanks" was swallowed up in the overall din from the rodeo fans. Clearly, Julie wasn't the only spectator who had been favorably impressed.

He knew he should immediately report to the area behind the strip chutes and pick up his rigging. And he would. In a few minutes. As soon as he'd spoken to his newest fan.

Don't miss the romance between Julie and rodeo hero Ryan in HER MONTANA COWBOY by Valerie Hansen, available July 2014 from Love Inspired®.

LIEXP0614R

SPECIAL EXCERPT FROM

Love Inspired
SUSPENSE

When a widow is stalked and taunted by memories from her tragic past, can the man who rescued her years ago come to her aid again?

Read on for a preview of PROTECTIVE INSTINCTS by Shirlee McCoy, the first book in her brand-new MISSION: RESCUE series.

"Who would want to hurt you, Raina?" Jackson asked her.

"No one," she replied, her mind working frantically, going through faces and names and situations.

"And yet, someone chased you through the woods. That same person nearly ran me down. Doesn't sound like someone who feels all warm and fuzzy when he thinks of you."

"Maybe he was a vagrant, and I scared him."

"Maybe." He didn't sound like he believed it, and she wasn't sure she did, either.

She'd heard something that had woken her from the nightmare.

A child crying? Her neighbor Larry wandering around? An intruder trying to get into the house?

The last thought made her shudder, and she pulled her coat a little closer. "I think I'd know it if someone had a bone to pick with me."

"That's usually the case, but not always. Could be you upset a coworker, said no to a guy who wanted you to say yes—"

She snorted at that, and Jackson frowned. "You've been a widow for four years. It's not that far-fetched an idea."

"If you got a good look at my social life you wouldn't be saying that."

Samuel yawned loudly and slid down on the pew, his arms crossed over his chest, his eyelids drooping. The ten-year-old looked cold and tired, and she wanted to get him home and tuck him into bed.

"I'll go talk to Officer Wallace," Jackson responded. "See if he's ready to let us leave."

"He's going to have to be. Samuel—"

A door slammed, the sound so startling Raina jumped.

She grabbed Samuel's shoulder, pulled him into the shelter of her arms.

"Is someone else in the church?" Jackson demanded, his gaze on the door that led from the sanctuary into the office wing.

"There shouldn't be."

"Stay put. I'm going to check things out."

He strode away, and she wanted to call out and tell him to be careful.

She pressed her lips together, held in the words she knew she didn't need to say. She'd seen him in action, knew just how smart and careful he was.

Jackson could take care of himself.

Will Jackson discover the stalker and help Raina find a second chance at love?

Pick up PROTECTIVE INSTINCTS to find out.
Available July 2014 wherever
Love Inspired® Suspense books are sold.